Castle Crespin

By the same author

The Pig Plantagenet

Castle Crespin

Allen Andrews

Hutchinson
London Melbourne Sydney Auckland Johannesburg

Hutchinson & Co. (Publishers) Ltd

An imprint of the Hutchinson Publishing Group

17–21 Conway Street, London W1P 6JD

Hutchinson Group (Australia) Pty Ltd
30–32 Cremorne Street, Richmond South, Victoria 3121
PO Box 151, Broadway, New South Wales 2007

Hutchinson Group (NZ) Ltd
32–34 View Road, PO Box 40–086, Glenfield, Auckland 10

Hutchinson Group (SA) Pty Ltd
PO Box 337, Bergvlei 2012, South Africa

First published 1982

Set in Linotron Bembo

Printed in Great Britain by The Anchor Press Ltd
and bound by Wm Brendon & Son Ltd
both of Tiptree, Essex

ISBN 0 09 147650 X

Contents

Author's Note

At the time in which this story is set the articulate world argued about Love to a far broader extent than in the present. The Church had already pronounced its dogma, still sounded today, that passionate physical love between married people was adultery. The aristocracy of Aquitaine, which had all gone into marriage for money, was briefly happy to accept the advice of its troubadours and commit flagrant and more traditional adultery, until the fashion changed and Courtly Love became a barren intellectual exercise. Meantime, the recognition of a wider love, passionate in many senses except the sexual, was being spread by Francis of Assisi.

Francis, who was not a sentimentalist, gave a greater importance to the individuality of animals than his orthodox contemporaries, though many more unorthodox religious thinkers assigned them souls. The world of the forest in which free animals lived, often a far greater area than neighbouring tracts of civilization, was rightly held in awe by most humans.

Animals have always been able to communicate, though they have rarely been translated. Occasionally the capacity to understand them is conveyed to a human. The author takes no credit for possessing this fortuitous gift.

It is a fact of historical accuracy that the Order of Teutonic Knights was permitted to conduct organized man-hunts of pagans or heretics as sporting occasions.

1

The Ingenuity of Fulgent the Fox

Poitou, France, 1225 AD

Fulgent des Saules, prince of the foxes, lay like the lord he was, asleep in the sun. It was not a strong sun, but the best St Martin could provide for his mid-November summer. For a short time, carefully calculated even in the depth of his drowsiness, Fulgent exposed himself so vulnerably as to lie on his back, his black-tipped paws drooping over his white chest in a cubbish posture so appealing that any woman might have been tempted to pick him up and cradle him; but he was nearly twenty pounds in weight and a yard long, not counting his tail, and certain scent glands made him as distinctive, if not positively unpleasant, to any lady stooping to lift him as the modified sweat glands of the lady made her distinctive, if not unpleasant, to him.

Fulgent rolled over, stood up, and followed his tail for two tight circles – rotating widdershins as always to express his aristocratic contempt for the superstitious hunting dogs, who followed the path of the sun 'for luck' when they wheeled in the same motion before settling. He subsided neatly into a flaming cushion of red and tan, dappled with black and the startling white of his jowls and tail-tip, yet curiously merging in a broken camouflage with the dead bracken in which he was lying. He arranged his glorious brush to catch the sun without shielding his coat or tempting him too strongly to bury his nose in it. For survival depended on suppressing all let or hindrance to the detective functions of smell, sight and hearing concentrated in the lean mask of his skull. He was sunning himself to dry out his pelt after an arduous swim across the currents of the river Guirande, swift and brimming with the autumn rains. Although it was his habit and preference to work by night, his present hunting formula was forcing him to delay the water crossing back into home ground until well after dawn.

In his own country, here on the forest side of the river among the willows from which he took his title, he had sensed the beginning of a fine day when, very deep in his earthen den, he had awoken with the shivers after his first deep sleep of gluttony. But he would never have committed himself to the daylit open in a season when the cover was bare if he had not been sure of the company up there of his particular friend Grondin, the black wild boar.

Dog-foxes and boars have an affinity. They are independent, even solitary, creatures for much of the year, until the surge of the mating months changes the rhythm of their life. But a boar, even while avoiding other boars in the gloom of the forest where he spends his day, will tolerate a lone fox on his territory, and with Grondin and Fulgent the toleration had warmed into intimacy. Grondin's mating season was some two months in advance of Fulgent's, and when he passed the time of day with the somnolent fox as he paused to cast a gourmet's root-calculating eye over the bracken in the bed, the sensitive Fulgent observed some signs of restlessness.

'You're not yourself, Grondin. Are you sickening for something?' the fox asked in a tone blending genuine sympathy with the male snigger to a degree which pleased him by its finesse.

'I've got the Curse coming on,' said the boar gloomily.

'Not the glorious urge?' said Fulgent, perking up his head with bright interest.

'Glorious!' scoffed the boar in what was intended to be a delicate sniff of world-weary disdain. Because his vocal engineering was not designed for subtlety it registered a snort which shook Fulgent like an earth-tremor. Grondin resolutely buffeted his way through the lapse of attention. 'Glorious!' he repeated. 'I've got to spend the next few months of my life charging like a mad thing at brother boars with whom I haven't the least quarrel today, all for the dubious pleasure of asserting my right to tup. I've got to tear my finely adjusted tusks up the tough briskets of gentlemen who normally behave as gentlemen should, not speaking till they've been introduced, when I've spent half a year developing these remarkable canines into the most efficient all-purpose agricultural machines in forest or arable – not swords but ploughshares.'

Fulgent murmured with understanding, though he reserved his open approval. Personally he had a better use for canines and envied the boar for his magnificent tusks. But Grondin was not angling for assent, and plunged on like the river in spate.

'And all for nothing. For Hecuba – by which you will understand my late unlamented and, I fear, future lamented mate, the ever-loving and unfortunately ever-living Dame Albaine. My intended! *She* intends it, I don't. She believes in perpetual pairing. I don't, and there's no law in the forest which says that a boar should. She's lived too long near Hurlaud and Pernale. "Such a devoted couple!" she simpers. "They've been together all their lives." I dare say they have. It's all right for wolves. It's downright unnatural for swine. It's all right for owls. We did ourselves a bad service when we elected Uhlan le Sage to be President of the Council of Animals, and he's a merry old widower owl by now. But owls are with us to be observed, not imitated. I don't sprout wings and go hoo-hooing all over the forest. I see no reason why I should come back to the herd after a good solitary summer and owlishly nominate my mate in advance when the whole business should have the uncertain glory of an April day. You must feel the same, Fulgent?'

'It's not as if we fail in our duties once we're embarked,' said Fulgent. 'I shall soon be press-ganged into procreation like everyone else, and from that moment I shall be dominated by a female who will ride me much harder than you are likely to be treated by Dame Albaine or whichever light-o'-love falls to you if you can rig matrimony back into the lottery it should be. Call it devotion or call it slavery, but I am bound to my vixen and cubs, fetching and carrying, expelled at will from the nuptial couch, foraging and feeding, often with considerable loss of personal dignity.'

'That is the law of the forest and we observe it,' said Grondin sententiously. 'The female has been given the privilege of enforcing it more rigorously. The trouble comes when she gets ideas above her station and goes all inflexible. That stubborn moon-eyed sow doesn't recognize that there's one law for the wolves and one for the swine. But I won't go on. Thanks for listening. It does a chap good to get a thing off his chest. How are you in yourself, Fulgent? I must say I've never seen you in better shape. I was remarking on it to Hurlaud and Baclin only the other day. Fit and fine, fit and fine. Where are you hunting these days?'

The fox rose and stretched indulgently, but did not answer the question. He was indeed in splendid condition, his muscles rippling under a thick coat which shone with well-being. He turned his keen face towards the boar and spoke to him warmly, without excessive flattery.

'I've always considered you one of the most impressive animals in our forest. Why do you forever underrate yourself? Black, monumentally square-fronted and delightfully devil-may-care. I'm built for slinking, but you are nature's charger. You should charge more often, and swear horribly as you do so. For when that great black muzzle opens and the red flesh throws those terrible tusks into proper perspective you are utterly majestic. Have you ever considered that this impending mating circus which you regard with so much diffidence sets you up to the pitch where you're at your most magnificent?'

Grondin's answer was short and decisive. 'No,' he said. 'Where did you say you were hunting these days?'

'Oh, here and there,' said Fulgent vaguely. 'Wherever it's convenient.'

'It's not going to be so convenient in the future around Henriot's farm at La Fiallerie,' said Grondin. 'They're under siege orders there. Triple defences and an all-night watch when they can muster it. I've been talking to my cousin Plantagenet at La Tranchée. He says Henriot is trying to get his neighbours to go on a roster to spend the night there, which includes Maister Brémand and the beagle Rupert. I'm told that the last straw for Henriot was when he found that some marauder had actually marked out the farm as his own territory. I'm just passing on what I hear. Ah well, it's good to have talked to you. Don't take my moaning too seriously. I'm no more depressed than usual. Or not much more. Now, I promised myself a look at a favourite chestnut tree after last night's timely gale. Good hunting.' The boar moved solidly away, nonchalantly treading down an oak sapling that had sprung from an acorn he had overlooked in previous years.

'Damn!' said Fulgent, gazing at his retreating rear. He

realized that Grondin had signalled the end of a highly successful offensive in the fox's autumn campaign.

Fulgent had put into operation, some time earlier, a series of risky patrols on the other side of the river, prospecting the tract farmed by Maister Henriot at La Fiallerie. The land was not worked so well as was the model farm run by Maister Brémand at La Tranchée, where Grondin's cousin the pig Plantagenet was in residence. But one aspect of it interested the fox deeply. The geese being raised by Henriot seemed of superb quality. Fulgent concentrated his attention on them with the intensity of a connoisseur. They were as plump as could be wished. Wasn't Henriot bringing them on a little too fast? Wouldn't they be past their prime if one waited until Christmas? Soon Fulgent's palate confirmed his sound judgment of livestock-breeding. He was a skilful predator and he mounted a number of successful raids, varying his tactics and methods every time. Definitely this was a vintage that should be tasted young. With such a fine and early start it promised to be a glorious winter. Unfortunately, although Henriot had been very badly educated, he could count. He was aware that his flock was diminishing. And the clusters of feathers, with certain physical traces which Fulgent was unwilling to cover up, showed that the raider was a fox. A fox tends to deposit its very identifiable droppings, with a characteristic pinch at the end of the stool, blatantly on open mounds as a clear sign to other foxes of the boundary-stones of its territory. Fulgent had thoughtlessly followed the same practice within the farmland of La Fiallerie.

Fulgent now realized that this had been an unforgivable *folie de grandeur.* He retired from the sunlight and went back to his earth to ponder, relying on his old instincts to prompt some adaptation of his hunting. That night he went out, determined to curb his overweening appetite. After an adequate meal of fifteen mice and a few clusters of berries he swam across to Henriot's land for a reconnaissance in depth.

He was aggrieved to find that the entire Henriot farmstead was ringed by the smell of man. Men had been recently working there, and their scent was almost unbroken. Stepping very gingerly, and never approaching too near, Fulgent perceived half-buried objects and traces that the earth had been lightly trenched between them. From a few points in the middle distance came the enticing whiff of carrion, but slightly stale carrion, killed at least eight hours previously. The fox's keen ears registered an occasional windblown clatter, like a small cracked bell or pebbles rattling inside a crock. Where the wind hissed over the grass his eyes caught faint undulations on the ground like long worms heaving, and he saw that lines had been laid connecting some of the unnatural objects projecting from the soil. The farm had in fact been virtually encircled by a network of traps, poisoned bait, tripwires and crude alarms set off by twine.

'This man Henriot must be out of his mind!' Fulgent commented to himself with pious disapproval. 'An extravagant expenditure of labour, time and material! Sheer economic madness.' And with a sapper's eye he selected the most favourable place to mine.

Tunnelling fast and skilfully, he passed under the outer defences. He climbed the farmstead wall, which Maister Henriot correctly assumed was unassailable by any normal fox, by a series of zig-zag leaps which he had long perfected. He made a successful entry into the fowl-houses in an area where he knew the guineafowl were clustered. He selected a bird of small size, not so much for the modesty of his ambitions as because he wanted to take his prize home with him for a more leisurely meal. He leapt, quickly silenced the bird, and carried it over the wall, finally dragging it back through the tunnel. Later, at peace in his earth, he composed a short collect praising the Creator for the evolution of Staff-work and Planning.

The next night he chanced his luck again, and only narrowly escaped being pinned by the snap of a spring-trap that had been placed in the tunnel. This counter-measure was not wholly unexpected, and he retired intending a later reconnaissance in full light. Rain fell persistently throughout the following day, and Fulgent lay in, contenting himself with a supper of a few frogs which had interpreted the weather signs too optimistically and a blinded rabbit which he skilfully filched from under the beak of the crow that had maimed it.

When the fox was finally able to survey La Fiallerie in daylight he found an extraordinary transformation. The farmstead was completely surrounded by a new defence system. At some distance from the wall a plough had been used to cut half a dozen furrows in concentric circles. Behind the innermost furrow an erection of hurdles had been built up into a low fence. The furrows were clean and entirely unbroken by obstructions, so that not a single trap or alarm was visible, although what lay inside the hurdles could only be guessed. But an astonishing array of lines and strings was laced in a massive tangle from points at the top of the hurdles to beds below the surface of the furrows. It was impossible that every line could be attached to an engine of destruction, but equally impossible to determine which cord led to a trap and which was merely a deterrent.

'Budgetary suicide!' fulminated Fulgent, more in jargon than in anger. 'A crisis of management! Debit the man-hours required in a labour-intensive industry to set up this elaborate charade, plus the cost-correlative of iron traps in an economy where metal is at a premium. Balance that against the trivial advantage sustained through the survival of a handful of geese. The man is a fiscal nincompoop.

'Or am I completely at sea?' the fox grudgingly added with a hypocritical bob towards economic reflation.

Like other dogmatists, he was of course at sea. Henriot was at war with a fox, and the satisfaction of waging that war could not be expressed in monetary terms. Much more important, Henriot's wife, Dame Blanche, was at war both with the fox and with Henriot, expressing grievances based as solidly in the feudal system as in the predatory nature of vulpines. Since she could not belt the fox she gave Henriot a daily double whipping. Her only wealth, the sole personal return which gave a farmer's wife any emancipation, lay in the poultry which she traditionally raised as her private interest. Almost as fast as she was raising it Fulgent was lowering it. Henriot was little more than the bloody scales recording the latest transaction. The daily confrontation between husband and wife plumbed the depth of male humiliation. Henriot was passion's slave, a condition which makes no obeisance to economics.

Fulgent, skulking on a thistle-grown molehill where he was with difficulty refraining from depositing his droppings, saw carts suddenly emerge from the main gate of the farm. They were escorted by a handy group of men and women, nearly the total workforce of the farm, Fulgent estimated. Some of the men removed two aligned hurdles to let the carts pass through the new perimeter. From the careless way in which they handled the lines the fox was fairly sure that that particular area, though ploughed, had not been mined or tamponned with springtraps. It was a detail to remember. The carts went out to a distant field and the workers bent side by side as they dug up rows of vegetable growth. Clearly it was time for one of the root harvests, probably turnip.

A wild temptation seized the fox to raid the relatively

deserted farm in full daylight when all the poultry were unconfined and unsuspecting. Fulgent resolutely applied his realism and repressed the urge. Instead, he planned ahead and found an old badger-set to sleep in securely.

He emerged in the late afternoon when the light was lowering. Using masterly concealment, he stalked as far as the harvesters and sprang lightly into one of the carts which had been ferrying roots from the field to the barn all day. Once inside, he burrowed fast and vigorously near the top of the heap. He contrived to disappear without being smothered, and shortly afterwards was driven back to the farm like a king in a chariot. Through the furrows, past the hurdles, over the cobbles he was conducted. The portals of the main gate slammed behind him. The field was finished, the harvest was home, night had fallen, and Henriot sent off his workers to clean themselves up before supper, leaving the last load in the carts to be stacked in the morning. Fulgent waited until he heard the whoosh of crocks being filled from barrels and cheery voices raised in song around the table after hard work well done. Then he emerged from his barouche, soundlessly infiltrated the fowlhouse, chose and silenced the sacrificial bird, gripped it firmly and ran to his personally expropriated section of the wall. He clambered over and sprinted round to the outside of the main gate, charged down the cart track, leapt with light unconcern over the hurdles into the innocuous furrows, and went home to enjoy his dinner.

The ritual lashing of Henriot began at eight o'clock the following morning when the larceny was discovered.

By the time of Angelus, the suffering siege-captain was ostentatiously reorganizing his defences. A considerable proportion of his men were digging up and replanting sinister objects into the strip of land which previously had been neatly ploughed. Not all the workforce was visible, Fulgent observed, and he was curious as to what the men were doing, for no one was working in the fields. That evening the fox had a quiet word with Puissard the sparrowhawk, who owed him a favour.

Next morning Puissard flew over the farm and reported back to Fulgent.

'More than half the men are still working outside,' he said. 'They're digging up whatever it was they planted yesterday, then putting the things back in other holes they've dug nearby and rearranging all the lines. The rest of the farmhands are busy in the courtyards. Some of them are trenching and planting. The others are just whittling.'

'Whittling?' asked Fulgent.

'Just sitting around with knives, carving wood.'

'Carving wood into what? Portrait heads of Henriot? Busts of his wife?'

'The shapes are the same as traps. They're burying some inside and sending the rest to the hurdles.'

'Wooden traps? Do they think I'm a mouse?'

'I'm only telling you what I saw.'

'They're dummies!' exclaimed Fulgent in a burst of revelation. 'Decoys. Every line will be attached to *something*. I can't spend all night on trial and error. These people are really set on making it difficult for me.'

'They're obsessed by you,' said Puissard. 'Don't be obsessed by them. They're wasting their time, don't let them waste yours. Concede them a victory.'

'Those that seek my soul to destroy it,' said Fulgent with an intensity of superstition that could pass for fanatical piety, 'shall go into the lower parts of the earth. They shall fall by the sword, they shall be a portion for foxes. Psalm 63.'

'The fear of the Lord is the beginning of wisdom,' said Puissard. He knew very well that Fulgent had been to church only once in his life, by accident, and, trapped in the belfry with Uhlan the owl, had chanced to hear

Psalm 63, which he used ever after as a lucky charm once Uhlan had explained it to him.

Puissard was a military type with a respect for hierarchical discipline, and although, like everyone else, he quoted only the Scripture that backed his views, he went to more trouble to verify his sources. To score one up on Fulgent he repeated his text in Latin, but with no discernible tone of superiority. '*Initium sapientiae timor Domini. Proverbia.* I quote, of course, from the Vulgate of blessed Jerome with Lanfranc's revisions.' And with a soldierly, moustache-settling twirl of his red cheeks he beat his wings rapidly, sailed over a bush and took a rosy bullfinch. It was no mean feat to catch this evasive, security-conscious bird, and the sparrowhawk relished the neat finality of such an impressive operation in front of the fox.

'Save me the core,' said the fox sardonically, as Puissard tore and swallowed the warm flesh.

On the following day Fulgent again took up his observation of the farm. The men were once more digging up the perimeter, changing the position of the sunken objects and reburying them. More and more of the traps seemed genuine rather than dummies, for an alien oxcart had been driven up to the farm and ominously clanking apparatus had been unloaded from it. Next day they repeated the task. It seemed that Henriot's sole purpose in life had narrowed into intensifying his hardware and confusing his enemy about its location.

'He has still to get in the rest of his root harvest,' moaned Fulgent with professional concern. 'There is hedging and ditching to be done. Those new traps cost far more than he can afford. To feed and keep his men is only cost-effective if he can use their labour for productivity. He is diverting his entire gross output to defence expenditure.

'And all in vain,' added the fox. 'For I shall now make a pact with Picot. I shall bring on the clown.'

Picot was a purple heron, with little of the grace of his grey cousin. Nature had cruelly given him a neck which a besotted poet might conceivably describe as sickle-shaped, though harsher observers would nominate it as the biggest Adam's apple in creation: his gullet seemed to have lost all sense of direction so that it sprouted upwards into a grotesque question mark. Like many involuntary laughing-stocks, Picot was by disposition humble, gratingly suspicious and opportunistic.

He was allowed the indulgence of a limited access to Henriot's farm. He did not press his luck, but used his privilege modestly. In times of hunger he would fly in and feed off a few scraps of offal on the rubbish heap near the kitchen. Usually he was left in peace. Peasants, unless they preserve stock in a fishpond, generally consider herons useful and inoffensive. Buffard, the general labourer among the farm dogs, had made an effort to go for him, but the farm servants and even Dame Blanche intervened, and Buffard had taken a hiding. So Picot, muddling through with his awkward flight and freakish aspect, was habitually tolerated when he flipped over the gate at La Fiallerie under the smouldering eyes of Fulgent, who was kicking his heels in a thicket on the outfield.

Having decided to recruit Picot, the fox called on the heron in the watery ditch where he spent much time gazing dejectedly at his feet, and gave him the glad news of his promotion to quartermaster general in the newly raised Fulgent's Foragers.

'No go,' rasped the heron. 'I do pretty well on Henriot's garbage.'

'Skinflint!' hissed Fulgent to himself, then expanded into more persuasive arguments.

'Come off it, old man, you're not going to tell me that

those throw-outs are enough for you? Look at yourself, dear boy. You are pretty thin. I see a tremor, too. You can't be doing yourself any good by trying to live on a diet of muck like that. In the long run you could well catch Lummock's disease.'

'Great God, what's that?' asked Picot in alarm.

Fulgent stared long and hard at the tapering beak of the spindly bird, then shifted his gaze to the skull. He toyed with the idea of giving himself the pleasure of crushing the bony head with one snap of his jaws. But the appearance of that frightful, shrivelled thorn-bush gave him immediate heartburn. Picot would make only one meal, and hard tack at that. Fulgent confirmed his decision that a more ambitious social role should be reserved for the bird.

'Lummock's disease,' he explained in confidential tones, 'is an illness which attacks creatures who feed too long on vegetable parings and festered cartilage. It starts with colic. It doesn't seem so bad at first, but it gets more serious very quickly. If the patient persists in feeding on that sort of stuff he is soon overcome by a fever and he can die in a week.'

In dismay Picot let his spiny bottom fall on to a sodden log, which moved away as if not relishing the contact.

'Pull yourself together, Picot. You haven't reached that stage yet. But by the look of you I reckon it's high time you did something about it.'

'Nothing quite like that has happened to me yet,' said Picot uneasily. 'But it is true that from time to time I come out in cold sweats.'

'Look, old friend,' said Fulgent in his best bedside manner. 'Let me prescribe for you. You're proper poorly. What you need is a leg of goose from day to day to restore your strength. We have got to think of building up your resistance now to get you through what is to come. After all, the winter is only just starting. But of course it's your business.' Fulgent went through the motions equivalent to packing up his instruments before going on another call.

'For Nick's sake stay a bit longer, you're not in such a hurry as that,' said Picot piteously. 'Look, the fishing is poor here and the frogs have started hibernating. You know very well that I could go a bundle on a bit of fresh meat from time to time. But see how I'm situated. I can't go for geese or ducks. I'm tolerated at the farm, no more. I can't let myself get into trouble.' He thought for a moment and looked cunningly at the fox. 'I'd like very much to help you, Fulgent, but it's not easy. I've built myself up by my own efforts into a position of trust there, and it's just not honourable to let the side down. At least, not unless I know what's in it for me.'

Fulgent sat down in apparent hesitation. He sniffed the air, nodded his head and hummed a little as he stared into Picot's beady eyes. Then he spoke: 'I'm asking nothing really, old man, I'm only concerned with getting you back into fighting form. I'll do all the work and I'll look after you. Carry on as usual. Don't change your routine. Just keep an eye on Henriot and his men. Make a careful note of the places where they set traps and alarms, particularly inside the courtyard. Meet me every night at this spot and give me an accurate report. That's all I'm asking. For this little service I'm offering you a wing. . . .' Picot's eyes suddenly narrowed. 'Did I say a wing?' Fulgent continued hurriedly. 'I meant a leg. I'm offering you a leg of prime goose paid down on the spot at the end of every successful trip.'

'Done!' grated the sour voice with the conviction of having struck a rare bargain. 'And Devil take the one who goes back on it.'

'Done!' agreed Fulgent indulgently, with a voice as bored as a bishop.

This was the beginning of a highly effective collaboration between Fulgent and Picot. Every alteration in the location of a trap, every change in the routine of the defenders and the patrol-times of the sentries, every setting of poisoned bait, was scrupulously reported to Fulgent, who altered his plans accordingly. The fox kept his word and made over to Picot the agreed share of the spoils.

Henriot reacted vigorously, strengthening his outer defence, setting more traps and alarms and bringing in fresh dogs. He organized the night watch he had long been planning and, lacking sufficient personnel, called on his neighbours for help. They came on a rota system with mastiffs and bulldogs, and Maister Brémand of La Tranchée brought Rupert the English beagle, and basked in the admiration which the dog inspired as a distinguished foreign visitor. Some of the hounds were left at La Fiallerie during the day. It was this last invasion which settled the matter. Picot had increasing difficulty in penetrating the farm without being set on by fresh dogs which had not been schooled to disregard him. Maister Henriot was constantly rescuing the heron, but finally he bowed to the inevitable. He decided to exile Picot to a ditch well outside the farm, and he had a few scraps regularly taken there. 'We can't destroy such a useful creature,' he said. 'Hey, hounds, leave that bird alone.'

Fulgent perceived that the alliance was over. He regretted it particularly because he had begun to bring presents of game to the vixen he was courting and mating. But the raids would have to be called off. He decided however to crown the campaign with one final sunburst coup, operating alone, as prince of the foxes.

By this resolve the fox was to have a critical influence on the fortunes of many animals and the lives of many humans among the different feudal orders linked in the web of existence in Poitou. It was not a remarkably complicated decision, merely the expression of a creature's strong determination to survive and breed, with a certain additional element of pride, self-assertion or machismo.

Pride, self-assertion and machismo are qualities which we are strictly warned by one puritan school of thought not to ascribe to animals, although their will to survive is conceded. But realists, who have learned to know animals intimately if only because they profit from betting on that knowledge, do not hesitate to judge individual animals by their degree of pride, self-assertion or machismo. The puritan theory may be dismissed from the academy of philosophy in the same words that have been used to withdraw steel-spurred roosters from the cockpit and a king of England from the constitutional battle-order ranged to contest his abdication. The text is taken from the Book of Beaver given to the Squire of Chartwell under King Edward of Windsor in the 320th day of his reign: 'Our cock won't fight.'

Fulgent did fight, and by fighting he encroached on the lives of humans in the County of Poitou, from the castle to the cottage.

2
Hearth and Home

From outside the unshuttered windows of the cottage the red glow of a high hearth-fire waxed and waned with the movement of heads and shoulders like clouds passing fast across the face of an igneous moon. Nails and knuckles beat out the tripping introduction to a dance tune on the stretched parchment of tambourins. A small horn announced the air, soon sweetened by the plucked strings of vièles. A chorus of voices took up the tune, singing roughly but seriously with accurate attention to the rhythm. The fire-glow on the night air began to dip and rear with the regularity of waves on a lake as the gliding dancers found their unity, and in the brief intervals of rests in the flow of the music there came the soft sweep and stamp of feet on the rush-strewn earthen floor. When the dance ended there was cheering and laughter, the clinking of metal pots, and an occasional shriek and cascade as an earthenware crock was clumsily shattered. Men began to bay with the endless vacuities of concupiscence – 'You know what I mean? Course you know what I mean. What you think I mean?' – and were answered with shrill giggles of embarrassment or provocation. There were the clicks of inner doors being unlatched and the thud of couples falling among the barrels. Amid ribald acclamation someone proposed a round game, a foolery which would end with spectacular forfeits. In the tumult of its climax the drums and strings paraded more music. The grave and graceful undulation of heads once more rippled against the fire-glow.

It was a customary wake, and yet it was not an ordinary funeral. The village remembered it long afterwards with a shaking of heads that conveyed a passing tribute to conventional shock and a deep sense of sly nostalgia. Even the priest salted his formal criticism with a pleasantry. One of the boys born after the appropriate interval, later a devoted server at Mass, was always referred to by Sir Bernard as Vigilius. The cleric used to say it was in tribute to 'the famous Pope', but Pope Vigilius had been dead for nigh seven hundred years and no one was surprised when Sir Bernard, whose memory of ecclesiastical history was as sketchy as any other parish priest's, failed totally to define what the previous Vigilius was famous for and whether he ruled from Rome or Byzantium. The certain facts were that the boy was one of a clutch of babies born in the village – fortunately all to married women – at a matching time; that his mother, one of the sweetest voices in any village chorus and a stalwart organizer of the banquet at any village funeral, discreetly reserved all comments about his conception; and that the priest was present at every phase of the vigil, complementing his liturgical role with his pastoral and social presence and affably received in all his functions. And if, with excess of zeal, he had striven too energetically in his mission of comfort and yet had caused no offence, there were few who would hold it against him. For there were vows taken by some men in brief ecstasy that were little better than self-mutilation, and there were times like two in the morning of a monumental wake when charity demanded that a grievous ache should be eased, and the only vow worth remembering was the pledge of the troubadour in the dawn-song styled the Aube:

> Here in my arms I hold my lady naked,
> Snug midst the din her jealous lord has makèd.
> Silent within, till all our thirst is slakèd,
> We vow to love till dawn.

Certainly it was the Church, by its rigorous extortion, that had provoked the resentment which underlay the reaction of the memorable excesses of this wake, but no ill feeling was directed against the amiable priest in residence, only towards the distant bishop who had ruthlessly exacted the death-tax known as mortuary.

The woman whose death had occasioned this emotional stir had presided quietly over the first mourning ritual of her vigil, lying on a trestle table set up in the hearth-room of her cottage. Later, when the fire burned hotter and the company moved more awkwardly, she had been taken to a bed in an adjacent room. But through the afternoon she had lain in dignity, tightly shrouded to the shoulders but with the linen loose over her face, so that the cloth could be set aside for newly arrived participants to gaze on her. Often the covering was not immediately replaced, and her sharp, rather youthful face gave the impression that she was listening companionably to a neighbourly conversation which she might interrupt at any moment. From time to time a boy, a youth, a dwarfish young man – his face and figure were continuously deceptive about his age – came up to her, uncovered her face if need were, and caressed it with no great subtlety, following the contours like a pawing puppy that cannot moderate its strength. His hands and fingers, small and crude, could neither remove nor replace the shroud with delicacy or precision, and when he touched the face the flesh of the thin cheeks was depressed into furrows and even the tip of the pointed nose was displaced. The youth did not weep. His eyes, set small and slanting slightly upwards and outwards in a broad head, seemed shining pools of deep, affectionate compassion for everyone he looked towards, with no regard for himself. The only vocal sound he made was a repeated *Mu-mu-mu-mu-mu* every time he came to the shrouded body and touched the face. Once when he made this communication a pear-drop of saliva fell from the corner of his mouth on to the cheek of the corpse. He bent swiftly to brush it away, with his face not his hands, and, as if thrown out of control by the novelty of the movement, he began to kiss the cheek and the mouth with a kind of desperate greed. The sitting mourners, genuinely distinguishing his purity in the seeming indecency, rose and led the lad away from his mother with soothing explanations about respect for the dead, which he seemed to understand.

'Poor fool,' one villager commented to another. 'He is to lose all his possessions and the fire will be put out in his home. And I'll tell you a strange thing. You know we can understand most of what he's trying to tell us with his Moo-moo-moo's and his Mee-mee-mee's once we've got to know him? Now there are only three words in the whole wide world that he can say properly and distinctly. Well, I've heard him say another set of three recently, though these are the first and foremost. And those three words are "hearth-and-home". Now what do you make of that?'

Hearth and home were exactly what the youth was about to lose through the accidents of untimely death and unyielding feudal masters. He was an only child. His father had died less than two years previously. The lord of the manor, acting through his local agent the bailiff, claimed from the possessions of his serf the death-duty called heriot – theoretically, the accoutrements of war provided by the master to his man so that he was fit to be mustered for military service at any time. Since the man was dead he could no longer use arms and armour, and they had to be returned to the lord. But in this village there had been no issue of arms and armour for a number of generations. An equivalent had therefore to be levied from the dead man's possessions. The levy had been fixed, by manorial custom over the same number of generations, as the commandeering of the man's best beast, best chattel (preferably a cart), and a generous selection from his other livestock and deadstock with a keen preference for implements of metal. When the demand for heriot had been settled, the Church lodged its claim for the death-duty called mortuary. Theoretically, and perhaps realistically, this was a levy on the dead man's possessions in lieu of that proportion of the tithes and other church dues which he had successfully avoided paying in his lifetime. Mortuary took the pick of what was left after heriot.

The taxes demanded at the death of the boy's father crippled so gravely his mother's ability to run her tiny agricultural holding that the lord of the manor relented. He ordered his bailiff to return the impounded ox and tumbril and to give the widow until the following harvest to pay the tax in coin. And this was done. But, on the widow's death an unseasonably short time afterwards, the gates of mercy were barred shut. Having ascertained that the bishop of the diocese would under no circumstances forgo his right to mortuary, the lord calculated that with the meagre remaining equipment neither the house nor the holding could be managed by a competent rustic, still less by a babbling idiot. He informed his reeve that both house and holding were to be resumed – merged back into the manorial estate – and ordered his bailiff to eject from hearth and home the useless survivor of this wretched family.

The lord's reasoning was, as it happened, in error

because his facts were wrong. But, since he was not in the habit of giving any reasons for his decisions, no one could correct him. The holding had been farmed satisfactorily by a primitive co-operative through the last months of the widow's life. A pair of ragged Grey Friars had come into the district and had squatted in an area of no man's land in the outskirts of the forest. They occupied a derelict building, at first little more than the skeleton of a house. But they had planted sticks and had woven twigs to support clay walls, and they had cleared land around the retreat, giving the dell a sort of permanence as if they intended a long stay. They revealed the purpose of their arrival with artless transparency. They had come, they said, to live like Christ, in the poverty and humility which he experienced, to preach repentance, to serve the sick and the poor, leading people by their own humble example to acknowledge that God is simply love. They rarely mentioned happiness, but the two poor friars seemed often to be not only deeply happy in themselves but the source of happiness in others.

One of the first to be attracted to their retreat was the widow's son, who had habitually spent much of his free time in the forest, attentively looking and listening and learning in his own way, so that he was more familiar with the wild life of the woods than any other creature in the countryside. There was no bird-song heard in that champaign that he could not faithfully reproduce. The Grey Friars had welcomed him and talked long and patiently to him as an equal, without ever catechizing him at the end of a session like schoolmasters demanding proof that he had understood them, and without requiring repetitions of his babbling to be sure that *they* understood *him* – a happy issue which was accomplished within a few weeks by dogged love. The friars directed and helped the lad in the daily work that needed to be done in his sick mother's farmland holding, where the widow had to raise on her sections the same crops which the other villagers did on theirs. They also supervised the son's tasks in the private garden round her own cottage where the widow grew vegetables and herbs for the pot, some fruit and even a flower or two. The lad was a good worker so long as he was given encouragement and friendly overseeing, and, though he spent less time in his forest school, his mother's plots of cultivated land did not really disgrace or impoverish the village.

However, all this attention pushed the level of subsistence of the ingenuous Little Brothers below the local poverty line. They had no possessions, because their last worldly action before joining the order of the Friars Minor had been to obey Christ's bidding and sell everything they had, to give it, not to the Church, but to the poor. From that moment, under vows to strive for a true imitation of Christ, to accept humility and to revere 'our lady Poverty', they handled no money. Jesus had sent out the apostles to preach without provision for money in their purse, and the Little Brothers supported themselves by working in the fields throughout the day in exchange for alms in kind, such as food, but never for money. They evangelized as they worked, but by concentrating on the land held by the perilously ailing widow, from whom they would accept very little, they made fewer contacts than could sustain them.

Not only their nutrition suffered, but also their evangelism. The widow's son seemed their only undoubted convert. Brother Sylvester, who was endowed with less patience than his colleague Brother Robert, sometimes questioned whether God in his accounting would credit them sufficiently for the adherence of such a simple fellow to his flock. 'The lad is not even a leper,' he objected.

'I've no doubt,' reasoned Brother Robert, 'that we should earn more instant acclaim if our first acknowledged convert was a hard-used leper. But we settled here in good faith and the local leper colony is some distance away. This lad is a son of God and now he recognizes his father with all his heart and with what mind God gave him. He is a very happy fellow and he's a good start for us. We can't always go for the dramatic.'

'Francis is dramatic,' argued Sylvester. 'Francis is spectacular when he makes his point. The first thing he did in Assisi, even before he stripped himself naked in front of the bishop to hand back all his clothes and his money to his earthly father, was to go up to a leper and kiss him. And he was *revolted* by lepers. Still is, really.'

'He didn't convert the leper,' commented Brother Robert in the no-nonsense tone of voice he sometimes adopted towards Sylvester. 'He *showed* God's love, but he has never said that the leper saw it, and we've done better than that with the simple lad. The leper was *used* by Jesus to help Francis. I quote, dear Brother Sylvester, and you'll concede that I have an excellent memory: "This is the task the Lord set me, me, Little Brother Francis, as the beginning of my repentance. Formerly, when I was in sin, I could not endure even the sight of lepers. So the Lord sent me to mix with them. And I greeted them as my brothers under God. After this experience I was changed. What had seemed to me disgusting now filled my body and soul with a new fragrance." The drama is what happened to Francis, and what happened to Francis is the seed of what has happened to us and to the thousands of our brothers who have come into the order partly because of Francis' flair for the spectacular: a flair, Sylvester, which he uses as Jesus used parables, to clinch a lesson unforgettably.

'Let's leave the colourful side to Francis, and the Lord in his good time, and not be discontented with changing the life of a simple lad. We can't deny that he is happy. And he sings divinely.'

The lad at that moment, while building a dry-stone

wall as the beginning of a stockade protecting the clearing, was singing the song of the blackbird, liquidly clear and, to humans, entirely unmenacing, perhaps the sweetest music in all the forest.

Brother Sylvester listened, and his heart melted with pleasure. 'Do a lark,' he called. 'Do a lark. I love larks. So does Francis.'

'La-la-la? Far-far-far?' queried the lad.

Sylvester crouched on the ground, then sprang up. He was thin but wiry, and as he went upwards with his arms stiff by his sides he mounted straight and vertical like an arrow. At the peak of his leap he fluttered brown hands in the sleeves of his grey robe and voiced a clear ecclesiastical chant like the beginning of plainsong.

'Lark, skylark,' he said. 'For Francis.'

The boy smiled in understanding. Effortlessly and without any distortion of his face he sang the high coloratura song of the lark ascending. It filled the air with an extravagance of notes, an impromptu that yet seemed to transmit the most shapely design. The singer's head was thrown back, his eyes wide open but far-focused as if he were searching the limits of the sky. After long minutes of pure sound he let the notes die in the distance.

'Beautiful,' said Brother Robert. 'Now, have you said your prayers yet?'

The lad shook his head. 'Naw-naw,' he said.

'Say your prayers, then. Talk with Jesus.'

Simply, the boy obeyed. He talked to Jesus and echoed what, it could only be presumed, Jesus said in reply to him. For on these occasions nobody could precisely duplicate him at all. He abandoned the repetition of his tripping monosyllables and reproduced a scrambled version of animated human speech. It was constructive mimicry as original as his version of the skylark's song. He had a very exact ear for the intonations of vocal intercourse, the rise and fall of conversation, the peremptory accent of a question, the reasoned reply, the patient explanation, the occasional tone of humorous absurdity which finally disposed of an objection. It was entirely acceptable as an overheard dialogue except that it used no recognizable language. He spoke to Jesus as if narrating the events of the day, asking confidently for approval on some points and diffidently for guidance on others, occasionally expressing frustrated bewilderment at reactions he had provoked. Jesus spoke short sentences of encouragement at the beginning, and gave longer answers as the number of questions began to mount.

It sounded like an easy communion between father and son heard darkly through a closed door until it ended unmistakably with a blessing and 'Good night'. If the tones which the boy gave to Jesus were clearly reminiscent of the pitch and intervals of the voice of Brother Robert, that was understandable enough, on the premise that Robert was the nearest to Jesus of all the acquaintances the lad had yet made.

The friars added their own good-night blessing and sent the boy home.

'His mother will soon be dead,' said Brother Sylvester.

'Then we shall be all that he has on earth,' answered Brother Robert. 'Come now, it's time for meditation.'

'We shall do our best,' he added after a long pause.

'Is that what you were meditating on?' queried Sylvester with a tinge of accusation in his voice. 'Is it allowed?'

'Of course it's allowed.'

'Good. Because that's what I was meditating on.'

'I think we'd better pray,' said Robert hastily, and he began loud and fast before Sylvester could comment. 'Dear Lord, we need your help more than some of our brothers because we are comparatively new in your service and haven't really got the hang of how to start a meditation. Our trouble could well be that through regrettable inattention during our induction course we lack sufficient conviction that meditation is worthwhile. One of us is a very practical person, formerly a mercenary soldier as you well know from the occasion when he surrendered his arms to you. He is still very good with his hands and has been positively straining to help others for the love of you since he joined your colours. The other only played soldiers, dreamed of being a knight and, when he found more discomfort than glamour there, dreamed of being a scholar, even dreamed – it was only a dream – of doing good. But you found us both and we found you through Francis, and you showed us a hard life but a life worth living. The trouble is that we can take the tough stuff – getting beaten up as Waldensian heretics and all that – though going without shoes, as you may have gathered from the entirely impersonal curses that possibly attract your attention from time to time, is still quite a strain because one of us has very tender feet. None of these pinpricks, we realize, deserves to be mentioned when we think of the agonies you had to suffer. So, physically we're in fair shape, and if we're slow but sure in preaching your way and your truth we do our best to live your life of humility and love. But we do come a cropper over this business of meditation. Sylvester can't get started on meditation because he wants to be up and doing all the time, and Robert too easily gets side-tracked into daydreams. Perhaps if you could show us that meditation really gives us the necessary strength for action, like eating our emergency rations before battle under captain's orders, we'd see the point of it all rather better. Would you try to do that for us, dear Lord?'

'That's a good prayer,' said Sylvester. 'I like that bit about enlisting in the Lord's colours. And "emergency rations", that's right on the mark.'

'Then start meditating,' said Robert.

There was an uncomfortable pause.

'I should have seen it before,' said Sylvester with sudden decision. 'We've got to have a drill. Everything comes easier when you're following your drill. Now here's a drill. *You* start by saying our dear Lord's words when he sent the apostles out on their first mission. You know very well what he said. Go on, something is sure to come from that. Do begin, Brother Robert.'

' "As ye go," ' said Robert slowly, ' "preach, saying The kingdom of Heaven is at hand. Heal the sick, cleanse the lepers. . . ." '

Sylvester raised his head as if about to say, 'I told you so,' but was stilled by Robert's unyielding eye.

' ". . . raise the dead, cast out devils. Freely ye have received, freely give. Provide neither gold nor silver nor brass in your purses, nor scrip for your journey, neither two coats, neither shoes nor yet staves, for the workman is worthy of his meat." '

There was a silence.

'Is it all right if we meditate aloud?' asked Sylvester.

'I should think so.'

'What was that bit after . . . you know . . . "cleanse the lepers"?'

Robert paused, because a sudden intake of breath had stopped him speaking.

' "*Raise the dead*," ' he finally said.

'Do you think we could?'

'We could try,' said Robert with a tremor of fierce excitement in his voice.

Sylvester looked at his brother with simple enthusiasm and quite without irony. 'It would be spectacular,' he said.

On the morning that the news was brought to them of the widow's death the Little Brothers continued working for some time on her holding in the field. A woman had come down from the houses to tell the menfolk of the village, and only later in the day was the further news given that the lord was repossessing his fief and ejecting the boy. But still the friars were inhibited from going into the village though they yearned to get to grips with resuscitation at the earliest possible moment.

They maintained relations of friendly unease with the parish priest, Sir Bernard. The Friars Minor had been licensed by the Pope to preach, provided that Francis or his provincial deputy personally approved the preacher. But Pope Innocent had restricted them to the preaching of repentance only, not of doctrine. 'Very proper!' Francis had commented, smiling when he commissioned Robert and Sylvester to go into France, and appointed Robert a preacher. 'Sylvester knows no doctrine. Robert has studied too much and still is sure of nothing. But you both have enough acknowledged sin in your record to be dab hands at repentance.'

But the awkward immediate fact was that Sir Bernard never preached at all in the parish, finding it very difficult to compose and expound a sermon even when his bishop urged him to be more lively in propagating faith and doctrine. The continuing mundane demands on him as a mediator in village life, and the daily celebration of the mysteries of the liturgy, were overwhelming enough.

Robert and Sylvester judged that they could not intervene in the widow's house before the completion of the traditional wake. And they shrank from the participation of a large congregation of spectators goggling at an attempt to perform a miracle which might not succeed. They therefore got Sir Bernard's permission to say a few private prayers in the presence of the dead woman on the following morning. Soon after dawn they left their retreat and began walking to the village, very tense with excitement and anxiety.

'The important thing,' said Sylvester as they trudged barefoot through the dew, 'once we are alone with her, is to attack immediately, make no feint to right or left, advance irresistibly and rely on the advantage of surprise.'

'Whom are we surprising?' asked Robert. 'We are not taking God by surprise. He must have known all about our plan of campaign since we first meditated. Are we taking the widow by surprise? If she is going to be surprised we needn't bother, for she can't be dead.'

'We are going to take Death by surprise,' Sylvester answered confidently. 'And Death will be swallowed up in victory.'

'One thing I do ask,' said Robert, 'and that is that we try as far as possible to use only the words that the Lord Jesus used on these occasions, as we know them from the Gospels.'

'Why? Are they magic spells?' objected Sylvester. 'That gives you an advantage, because you remember the sentences of the Lord better than I do.'

'I'll give you one to start with. "She is not dead, but sleepeth." You can hold on to that one like a password.'

'We don't need words so much as faith,' Sylvester declared. 'If you have a kernel of faith no bigger than a grain of mustard-seed you can face a mountain squarely and order it: "Hey, you! Mountain! Pick up your accoutrements, leave this post, and go on picquet over there. Move!" And it will move.'

'That's very true. Thank you for saying it, Sylvester,' said Robert with genuine humility, greatly impressed. 'But don't forget prayer and fasting.'

'We've done all that,' Sylvester replied impatiently. 'Now's the time for action.'

They stood in the dappled daylight in the hearth-room of the cottage, which had been effectively tidied. The widow had been placed again on the trestle table. The doors were shut, but the friars knew well that they were not soundproof.

' "She is not dead, but sleepeth," ' said Sylvester in a hushed, deep voice.

"*Talitha cumi*," said Robert. ' "Damsel, arise. Take up thy bed and walk." '

' "She is not dead, but sleepeth." '

The widow lay still.

' "She is not dead, but sleepeth," ' Sylvester repeated, beginning to go red in the face from a variety of emotions.

Robert spoke with deliberation but with great urgency: 'Jesus said to her, "I am the resurrection and the life. He that believeth in me, though he were dead, yet shall he live, and whoever liveth and believeth in me shall never die." '

' "She is not dead, but sleepeth," ' Sylvester insisted.

A small sound came from the body. Robert and Sylvester gazed at the widow, and then at each other, with sudden wild hope. But nothing further happened, and they were experienced enough in mortality to recognize the settling of tissue in corruptible flesh.

'Prayer!' said Robert savagely. 'It doesn't matter about the words.' The friars dropped to their knees facing each other, and with a single impulse they reached up their hands, not with the palms closed but each gripping the fists of his companion, the tendons straining so that the hands shook, while they glared into each other's faces in agonized concentration.

After an interval they breathed out forcibly, and then with a swift intake stretched wide their arms and bodies to the quivering tautness of bowstrings as they strove only to listen and distinguish the flutter of returning breath. They scrambled to their feet and looked down at the dead woman. Nothing had changed.

' "Father," ' said Robert in utter resignation, ' "all things are possible to thee. If it be possible, let this cup pass from me. Nevertheless, not as I will, but as thou wilt." '

Then, in a roar of final desperation at the exhaustion of all his repertoire, he bellowed almost bitterly:

' "Lazarus, come forth!" '

The door opened and a shrouded figure stumbled into the room. It made its way uncertainly towards the friars, who stood transfixed with the beginnings of terror. The shroud dropped from the face and shoulders, and revealed the form of the simple lad. It had occurred to him that it would be no disrespect for the dead if he dressed up to look like his mother. He came forward with his eyes shining and removed the linen from the woman's face. The cheeks were livid, altogether unlike the features he had known, and he made no movement to kiss them but looked up, still smiling shyly, towards the brothers. They had seen in his entrance some form of a sign and, the one after the other, they enfolded him in their arms.

Robert was still trying to interpret the sign when Sylvester later commented wryly: 'So much for our apostolic mission.'

'Don't be unduly cast down,' said Robert with gentleness and serenity. 'It has occurred to me that Francis did not cleanse the leper he kissed, and he has never said that he even tried to. But Francis is an apostle. We don't question that.'

Sylvester's face creased in a momentary passion very near to hatred. 'Coward!' he said. 'Runaway! Faintheart. You lack the faith.'

'What do you mean?' whispered Robert in amazement and some fear.

'Has it really just "occurred to you"? Or did you have it in the depth of your mind all the time as an excuse to fall back on? It's all words, isn't it? Your trouble is words. You build them up, and if you don't like what they say you change their position – it means something different, but you soon get used to that. You scholars think too much. You think and think until you falter. You lack the faith. Has Francis and the leper really "just occurred to you"?'

'No,' said Robert in miserable shame. 'It has been at the back of my mind long since.'

'You're honest,' said Sylvester. 'We stay together. Pardon me as freely when I need it.'

Later in the day the widow in her cerements was carried on a hurdle to the graveyard enclosing the parish church, all the people following. With tacit acceptance the Little Brothers supported the son, leaving Sir Bernard an untrammelled stage on which he could perform without corrival all the dignities of the major funeral rite of the committal.

The four men who carried the hurdle, swinging it easily at hip height for it was not a heavy burden, were flanked by two groups of women who began to wail in a businesslike fashion as soon as the procession formed and moved. They were not professionals, but village friends of the dead woman, determined to give her a good send-off since she had no female relatives to perform this public lamentation for her. Their high wailing and keening startled the widow's son, who was walking between the two friars closely following the bier. But it provoked a resonance among the women in the main party behind. There was a space of time no longer than the interval between throwing a ruby of charcoal on to dry kindling and seeing it burst into flame. Then there came an explosion of lamentation so sudden that two horsemen who were riding on the road well ahead of the procession turned their heads, urged their horses to mount a knoll, and reined them in to wait in curiosity for the funeral to pass.

The sound swelled until it became a living chorus

entirely superseding the individuals who were making it. It was corporate mourning, a primitive alleluia of the fulfilling affirmation of bereavement, a cauterization into temporary purity of all the single lives that had stumbled blindly through the wake seeking an expression of the acceptance of death. It ended unexpectedly, clearly much more swiftly than the participants had intended, as one by one they yielded to the domination of a new sound, an insistent recognizable call of far greater musical discipline.

The simple lad was singing the song of the nightingale. He was plunging forward behind the moving bier, the friars firmly holding his arms, for his eyes were turned to the sky and he took no care as to where his feet were falling. He began with repeated high notes of extraordinary power, and these stilled the wailing. He broadened his tone into the honeyed bubbling of that passage in the bird's song which purls like the echo of a rivulet in Arcadia. The rippling melted into an unforgettable, perhaps unrepeatable, sequence – a virtuoso scattering of notes in prodigal sprays which no countryman could be sure he had ever heard before, yet which faultlessly presented the essence of the liquid song. The cadenza flowed to a natural pause and shifted into the familiar slow, repeated double call heralding the finale. The great fluting crescendo rose in phrases intensifying in pitch and volume and brilliance like waterdrops in a high fountain, and then the song was ended.

The horsemen had sat motionless while the procession passed and the boy sang. One of them, to uncover his head in deference to the dead, removed a stiff cap shaped like a crown. As he replaced it his glance swung with surprise from the entranced face of the singing lad to his grey-gowned escorts. The riders eased their horses down the slope and followed the funeral. The man with the crown gestured to his companion, who loosened sling-straps from his back and passed him a harp, a ten-stringed instrument in a frame as wide as a man's shoulders. Dropping his reins and sitting easily astride his gleaming chestnut mare, the man with the crown followed the lad's lament intently to its end, then plucked the strings of his harp and sang in a clear, warm voice as he rode at the tail of the funeral:

> Breast against thorn, the nightingale
> Bleeds out his heart, and drowns the dale.
> Song against scorn will not prevail,
> Lady, Lady, Lady.

He sang the last 'Lady' in a long cadence of caressing notes as if he would not loosen his hold on the word.

> Scorn may be counterfeit for dread.
> Fealty's vows may soil your bed.
> How pure alive, how purer dead,
>   Lady, Lady, Lady.
>
> Halberds, not thorns, assail your breast.
> Jealous that you should be possessed,
> Death makes the ultimate arrest,
>   Lady, Lady, Lady.

The cortège reached the graveyard and Sir Bernard came from the church porch to meet the body. The horsemen did not dismount, but remained outside the low wall, near which a grave had been prepared. As the followers grouped themselves around the pit the man with the crown called quietly:

'Robert.'

'Gérard,' said Robert in acknowledgment, without enthusiasm.

'I never thought I'd see you tonsured.'

'I never thought I'd see you so well mounted.'

'Gifts that God gives,' said the rider. 'Tricks of the troubadour's trade. I'm working the top circuit of the great halls of Poitou. These lords are very competitive. If they don't like your horse when you come they give you a better one when you go. It's a way of saying "Beat you!" to the last impresario and "Beat that!" to the next. Pecking order in the same poultry-yard, really, nothing to do with talent, though I'm in good form these days.'

'Where are you booked into next?'

'Château de Crespin. Messire le Vicomte de Frébois. He's an independent thinker. A friend of yours?'

'He's no friend of this lad,' said Robert. 'He has dispossessed him.'

'Pity. He sings like an angel.'

'He may be an angel.'

'Then stick to him. He could bring you salvation. You were always groping. Who's he mourning?'

'His mother.'

'Lady, Lady. God rest her soul.'

'*Requiem aeternam dona eis Domine, et lux perpetua luceat eis . . .*' Sir Bernard began to intone.

'We'll meet again perhaps?' asked the troubadour Gérard.

'Perhaps,' said Robert.

As the earth was being shovelled on to the body the lad stood on a pile of clods at the foot of the grave to see better what was happening. Since he had a higher footing, the brothers held him between them shoulder to shoulder. At first he was shattered by surprise at what he saw going on, and then, for the first time in all the crowded sequence since the death of his mother, he was deeply angry.

'Naw-naw-naw-naw-naw!' he protested, as the grave-clothes flinched under the fall of the earth and the body became a contour in the pit.

Robert made an unrehearsed gesture which was as

graceful and informative as a Saracen dancer's, diverting the lad's attention from the grave to the sky.

'She is happy with Jesus,' he said.

The lad seemed to understand and his face softened. But there was something in what Robert had said that he still could not fully accept.

'Naw-naw-naw,' he said without anger, in a very reasoned tone of voice as if he knew better and would explain if necessary. 'Me-me-me-me-me happy with Jesus.'

'*You*?' asked Sylvester.

'Me-me-me happy with Jesus.'

'*You* are happy with Jesus?'

'Um-um-um.'

'You have said it,' pronounced Robert in a sudden eagerness as if he saw the sign more surely. 'You are happy with Jesus. In the name of the Father, the Son and the Holy Ghost I baptize thee Happy-With-Jesus.' And he moistened his finger with his mouth and traced the sign of the cross over the forehead and the eyes of the boy.

'Now you are coming to live with us,' he said. 'Come home, Happy-With-Jesus.'

'Hearth and home?'

'Yes.'

'Happy-With-Jesus, hearth and home.'

They left the graveyard without a backward glance and went along together.

And at the retreat Adèle was waiting.

3

Grace at Eventide

'It's Adèle, and she seems to have brought the family,' said Sylvester with gruff pleasure. He was looking towards the clearing across the shallow combe, hatched with the light and shade of brushwood, which marked the beginning of the forest. A boisterous wind kept the far foliage shifting and shimmering. In the dell, exposed through the gap in the unfinished wall, the motionless forms of a girl and some animals teased the eye, the pointillist effect of distance and background confusing their outline. Then the girl waved. It was easy to distinguish Adèle, for in a bonneted age she rarely wore any head-covering, neither cap nor coif, snood nor wimple. She came forward a little way to meet the brothers and their ward as they climbed the last slope of the combe, Robert treading as delicately as he dared without making too ludicrous a display of his determination to espy and evade the creeping brambles. The darting wind tore at Adèle's hair, but did little more than ruffle the twists and wisps that haloed her forehead. Beneath a tremulous spray of gossamer her tresses lay shining along her back, heavy like ebony, as she bent to kiss the hands of the friars.

She stood erect and took Happy-With-Jesus by both his hands, holding them for a long interval and smiling into his eyes without speaking, a nut-brown maiden whose cheeks still soared into a carmine appleglow to round the tan. With great gentleness and reasoned continuity the lad said something which the others did not comprehend. 'Thank you very much,' said Adèle. 'It is a pretty thought, and it's something I shall never be able to prove. I doubt if even Narcissus could prove such a thing. Narcissus was a silly young man,' she added in explanation. 'He was very beautiful but he thought only of himself and never of others. He was not like you.'

'Happy-With-Jesus,' said the lad.

'It's his new Christian name,' beamed Robert. 'He chose it and I baptized him.'

'Who was his godmother?'

'It was all rather hurried,' Sylvester broke in with some embarrassment. 'He hasn't a godmother.'

'You were waiting for me,' said Adèle cheerfully. 'Happy-With-Jesus, your godmother is Adèle.'

Robert made one of his large expressive signs and it was clear that God embraced the boy through Adèle.

'I see you've brought the family,' said Sylvester to relax the sacramental tension. 'The Three Pioneers?'

There was a stir from the three animals who had been watching quietly from the dell. They were a slim boar of athletic build widely known as the pig Plantagenet, a donkey named Sobrin of impressive benignity, and a low-slung beagle called Rupert with a look of authority in his eye and a remarkable lack of doggish obsequience in his general bearing.

'Family!' Adèle repeated, raising her eyes to the Heaven whither Robert's God had just retired. 'Pioneers? Privateers, rather! There's precious little about them at the moment that makes them want to run in any family. Headstrong, wilful, set to embark on any impractical adventure without one thought of including me! Mutinies will occur in the best-adulated families and I expect a declaration of independence at any moment. Meet the Three Mutineers. No, perhaps that's not fair. They did want to give you a welcome and bring you your supper. Today, by special indulgence, they're my Three Volunteers.'

Happy-With-Jesus saw sufficiently through the verbiage to recognize that it was word-play and there was no serious quarrel with the animals. He voiced a vibrating musical call to Rupert which the beagle companionably returned. This was neither a bark nor a bay, but the singing salutation which a hound makes when it is contented, the equivalent of a purr or a whinny, and the lad reproduced it with fidelity before greeting the others. The pig Plantagenet, though not pointedly uncharitable, acknowledged the boy with a certain reserve of dignity. The donkey Sobrin, with bland goodwill, momentarily stopped switching his tail over his rump and used it as a drooping pointer to indicate the pannier of food carried on one haunch, from which he had been ceaselessly discouraging the flies.

'A feast!' said Sylvester, his eyes brightening at the sight of the basket.

'Lenten fodder. You deserve better. But I passed under the yoke to bring it to you,' laughed Adèle, raising herself on demi-pointes and extending a dancer's toe towards two small leather buckets standing upright in the grass, thonged to the curved boxwood bow by which she had carried them. 'You must drink that, whatever your taste, if only to acknowledge my humility. Cool milk, and much too cool bean pottage. That needs reheating. Off with the turves and uncover your hearth.'

'Hearth and home,' said Happy-With-Jesus.

Adèle slapped Sobrin's buttock. 'This morning's loaf, cheese and eggs, and a pâté-en-croûte that I forgot to ask my lady mother if she would miss. To crown it all with a crown of thorns, a butcher's broom; because you're not paying sufficient attention to your floor. Ask my clean, trim, tidy pig, my salutary sanitary inspector Plantagenet.'

The lean pig flashed her a glance of mollified appreciation, and slightly softened the stare he had been directing at Happy-With-Jesus, who had already taken a great leafy switch from its lashing on the outside of the pannier.

'What is butcher's broom?' asked Robert.

'Knee holly,' said Adèle. 'Very good for sweeping. But if it sheds any spines be sure to pick them up, or you'll be dancing on the prickles.' She looked swiftly into his face to see if she had offended him and impulsively sank onto her heels, took his left foot and cradled it in her thighs, fondling and soothing it with her adept milkmaid's fingers. 'Tenderfoot, tenderfoot,' she said. 'Francis was doubly callous when he ruled out sandals for you.' She kissed the instep, eased the foot back to the ground, and leaned forward to kiss the other instep.

'That is where the nails were driven,' she said. 'Rocks and brambles are no great agony compared with His. But wash them often,' she commanded, rising to her feet. 'Scrape limestone into the water, for the chalk is good against infection, and wipe them clean with fiddle-dock leaves.'

Robert was gazing at her with a face all warm confusion, his mind outstripped by the mercurial variations in her tutelage. 'And don't forget to dry between your toes,' she added mischievously, allowing him no respite for adjustment and no pause for veneration. 'Now you must see to your suppers, for I have promised myself the luxury of an evening retreat with my father, enriched by the genial if clouded understanding of the triple entente.' And she gestured affectionately towards the animals. 'We meditate,' she explained to Sylvester, looking him full in the eyes with seeming innocence. 'We contemplate.

We don't very often hear trumpets, but, yes or no, we don't go over the moon or up the wall. Grace comes down, like eventide.' She turned and curtsied, flourished her arm in a swift, upward sweep that set the back hem of her skirt clenched in her teeth, and sprang for the shoulders of Happy-With-Jesus, leap-frogging across his head and high and wide over the croup of Sobrin where the empty pannier was still strapped, so that she landed perfectly astride the donkey's back with her hands on the ridge of his withers. 'Mutineers, march!' she ordered.

But after two paces she wheeled Sobrin and came back to the friars.

'Bless me, brothers,' she asked. 'As Francis blessed you.'

'The Lord give you peace,' said Sylvester.

'He didn't invent that,' said Adèle petulantly.

'He didn't invent peace,' said Robert. 'Are you in a difficult mood?'

'Restless,' admitted Adèle. 'Questioning. Mary, Mary, quite contrary. Don't take offence. It's my mind stretching. They're *my* growing pains, not yours.'

'He didn't invent peace,' said Robert. 'But he has accustomed people to call for it. Has it ever struck you that "peace" was an unnecessary word until they invented war? Would you like his prayer?'

'Yes, please.'

'It's the only one he taught us besides the Paternoster. It doesn't ask for anything. We adore thee, O Christ, here and in all thy churches throughout the world, and we bless thee because thou hast redeemed the world.'

'Has he redeemed the world, I wonder?'

'But he sacrificed himself on the cross.'

'He paid the ransom, but who imposed the ransom? Was it the right price? Was there a genuine pawnbroker holding something valuable to redeem, or was it a trickster offering a gold brick? Redemption is for slaves and serfs and lordly prisoners of war. It's the means by which they buy their freedom. There is always a chance that they *may* find the ransom. But *we* can't.'

Robert stared at Adèle with wary amazement. This girl, sometimes so darting and elusive that he could not focus, snap, catch her, was now a reasoning advocate deserving all attention. Robert was accustomed to the shocks of theoretical blasphemy in scholarly disputations among men. He had encountered women scholars, too, and by their worth and rarity they had been received with respect, rather than the scorn they would have incited if there had been more of them. The woman before him, restrained but vibrant with her olive-and-crimson skin and the two black bars of thickly plaited hair, was speaking with the lively gravity of a Greek goddess – before Time and the Turks washed colour and corporeity from the Greek divine and left it ghostly marble statuary.

'Redemption is not for us? Why can't we redeem ourselves?' Robert asked unprovocatively, like a chess player advancing a pawn.

'Because we can't find the ransom. Dogma has decreed it. We have been denied our liberty. It's nothing to do with Jesus or the Jews. Divine atonement was preached before them. Long before the Nativity religion insisted that mortal man is so hopelessly condemned by sin to slavery that he can never raise the ransom to redeem himself. He can never win his freedom through his own effort. Only God can do it for him, and then only by sacrificing God's own life. Or God's own son. With the concession of the certainty of resurrection. Suppose religion was wrong. Suppose religion *is* wrong. I don't love Jesus any less because he was mistaken or deceived. . . .'

Robert broke in: 'But what are you saying? Who could have done it? God cannot mistake or deceive.'

'God led Abraham into temptation and deceived him when he urged him to kill his son Isaac as a sacrifice to God. It's not impossible that he made the same mistake with Jesus. Plenty of kings in history have sacrificed their only-begotten sons to get themselves out of local difficulties, naming them offerings against the sins of the people. I refer you to Plato or, if you don't trust my reading in that pagan area, to the second book of Kings, chapter 3, the last verse.'

'Adèle, Adèle,' said Sylvester, not belligerently but in wonder. 'How and where did you read Plato?'

'In Latin, out of the Arabic, out of the Greek. In my bedroom, which I have occupied alone since my brother went away on the Children's Crusade against those same Arabs who translated Plato – but he didn't meet any Arabs, only Christian slave-traders, and quickly died.'

'God rest his soul,' said Sylvester. 'But where did you learn to read Latin, and where do you get the books today?'

'It's not important now,' said Robert. 'We were talking about salvation.'

'We were talking about sacrifice,' said Adèle. 'Dear, dreaming Robert, don't be so dog-in-the-manger because Francis has turned you against scholarship. *It was very important* to me to be able to learn.' She turned to answer Sylvester. 'I learned books at the Castle of Crespin. From when I was very young the Vicomte de Frébois told my parents that I should be lettered. I sat with the tutor to the Vicomtesse. She is a very well-read lady.'

'Why. . . ?' Sylvester began again, but Adèle interrupted him.

'I don't question the Vicomte's charity. I was questioning God's charity to Jesus in giving him the hard choice between becoming the sacrificial or the scapegoat. I don't love Jesus any less if he was mistaken or deceived. His life was all love and his death was a slow act of love. I follow Jesus because his life and death kindle love in me. I kissed your feet, Robert, remembering his feet, and whether yours or his were hurt in error does not diminish my love. It's his love that gives me freedom. I choose to attempt my own redemption.

'For his sake but *on my own account now* I oppose shame and sometimes triumph. He does not dangle his death as my ransom. I see the love that ruled his death. I see right through the mirage in between – the scales of a nicely calculated sacrifice held up to insist that because he died, willy-nilly I must pay or be damned. I exorcise that phantom. The Judge at the far mouth of Hell is gone, and instead I have my near companion. In love I follow Jesus. And because it is Francis who has shown me Jesus laughing and dancing as well as teaching, a wedding guest as well as an outlaw, perplexed by injustice as I am but acquainted with peace as well as with grief, then behind Jesus I follow Francis.'

'She follows Francis,' said Robert to Sylvester. 'Make sure she never catches up with him. Or in the riptide of her rhetoric Francis will be following her. And then we shall all be burned.'

Adèle burst into laughter and there was a stir like a drunken stagger from the high dome of a sweet chestnut tree dominating the clearing: but only Happy-With-Jesus noticed it. 'Coward!' she said. 'You've run out of argument so you smear me as a heretic. You know perfectly well that you've taught me much of what I know about Francis. You're scared for your own skins. Now bless me decently. With Francis' proper words. Bless us all decently, including my three mutineers. Francis would never withhold it.'

'The Lord bless you and keep you. The Lord make his face to shine upon you and be gracious unto you. The Lord lift up the light of his countenance upon you and give you peace.'

'Amen,' said Adèle, and she swung homewards with the animals.

Chute-Feuille, the tawny owl named for his unnatural clumsiness on the succession of tall trees where he stubbornly roosted, opened his eyes and lifted his head again from the warm shoulder-feathers within which he had been dreaming. He lurched in a comical pratfall as if good-naturedly living up to his nickname but then, like the snap of a steel trap, his uniquely flexible outer toes swivelled backwards and his powerful claws, two fore and two aft, bit into the chestnut wood. He watched the little party move away while the men began to prepare their supper. Adèle's laughter had awakened him early and her departure snatched him from the additional doze he was coveting. But daylight was fading and he decided on the agony of a reconnaissance before serious hunting. To compensate for his uncoordinated balance he had become an enthusiast for fitness, convinced that no exercise was good unless it was painful, and a test flight even at twilight could be relied on to torture the eyes of this nocturnal bird as keenly as a kingfisher would be affected if he dared to stare out the noonday sun. Chute-Feuille cricked cautiously to his mate who was roosting in some nearby tree – they did not sleep together. There was no answer and he concluded that she was still drowsing. He launched himself stiffly, then came into his full inheritance of grace and sailed soundlessly over the homing group, idly registering certain vibrations of discord among them.

'What was all that about?' Plantagenet asked crossly as soon as they were out of earshot of the friars.

'Don't be sullen, Plantagenet,' Adèle countered. 'It was about our Lord, yours and mine, and it's no use your pretending you're out of the picture, because I distinctly caught you praising him for your sister Adèle after you'd had a happy little think on the way here.'

'Oh, I twigged the last bit,' said Plantagenet slightly more graciously. 'Make his face shine on you. I like that because it's what you do to me.' There was a pause, and the cloud which had lifted a little descended again. 'What you *used* to do to me more often,' he reflected glumly to himself – or believed he had only reflected.

'I heard you!' said Adèle, bubbling with laughter. 'We *are* sorry for ourselves today. Warn the gravedigger!'

They were speaking in the language used by all animals, which is as fast as thought and only slightly articulated. Plantagenet, absent-minded over details, was sometimes vague as to whether he had actually spoken or privately thought, and consequently was often constrained to curse himself for his bungling transparency. Adèle, with extrasensory percipience, could understand and speak this language, but the gift was rare among humans and full mutual communication was phenomenal.

When Adèle spoke her own language she was quite intelligible to Plantagenet, Rupert and Sobrin so long as she was speaking to them direct. An animal understood a human in proportion to the intensity of the emotional bond between them, whether it was love or hate. In general the talent was limited to domestic animals, who had more experience of these extremes of feeling than their cousins in the wild, and therefore had more practice in interpreting. But accuracy depended on confrontation. Eavesdropping was less reliable, and for a number of reasons Plantagenet had not understood all that Adèle had said to the friars. Chute-Feuille, who had excellent hearing, had dismissed Adèle's lively defiance of heresy and Robert's subsequent blessing as an undersong no more significant than the babbling of the wellspring near the friars' retreat which the owl himself patronized as a common utility. The free animals of the plain and the forest hardly bothered with human language except to mimic it with grotesque versions of the swearwords they heard. Though they often suffered violence from men the enmity was general rather than particular, based on blind genocidal fear, not individual knowledge. Since the men did not even know the proper names of the diverse creatures they were told they hated, they could hardly communicate with them in terms more explicit than the clichéd obscenities which they applied impartially to a lapsed concubine, a lame horse or a blunt razor.

Adèle urged Sobrin into a canter. Plantagenet, smarting under her call for the gravedigger, decided that Erebus or some other spiteful son of Chaos had decreed a punitive period of Nobody Understands Me. It was a state of mind he had once been well used to, but he had been hoping he had grown out of it. He grimly criss-crossed his short legs as he kept up with Sobrin's stride, running at the donkey's heels in a self-imposed martyrdom which subjected him to divots in his face and mud in his eye – but preserved him from any obligation to launch polite observations or absorb crude banter which might have arisen if he had trotted alongside. Rupert the beagle cruised steadily ahead at his usual pace-setting rate. The moat and wall of the home farm at La Tranchée came into sight and they pattered over the beams of the drawbridge. Without dismounting, Adèle called to her mother that she was home and rode Sobrin sedately round to the stables. In the cowshed she found an old skirt, smelling somewhat sourly of spilt milk, and threw it over Sobrin. She dunked his nose into one end of a very long, low hay-trough and half-heaved, half-bullied Plantagenet into the middle of it. She leapt into the length that was left and flung herself on her back along it, her hands clasped under her head and one foot wriggling companionably in a fold of Plantagenet's neck.

'Sky, loose your dragons and burn out the clouds,' she said. 'Sirius the Scorcher, cauterize the firmament. I want no cloud, rack, scud or nebula tonight. Tonight I shall lie here star-gazing and see seven bright jewels in one tiara: the six-point crown of Rigel, Aldebaran and Capella, Pollux, Procyon and Sirius, with Betelgeuse at the arch of the mitre and a hundred clusters in the diadem. Sky, loose your dragons and give me clear sight. A-a-a-a-ah!' In utter physical relaxation, without reflecting any of the drama she amused herself with in her words, she stretched in the hay and made small movements to snuggle down into it as she looked upwards.

'Oh, my oracular tongue!' she exclaimed. 'It's going to rain.'

The night was darkening fast. Remnants of ragged black cloud were passing indecisively across the face of the moon, but the weather was changing. The scurries of surface wind had died in the farmyard and the slowing of the tempo was matched in the sky. The tattered clouds halted and seemed to dissolve. The trees ceased their restless chattering in the wind and a brooding silence began a gradual domination. To the northwest a low, dark bank of nimbostratus was spread over the whole horizon and imperceptibly advanced as if the globe of the earth was slowly wheeling into it. This was where the weather was coming from.

The little group in the farmyard lay long without motion, separately, not as if overborne by a sweep of the wing of one enchantress angel, but like breathing statues each pondering an individual past and future. Then Plantagenet broke the stillness.

'What was that lad saying to you before you told him you were his godmother?' he rasped.

'He said that the skin behind my ears was as white as the blossoms of the blackthorn when they come in

March, all solitary on the black stem before the leaves appear.'

'Poetry!' said Plantagenet.

'I like poetry. So do you when you've thought of it yourself.'

'Anything else?'

'He said my hair shone blue like the sloes the blackthorn bears in autumn.'

'Blue hair?' said Plantagenet sarcastically.

'Black, really. You know the colour of sloes.'

'I've never much cared for sloes. Though I must say my friend Hurlaud seems to savour them.'

'Hurlaud of the Great Woods, lord of the wolves!' said Adèle in mock astonishment. 'And he's a friend of yours! My, my, we do move in noble circles. And how did this friendship come to be established?'

'Tha bugger!' said Sobrin in his first and only contribution to the conversation, and he was so overcome with the enormity of his remark that he hiccupped into a nervous bray which he suppressed after one hysterical hee-haw.

Plantagenet rode the whirlwind and redirected the storm. 'Did he say any more?' he asked Adèle.

'Who? Hurlaud?'

'That lad.'

'He said my eyes were green like the underside of lime leaves when the sunlight bounces from the foliage below.'

'*Is* the underside of a lime leaf pale green?'

'Yes. The lime is a tall tree,' said Adèle almost apologetically, because she sympathized with Plantagenet's occasional disgust at his hereditary short-sightedness. 'The leaves often don't start until quite a distance from the ground.'

'How did he manage to tell you all that rigmarole

about blackthorn and lime leaves? I've never heard him say much to any other human.'

'We understand each other,' said Adèle gently, 'much as you and I understand each other. We don't greatly need all those complicated syllables. You get on with him all right, don't you?'

Plantagenet did not immediately answer.

'Rupert does,' said Adèle, easing the dialogue into a more general orbit.

'Absolutely,' said the beagle. 'He's a very nice chap. Affable, distinctly affable. Good scout. No side. Knows more about us than most of the mandrakes put together.'

Plantagenet swiftly swivelled a shrewd eye towards Adèle, but could draw no conclusion in the gloaming. 'Mandrakes' was a term used by the free animals to describe humans, and Plantagenet and Rupert had picked it up from their friends in the forest. It was basically offensive, since it referred to the fact that the most frequent contacts between wild animals and humans occurred when the men were shrieking with passion or the Dutch courage of war-whoops, displaying the same implausible degree of overkill as the two-legged root of the mandrake was reported to register when it howled as it was plucked from the ground. Plantagenet was curious as to how Adèle would respond. She merely smiled.

'How could he tell that the skin behind your ears was as white as hawthorn blossom?' persisted Plantagenet in single-minded truculence.

'Blackthorn blossom. I suppose he saw it when I bent to kiss Robert's hand.'

'Why did you say you could never prove it? Who is this person Narcissus?'

'Narcissus was always admiring himself in a forest pool. Have *you* ever seen the skin at the back of your ears while gazing downwards into a forest pool?'

'Blackthorn!' snorted Plantagenet. 'I'd never compare anyone *I* liked with blackthorn. Does he like you? Blackthorn is what the mandrakes make cudgels from. You ask Sobrin. He's had his share of blackthorn.'

'Leaping-poles,' said Rupert in a gallant attempt to divert Plantagenet's ill humour.

'What do you mean, leaping-poles?' asked Plantagenet, falling for the beagle's ploy.

'The mandrakes use them for vaulting hedges and ditches. The best are made from blackthorn, though it's difficult to find wood of sufficient length. When I was younger, in England, and went out in a pack, the mandrakes used to follow with these poles, and the best of them could keep up with any horseman.'

'You went out in a pack?' said Plantagenet in a tone of total accusation. 'Did you hunt?'

'Yes, actually. I was brought up to hunt. My people always hunted.'

'What did you hunt?'

'Hare.'

'Did you like it?'

'Hare? Yes. Excellent.'

'Hunting.'

Rupert was becoming increasingly uncomfortable. Adèle intervened to rescue him. 'Rupert was young,' she said. 'All of us were silly when we were young. Anyway, don't start on this hunting routine. I have personally seen you in the farmyard stalking a week-old chick with intent to devour, and if you weren't approaching a private orgasm my bedroom window must be double-glazed with horn. Rupert is very brave to mention it at all. I can remember a pig who used to fall down in fright at the very mention of Hurlaud of the Great Woods, and he never speaks of that at all now.'

Plantagenet was saved from admitting his confusion by the arrival of Maister Brémand. Adèle's father was a stocky, muscular, well-weathered man who strangely combined a bustling manner with an air of deep pre-occupation. He greeted them all kindly, sat down and put his hand under Rupert's jaw to fondle him. The lower air was now completely still, although the black hood of cloud above came gliding on like a closing canopy. After a short time Maister Brémand shivered but, instead of drawing his short cloak more closely around him, he leaned forward and draped it over Adèle's body in the hay.

'Frost,' he said. 'You can feel it falling.'

There was another pause, then he stood up decisively. 'Supper,' he said. 'Rupert, don't stay but come in with Adèle. We have to go to Henriot's immediately afterwards.'

4

Conduct Becoming a Gentleman

When Adèle left the farmyard the beagle Rupert stood, looking quizzically at Sobrin and Plantagenet, and then followed her into the house.

Rupert was sensitive. He did not like to leave a party as part of a sheepish surge of guests. He held that a bung should never be yanked from a barrel when the tap could be delicately turned, and he appreciated how the tidying up of conversations, even including tolerant comments on departed company, amused, flattered and healed the hosts after the tension of hospitality.

Rupert had learned this delicacy of understanding from his own experience. He was a beagle. All hunting hounds are ultimately of French descent, but the beagle had been exclusively developed in England from French and Welsh stock for so many decades that, when Rupert arrived in Poitou as a solitary symbol of the cultural exchange between England and Aquitaine, he was regarded with snobbish adulation from one sector of his new world, though inevitably with chauvinistic disdain from another. Rupert, bred in straight descent from a proud line of long-accepted English hounds, was, like the humans of his country, a little standoffish but perfectly polite, and at heart a caring creature.

He had been a gift to Maister Brémand, as a token of

the lord's esteem for an excellent tenant, from Messire le Vicomte de Frébois, who from his castle at Crespin held suzerainty over a considerable part of Poitou, though he was deliberately vague as to where his own fealty lay. He had sworn allegiance to his overlord, the King of England and Duke of Aquitaine, when the new King was a boy of nine; but eight years had passed, the kings of France were dying with depressing regularity and their successors were each asserting with increasing force their sovereignty de facto and de jure over Aquitaine.

Brémand considered the acquisition of Rupert as a matter of great prestige, and he made sure that, whenever Messire de Frébois visited him, he should note the hound's good condition. Never before had a mere yeoman farmer owned so aristocratic a dog, and in unbounded pride Brémand considered nothing too good for Rupert. The beagle's lively eye and shining coat were the best witnesses of the golden life he led. He was housed in a comfortable kennel which was regularly repainted in the colours of the Seigneurie de Frébois. This miniature palace was blazoned with a leather plaque bearing the beagle's name set under the arms of Crespin. Rupert's collar, of red leather encrusted with golden studs, was the badge of his full membership of the household, for he was the only dog allowed inside at mealtimes, and Brémand always gave him the best titbits. None of this adulation unduly affected his vanity. Those who knew him well recognized him as an unaffected good friend. At first sight his characteristic reserve projected the image of a haughty seigneur, but anyone who bothered to establish a deeper relationship quickly discovered a perfect gentleman.

At the end of a belt-tightening supper, where Rupert accepted the usual meat offerings and first-fruits, Maister Brémand called for his horse Lancier, kissed his womenfolk, and set out with Rupert through the now dismal weather for the neighbouring farm at La Fiallerie. As he approached the gate he found himself barred first by the line of hurdles and then by an impenetrable cage surrounding the portals. It was made up of the interlocked shafts of boar-spears with sharp spearheads making a set of *chevaux-de-frise* above. He sounded a horn and waited. Lights appeared, and farm servants removed one hurdle from the defences, took three spearshafts from the stocks in which they were mounted and beckoned the visitors through. The mode of entrance was noted by an interested observer. This was the countdown towards the hour selected by Fulgent the fox for his final sally against Henriot.

The fox had chosen this black, sodden night as likely to discourage the guard from putting a nose outside. The angle of the windward quarter forced him to take a time-consuming detour. He advanced into the weather, and the wind bustled his scent behind him. Leaping, going to ground, gliding between tufts of turf and mounds of earth, he came within striking distance of the hurdle which had been moved for the entry of Brémand and Rupert. In the cold, brooding night nothing stirred or sounded except the breeze and the dull plash of rain which lapped into the ground. Then, very far off, he heard the cry of Baclin the wolf assembling his pack to go hunting. 'Ha!' he said to himself. 'Baclin is beating up the country near La Tranchée. I'll bet Brémand will be furious.'

Fulgent pawed the earth with a tense, trembling motion, then dashed for the hurdle, soared over it, and used his momentum to reach the base of the wall at his private point of access. The wind passing the top of the wall made a different purr from what he remembered. Looking up, he could distinguish a palisade of boar-spears. His secret entry had been discovered.

He moved back to the front portal. He leapt up on to a stone ledge supporting the frame of the main gate, which he had long marked out as commanding the means for a farewell assault on the farm when the evidence of his entry no longer mattered. Balanced on the stone, he hurriedly set teeth and claws to enlarge a gap between the sidepost of the gateframe and the mortared masonry chips of the surround. He freed the core of one segment of rubble and gently pawed it behind him to fall on the outside of the wall. He decided that the narrow hole he had excavated was enough. Carefully he stretched himself on the ledge, lengthening his body. His head passed through, then one shoulder and finally, by practised contractions of his muscles, his whole body. As softly as he could, he dropped to the ground and froze. There was no swift click of trapspring, and he allowed himself to breathe.

He made a mental note that he could never accomplish the return journey at speed with, for instance, a mastiff on his heels. In such a crisis he would have to go high, to somewhere like the roof of the barn adjoining the gatehouse, which would give him the best chance of a jump that enabled him to clear the outer ring of boar-spears without impaling himself. Fortunately they were all pointing outwards and he would not have to take them breast-on.

'We'll cross that aerial bridge when we come to it,' Fulgent told himself just inside the porch as, crouched very flat and with his eyes almost closed in concentration, he went over Picot's instructions about the traps set in the farmhouse area. One near the door on the left, one in the middle of the passage leading to the fowlhouse. He then had to follow the gutter of the drain emptying the cowsheds. There were two traps by the wall, some four fox-lengths apart, another hidden under some hay in a shallow hole by the opposite wall. Finally there were two portable springtraps just in front of the door of the fowlhouse.

One by one, Fulgent checked and avoided the traps in the passage, and as he moved slowly along he smelt every inch of the ground to detect any other contraption which the men might have set there since Picot had made his last observations. By this means he was able to locate a string that was attached to an alarm bell and fixed at half-height across the passage which gave the only possible access to the gutter. He lightly jumped over it, and spared it a smile. Using even greater care immediately outside the fowlhouse, he assessed all the features he could see and then quickly jumped high to the sill of a dormer window ventilating the fowlhouse. The window was fortified by flat bars topped with spikes, but Fulgent managed to pass between the bars.

Below him there was a living, pulsating silence, as deep as down, as all the birds slept with their heads under their wings. In the gloom the fox could distinguish vague white shapes roosting on the wooden perches inset into the walls. He held his breath for a moment, then hurled himself at one of them and rolled with it on to the damp straw below. The hen he had aimed at did not utter a sound. Fulgent had stunned it with the fall and with one snap he ensured permanent silence. Nothing stirred, only the feeble flutter of wings quickly fading. Having completed his contract he devoted his attention to getting out of the place. The inside sill of the dormer window was narrow, and after two jumps upward with his prey in his mouth Fulgent gave up the attempt.

And now all around him there began to dawn a muffled agitation as the birds slowly swam up to consciousness from deep sleep. The spread of the fox's smell began to provoke half-automatic convulsions of panic. Fulgent decided that since he could not escape while carrying his prey he should devour it on the spot. He dragged it into a more remote corner between two bundles of faggots which had been dropped and abandoned there. By rights this should have been a royal meal. But the fox had a dry throat and a constricted stomach, his mind constantly on the qui vive for the least movement around him. He realized that time was against him. He had been impractically long on his approach, unavoidably long on his entry. The stealthy detail of inspecting the traps and getting into the fowlhouse had been a matter of life or death, but it had taken its toll of the night. Now, by the time he was polishing off the fowl's heart, day was breaking. He decided to show the *métairie* of Maister Henriot a clean pair of heels.

With a bound he reached the sill. He squeezed through the bars, though with more difficulty than before. He jumped neatly down into the courtyard. The rain had stopped and in the wan light of a winter dawn he could distinguish the traps that had been set for him. A shiver ran through him as he saw a wolf-trap that had been set just under the dormer window. Picot had not warned him of this, and no doubt it had been positioned after the heron's last visit. On his take-off to jump upwards he had missed setting off the mechanism by the width of his claws. Jumping down, he had landed far beyond it. He bowed to his guiding star and, springing nonchalantly past the other traps which were now clearly visible, he soon reached the main gate. He went through his muscular diminishing exercises and started the passage through the wall-entry. Halfway through he realized that his belly, unconscionably swollen by his full meal, refused to follow his head and shoulders. He was wedged, unable to go forwards or back.

'Here a sheer hulk lies poor fox Fulgent,' he sighed to himself. 'What a death, stuck in a cat-hole to be eaten by mangy dogs!' Elongating all his sinews, he stretched himself carefully forwards, then shot violently backwards. He had got free. But the noise of his effort had awoken Cornet, the guard dog on duty near the gate. He began to bark. 'A fox! A fox in the courtyard!' With panic speed Fulgent turned and streaked across the space between the gatehouse and the door to the barn. Behind him a wild tumult was swelling.

'In the barn!' shouted a varlet who had tumbled out of a hay-bed. 'I saw him go in the barn.'

Maister Henriot almost fell out of the farmhouse door. 'Surround the barn. This time we've got him. Come on, men, I want his red bloody skin!'

Maister Brémand tumbled out after him. People were running everywhere. The dogs were unleashed. The beagle Rupert followed Brémand at a short distance, with an air of lordly unconcern. Fulgent scrambled up the bales of hay to the top of the barn, and dived through an outlet to the outside of the roof. He ran from one edge to another, poised to jump, then was suddenly overcome by a crippling fit of dizziness. The dogs had marked him on the roof and began a frightful baying below. Maister Brémand, scarlet with excitement, rapped out inconsequential orders. Henriot shook his fist at Fulgent and yelled: 'Raoul, Raoul, fetch a ladder quick. I'm going up after him.' A ladder was set against the barn. Raoul and Brémand held the foot. Henriot began to climb, with an iron-tipped club in his hands. For a moment Fulgent believed it was the end. Then, as Henriot's cap rose over the edge of the roof, the fox's mood suddenly lightened. What was the point in allowing this balk of a man to hoist himself on a barn roof twirling a murderous club with the sole object of finishing off a fox who had committed no crime beyond following his natural instincts? There was no future in that at all.

At the same time there was a thunderous knocking on the main gate. The furious barking of the dogs had been carried on the wind to a neighbour of Henriot, who knew his way through the hurdles and spears and was demanding to be let in on the kill.

Henriot put one foot on the roof. To keep his balance he put down his club in the gutter and heaved himself over with both hands. Fulgent took off from the peak of the thatch and charged. The shock was violent. Fulgent had connected with Henriot's thigh, and bit deeply into it. Henriot shrieked with pain, slipped on the slope, and shot down the ladder, bottom first, in a classic 'no hands' position. He hit Raoul and Brémand, who collapsed like sacks. The ladder veered sideways and pole-axed two men and a dog. The iron-bound club teetered in the gutter and fell vertically with the majestic finality of a thunderbolt, accurately crowning Henriot. Fulgent, with his teeth still deep in Henriot's thigh, allowed the farmer to cushion his fall, then streaked for the open main gate. Ahead of him was the palisade of boar-spears. He gathered himself, leapt like a rocket and soared over without touching the points. Never had he believed he could bring off such a jump. He raced across the open country and dived into a thicket. He estimated that he had three more bursts left in him, and he put two further thickets and an exhausting tract of marshland between him and the farm before, safely in the skirts of the forest, he could draw breath and plan a more methodical retreat. Fulgent was aware that he was in the near presence of some large manifestation of animal life, but it was not menacing, rather comforting, like the Rock of Gibraltar.

The uproar in La Fiallerie seemed not to have disturbed the forest. The white ground mist hung motionless. The gleanings of the night's rain slowly formed tears that dropped from the trees at measured intervals, like the dripping of stalactites in the cavern through which Orpheus drew Eurydice from Hades. Materializing in the haze there loomed the huge impermeable bulk of Grondin the boar, moodily prospecting for earth fruit and, like many bulky men at breakfast, constitutionally glum yet glad to welcome a reliable friend to relieve his solitude and absorb a pleasantry. Grondin had seen Fulgent cross the last brake like a ball of fire, and he now looked down on the wet and panting fox. He thought it would be rather rich to tax his friend with a hint that he knew all about Picot.

'Ho, ho, ho, Fulgent,' said Grondin. 'You look a little peaky. Are you sickening for Lummock's disease?'

'Tha bugger,' said Fulgent. 'Look out for yourself, Grondin. I have all Souligné, La Fiallerie and La Tranchée at my heels. In a few moments there will be an unholy crowd in this wood.' And the fox took up his mad dash again.

Grondin did not waste a word in reply. He doubled on his tracks and set off at speed, and it was a remarkable velocity he achieved. 'Glory be,' he grumbled, 'what sort of pickle has this scapegrace got into now?' A wild chorus behind him emphasized the prickliness of the pickle. No sooner had Grondin disappeared round the farther bend in the path to Grosses Terres than the first dogs in the pack streamed into the brushwood. Behind them rode a posse of horsemen. Henriot, crimson with fury in his face and with blood on his thigh, already outdistanced the rest. Brémand followed less energetically, incredulously rubbing his head and studying the thick silhouette of Henriot ahead of him as he asked himself how he could still be alive after taking that gut-sack on his head. Very far behind wheezed the two draught horses of La Fiallerie, on which two of Henriot's varlets were clumsily perched. Buffard and Cornet, two dogs from La Fiallerie, led the chase. As long as the trail was fresh they could keep going, but they could not be expected to keep touch for long. They were guard mastiffs, and rarely hunted. They led a dozen brawling curs as little gifted as themselves. Rupert trotted behind Maister Brémand with an air of distaste for the whole business. He had had a good laugh at the confusion Fulgent had wrought on the Henriot household, and regarded the fox with quiet admiration. He at least was a worthwhile opponent, clearly surpassing in dash and daring the gang of tykes who were chasing him.

Fulgent had quickly made up his mind that his only chance of safety was to confuse the trail and cross his tracks as much as possible. He covered considerable ground, turning on his tracks in thickets and clearings and penetrating very deep into the thick forest. After running three leagues he reached Malperthuis and again wheeled to cross the trail. Then he made straight for the river Guirande and swam across it. He ran back towards the edge of the forest for two leagues and then he swam across the river again. At this stage he decided to lie up, and he made for the lair of Hurlaud the lord of the wolves. In a state of fair exhaustion he came in at a jog-trot and asked if Hurlaud would extend his hospitality for a few hours.

He flopped down on a bed of dry leaves, breathing heavily. Hurlaud, good-natured, aristocratically hospitable but a little perturbed, waited until Fulgent had recovered his breath. 'It will take a clever fellow to find you here,' he told the fox when he had heard some of his story. 'But it was a bit rash to storm the farm like that. Don't get me wrong, I can't stand the sight of Henriot, still less of his curs. But you took a chance, old man. You might have lost more than your brush in those traps, and where would the next generation be then?' And he began to laugh. Fulgent joined in. They knew each other very well, and had even organized a few expeditions together. There is more than honour among highwaymen, there is a certain solidarity.

By now the hunt had long lost the scent. After two hours' punishing gallop through underwood and clearings, from thicket to high timber, they were hopelessly confused. Henriot caught up with his now spiritless mongrels and Brémand caught up with Henriot. At this point the dog Buffard was staring glassy-eyed and with lolling tongue at yet another crossed track, and simply lay down in disgust. Henriot almost had a fit. He screamed abuse and threats, thrashing around with one hand holding his iron-tipped cudgel while his other fingered the axe at his saddle. Brémand tried to calm him. 'We can do nothing for the moment,' he said. 'The fox has clearly crossed his tracks. But where is Rupert?' he ejaculated in sudden surprise.

Rupert was bringing up the rear with a more and more detached air as if the fury of this coarse and uncultivated master of hounds disgusted him.

'Ah, Milord,' said Henriot with ugly sarcasm, 'you take the matter lightly. Look at your fellows. Up till now they have done all the work. I should have thought that you would be the leader of this hunt rather than follow the coat-tails of your master. Is this how you earned the laurels you arrived with, or did you pilfer them from a gravestone on the way? You are hardly doing Maister Brémand much credit, and as for Messire de Frébois, I don't know that he'll keep your name on the rolls of the aristocracy.'

Rupert's only reaction was to sit down without paying the least attention to the taunts of Henriot, who promptly applied them direct to Brémand.

'We can hardly say your beagle's on form today, my friend. I don't know where these animals get the reputation that's handed out to them. It must have been lies in the first place and snobbery ever after.'

Brémand was very hurt. He bit his lips and said nothing, but he cast a look of suffering reproach at Rupert.

So effective was Brémand's silent plea that Rupert got

up in a bound, turned round on himself sniffing the wind, and plunged off purposefully the way they had come, sounding off from a find to a check, from a check to a view halloo which would have awakened any dead in the vicinity. This sudden voicing caused much confusion in the rest of the pack. Cornet, who still had a trace of the scent from the cross-point where Buffard had given up the ghost, began to bark again, more out of bravado than conviction, and launched himself with apparent great confidence on a track entirely different from the one Rupert had taken. The rest of the pack followed Cornet, baying dutifully as long as Henriot's eye was on them. Brémand looked at the two rival expeditions rapidly departing in different directions, and promptly followed Rupert. Henriot, who thought Brémand was severing relations with him because of his clumsy gibes at the beagle, followed Brémand to try to patch it up. The two horsemen were therefore following the solitary Rupert, who ran like the wind towards the Guirande. When they came to the bank they were astonished to see the dog plunge into the water and swim across. 'He's got it!' said Brémand in a voice half-strangled with sudden excitement. 'He's got the real trail, Henriot. Let's follow him from this side.'

With Rupert on the far bank, the horsemen on the near, the remnant of the hunt pounded along the Guirande for some time. Then, just as Fulgent had done, Rupert swam back across the river. He scrambled ashore under the noses of the two riders who were almost slavering with admiration. 'Hey,' asked Brémand, 'what do you think of him for a real hunting hound? The point is, Henriot, that these beasts are used only to hunt in good company. That pack of mongrels led him astray. Certainly he followed them, but only to please us. I'd put my hand in the fire on it, that scamp had his own ideas about the fox's whereabouts from the very beginning.'

Brémand was enjoying himself in getting his own back, and Henriot wisely said nothing. For a long time there had been utter silence from the rest of the pack. Cornet had in fact lost himself again. The dogs realized that none of their masters was following them and they took the first opportunity to call it all off and dribble back to the farm servants, who had long given up their draught horses and were following on foot a long way behind.

Rupert sniffed the wind again, checked it with the ground and darted into the forest. The farmers followed, but they were making very slow progress through the hawthorn thickets and the running snares of the brambles. Soon they had to dismount. Brémand proposed that they should tie up the horses in a clearing; he himself would stay with them to shout for Henriot to home back on him and, since this was Henriot's affair, his neighbour should follow Rupert and quickly settle his account with the fox, who certainly could not be very far from where they were. Rupert was to be relied on to bring him to his prey. A searing twinge in Henriot's bloodied thigh made him accept the proposal with zeal. He had enough endurance in his body and hatred in his heart to follow Rupert to the end of the world if necessary. Without a word more he unhitched the axe which hung at his saddle and trudged after the beagle. The going was very difficult. He sweated, snorted, cursed as he disentangled himself from brambles and stumbled over dead wood. He had to cleave with his axe and beat with his cudgel to clear a path.

For some twenty minutes Henriot plunged after the dog, who was giving good voice ahead of him. Suddenly there was silence. 'He's found him!' Henriot shouted aloud as he bounded forward. 'I'm going to kill that cacraminous pizzellopy, that jakesical . . .' and he began a list of earthy epithets which conveyed his passionate personal appraisal of the fox who had plagued him. The curses mounted into battle slogans, stoking up his fighting fury like separate tots of rum. 'Let me get at that blerblerblerblerbler, that sossossossossoss, that barbarbar. . . .' The last word suddenly stuck in his throat. In a tiny space of open ground ahead of him he saw Rupert standing stock still with his tail stiff. Three lengths ahead of Rupert, standing upright on his hind legs, with his front paws nonchalantly crossed on a dead spur low in the trunk of a larch, was the fox Fulgent, looking vastly amused. Covering him from right and left, braced ready to pounce, their bodies taut as bowstrings, their eyes flashing, were the wolves Baclin, Pernale and Hurlaud. Three of the most formidable beasts in the forest were ranged in support of the fox. Their appearance was infinitely more menacing than Henriot could ever have believed. His face convulsed and blanched, and the sweat on it ran icy as he gazed at the deep fangs Hurlaud was baring, and the fire in the yellow eyes.

Rupert made three steps to the side to protect the man who had followed him. Hurlaud registered the movement with his eyes but did not budge an inch of his body. He knew this dog Rupert. Though he was no normal menace to the wolves, a conscientious leader owed it to his pack to file intelligence on all elements of the opposition. The beagle was plucky, seemingly skilled as a tracker, but clearly no match for a wolf. Hurlaud accepted the fight that was now to follow as virtual single combat. His mate and his brother would not come in against the dog. The man with the axe was a feeble adversary. He was trembling with fear, and every one was aware of it.

For a few long moments the adversaries studied each other. Baclin made a feint to outflank to the right. Rupert bounded to face him, his hind legs tense, snarling in a subdued tone. Henriot felt the cold sweat seep into his temple. He wanted to call for help, but no sound emerged from his tightened throat. He had come across a wolf or two in the forest in his time, but never in full confrontation, and three was too much. Like a true peasant, he knew the saying: 'Whoever sees three wolves is a dead man.' He weighed up the size of the beasts, their wild eyes, their gaping jaws baring teeth and gums shining with saliva. There was silence all round, not a sound from the distant pack. Brémand might well hear him if he shouted, but certainly would have no time to reach him.

Very slowly, still facing the animals, Henriot retreated inch by inch, swallowing with difficulty. He reached the thorn bushes which he had just come through, then turned swiftly and dived straight into them, screaming for help as he ran.

None of the animals moved a muscle, save for a tic in the cheek of Hurlaud which might have been the beginning of a smile.

Rupert stayed to meet his fixed fate. His small build would not permit him to hold his own for long, one against so many. He rocked himself on his hocks and awaited the attack.

Hurlaud broke the silence. 'It is very imprudent of you to venture so far as here. You cannot be unaware that in these parts the law is ours and not your masters'.'

'I know that,' said Rupert in a level tone.

'You have therefore committed yourself deliberately, knowing that you could not hold out for long against us. Your friends recognize that the limit beyond which they dare not go is the clearing of Malperthuis, except under strong guard twice a year at the time of the fairs.'

'I know that, too.'

'So you are fully aware of your situation. You are lost.'

'So be it. I am at your disposal. *En garde*, Monseigneur.'

'Eh!' said Baclin with a grim chuckle. 'This good fellow is brave enough. Braver than his master.' And the other animals exchanged appreciative grins.

'I should be obliged if you would not refer to that man as my master,' said Rupert haughtily. 'It is true that he knows my master. I merely took it upon myself to lead him to you, Messire Fox.'

'Messire Fulgent des Saules,' interjected Dame Pernale somewhat punctiliously.

Rupert acknowledged her and continued addressing the fox. 'I believe he has some business with you. I have done what I set out to do.'

'And done it very well, to tell the truth,' said Hurlaud. 'You struck out on your own from that rabble of mongrels, and unravelled every trick of Fulgent. This is no small thing. I know Fulgent well. Before I had the honour of personal acquaintance with you I was not aware of anyone who could follow him so close for such a distance. You seem to me of very good breeding, Monsieur.'

'I am English,' said Rupert modestly.

'Ah, you don't come from these parts. I suspected it. Well, Milord, we wish to say that we don't seek any sort of quarrel with you. You realize that you have run very great risks, perhaps even have been foolhardy, in taking on this hunt for Fulgent so single-mindedly. But you ought to know, too, that we – the breeds of the forest whom your masters curse with such vigour and indeed obscenity – we pay a tribute of respect to your courage.

'Go your way, Milord, and may God keep you.'

Rupert bowed, and was about to withdraw when Fulgent interjected: 'I want to ask a small favour of you before you go.'

'Concerning what, Messire?'

'Oh, a very tiny thing really. You have led Maister Henriot to me. If I'm not mistaken, he just doesn't possess the mental equipment to learn the right lesson from the enormous, disinterested help you have given him – and since, as you say, this man is not your master you deserve even more credit for your action. What do you say to taking him a token tuft from my fur? He will certainly believe that you have killed me. You will enjoy a certain prestige from that. For my part I shall have peace.'

Everyone burst into sudden laughter. 'This devil Fulgent!' said Hurlaud, shaking his head in admiration. 'He can't get into any situation without making something out of it for himself.'

Fulgent bit off a tuft of his red hair and gave it to Rupert. 'I'm delighted to be of service,' said the beagle. 'I'll take it to the man you mean it for. You shouldn't have cut so deep, there's blood on this pelt,' he observed as he took the fur in his mouth. He made a courteous bow all round, and turned to go.

'There's no hurry,' said Hurlaud. 'Sit down. Have a chat. You must be tired. It's you who have been doing all the work lately. Even Fulgent has had a nap and a snack since he staggered in. Not that he had to work too hard for it, the baby snatcher. I don't think you've formally met my wife, Dame Pernale, my brother Baclin. Tell me – if you don't mind talking shop for a moment – tell me about this English craze for pack-hunting. It gives the hounds the élan of a squadron, but surely it saps a chap's individuality? Are they thinking of extending it to wolfhounds? They'd drop a terrible clanger if they did. I'm a pack-leader myself, and you might think I'm all for tightly drilled engagements, but we wolves work differently. I insist on a very high standard of independence and self-reliance in my chaps. Competence in tactical theory at staff level, of course, so that they know all the fighting options, but on the whole no brain-washing and very few orders – but when I do give an order in action I mean it to be obeyed *instantly*.' They discussed professional matters for some time, Dame Pernale herself being by no means reticent in military reminiscence, until Rupert finally excused himself and set off with his trophy to La Fiallerie.

In the farmstead there was an atmosphere of deep gloom and acrid bad temper. The menservants slouched around, cursing in antiphon against Maister Henriot who had sent them off over countless leagues in the forest without any provision for their sustenance. The motley pack of dogs lay around the courtyard in exhaustion. Cornet, with his paws swollen like flails, was morosely skiving under a cart. His mate Buffard, covered with the scratches he had taken in pushing through the thorn bushes, ostentatiously licked his wounds with an air of personified injustice. Maister Henriot was not in the peak of condition. His thigh was paining him but what smarted still more was the sting of unrequited hatred. He had managed to get clean away himself, no thanks to this rabble of hireling labourers who had lifted neither finger nor foot to help him deal with the fox. Dame Blanche was right. What a dreadful crew of layabouts he had signed on at Michaelmas.

Maister Brémand was in deep despair, sitting on the shaft of an empty cart, gazing at the ground and constantly sighing. He had not addressed the least reproach to Henriot, judging that it was not yet the occasion. But he reproached himself bitterly for having entrusted the fate of Rupert to this oaf. The poor dog was certainly dead by this time. He had given his life to defend his master's friend. What a magnificent hound he had been. Such grace, such elegance. Of course his very refinement had provoked jealousy, and no doubt there were some who were enjoying a secret smile at the news of his death. That only showed that sometimes animals were nobler than men.

He let his thoughts wander. He would take revenge. He would organize an individual battue. Of course he would be ridiculed for that. A battue for the sake of a dog, all the lords around would have a good laugh at such a suggestion. Well, he would do it on his own. He would mobilize his own men and go and teach these wretches the price of an attack on a member of the domain of La Tranchée. He would set about it no later than tomorrow. But in reality, who were the wretches? Who were the villains of the drama?

Brémand felt himself drowning in a grey flood of grief. In his active, detailed life as a practical farmer he had very rarely been touched by deep emotion. Now he was suffering in his innermost heart and he realized that he was on the verge of tears. How could one become so attached to an animal? he asked himself. Because its friendship is entire, asking nothing in exchange? Yet Rupert had his own dignity, he had not been slavish. Brémand sighed and beat his fist impotently on the shaft of the cart. What a fool this Henriot was, so dim and yet so obstinate that something of this sort was bound to happen. He could of course hardly be called a man of courage. But it is no small matter to face three wolves. Now he had put himself in the way of dining out on this experience for many years to come, no doubt discreetly omitting any reference to Rupert. But how dishonourable, to abandon a friend's dog when he alone had found the quarry; to run and leave the dog still face to face with the enemy!

All over the courtyard there was an air of sullen gloom. The men went about their tasks in a jaded and resentful way, with frequent curses and irritated gestures which conveyed a dull hostility to their master – and he was aware of it. Where there was known trouble they did their best to magnify it. One of the men who had been felled by the ladder in the dawn ambush was in a bad way, and his companions exaggerated his condition to the point of death. 'Oh, for God's sake, men, stop whining,' said Henriot in exasperation, and some shame. 'Wait for Ducquet the bone-setter. You can be certain of nothing until he has been.' Then he turned to Brémand, whose eyes were still fixed on the ground. 'Come on, Louis,' he said humbly. 'Come inside. The soup is hot.'

A sudden clamour arose by the porch and spread swiftly through the yard. 'Brémand's dog! Brémand's dog! He's come back!'

Maister Brémand was jerked in an instant out of his sombre thoughts. He sped to the porch with sudden energy. There was already a crowd there: farmhands, serving-women, dogs and even geese, attracted by the racket, were packed near the entry and formed a guard of honour. With gracious dignity, holding himself well, his tail stiff, his eyes level, Rupert advanced. The perfect gentleman as always, he took no notice of the cheers, or pretended to take no notice. He went straight to his master and dropped at his feet the tuft of hair which Fulgent had made over to him.

The watchers hushed into silence. Brémand felt his throat burn, his eyes brim with tears. He was not a man to demonstrate tenderness. He had been striving for some time to control himself, to show neither sorrow nor joy. If he had been alone with his dog, just for a moment, he would have welcomed him with an embrace. Now he held himself back. After all, Rupert himself was giving him the model for such bearing.

The dog set the tuft down in front of his master, then, without casting the most fleeting glance at the company around, still less at the stupified Henriot, he turned back towards the porch. He reached the gate, then nimbly came back, looking at his master as if a little surprised not to be followed. In the gaze fastened on him Brémand could read: 'With respect, Master, don't you think we have stayed here long enough? We really don't belong here. May I suggest, Master, that we go?'

Brémand's face set into a simple, natural resolve, uncomplicated by any suggestion of resentment or recrimination. Quickly he strode to the stables, unhitched his horse Lancier, mounted him and spurred him with both heels.

'Louis!' said Henriot, disappointed and confused. 'At least stay to supper, friend. It's being served now.'

'Thanks all the same,' Brémand replied with a smile. 'Georges and Pierre will stay. I'm off. I'm going home.' He turned at the gate. 'I have found Rupert,' he said.

At a steady trot Brémand disappeared with his dog into the underwood.

5
Summoned to Crespin

The skirts of the forest were cool but still luminous in the slanting light of a pale sun. There was the ripple of the voices of an infinitude of birds, not in congregation praising their maker nor pumping their lungs to trumpet territorial claims, but talking to themselves in the busyness of domestic evening activity. The year was young and, from his seat in the saddle, Brémand could see quite clearly into the forest as a vista, but with little security against predator animals, for the permanent tangle of underwood was thick at the height of a wolf's shoulder. Brémand kept to the drunkard's path on the border and the straighter track across clearings, if only to stamp down the fast growth that always threatened to mask a little-used way.

Lancier's hooves whisked and bruised the early-rising catkins of dog's mercury which were shooting from the creeping carpet of the plant. Rupert, who did not relish the smell of the milk from their crushed stems, ran wide on to slanting banks where the long runners of sweet violet were already thrusting, and brushed the fragrant flowers with his ears. A wood pigeon, which had been using the top of a bare ash as an observation post, waited until the party had passed, then dropped like a suicide from the crown of the tree, its half-spread wings inactive until it landed to claim beech-mast kicked up by Lancier's heels.

Brémand had a long tale to tell over supper in the farmhouse at La Tranchée, and he was looking forward to it, even rehearsing some details as he rode. For although he was a taciturn man he saw no intrinsic virtue in his nature. He was sparing of his words because little occurred to him which he judged to be worth talking about. Adèle led a no more adventurous life yet he delighted in listening to her. He recognized that her observation was keener and her imagination not only more lively but in better focus. She perceived and described daily happenings with relevant contrast, and had the same discernment, frankness and wit in narrating the sequels and contradictions that arose in her own mind. But tonight Brémand had a real *geste* to recount, from dawn drama to noonday suspense, afternoon tragedy and evening triumph. He greatly fancied the rare opportunity as he rode into his home yard, saw his family and dependents running to meet him, stiffly dismounted and gave Lancier's reins to his old manservant Edmond.

'What a day!' he said self-indulgently. And he got no further.

'What a day!' roared his wife, Dame Matilda. 'Where have you been all this time? The castle, the castle, Château Crespin. You're summoned. What have you done? Messire le Vicomte has always been so good to us. A noble gentleman, always drank your wine to the last drop. What have you done? Monsieur Jehan has been here. Drank your wine, too, in spite of the summons. Adèle, Adèle, she must go as well. What have you done? What's to become of her? She's to be married.'

'Married!' said Brémand, incredulous. 'She's been to the castle before without getting married.'

'She had better be married,' screamed Dame Matilda thickly. 'She was only a slip of a girl when she used to go for schooling. Can you trust that scum up at the castle? Dirty nobility! Drink our wine while they look over our daughter. I'm not saying the Vicomte. . . . He'd never. . . . Thank God for the Lady Eléonore. She'll see that our poor Adèle comes to no harm. Not that I trust her. Not as far as I can throw her. She runs a Court of Love at Crespin. So did her cousin, the other Eléonore who became Queen of England. Court of Love! Her grandfather set up a brothel in a nunnery in Niort with his own mistress as the abbess. Fancy our Adèle an abbess! I'd sooner she was married. But so was Eloïse. She was an abbess, and married too. What have you done, you lump, standing there and saying nothing! Why have you got to go to the castle with Adèle? Is it the Lady Eléonore making eyes at you now? She should never have let her cousin go to England. English vice! English vice! It's the English who are at the bottom of this.' Compensating for her emotional imbalance with an extraordinary physical equilibrium, Dame Matilda launched an astoundingly accurate kick at the rump of Rupert, who was forced forward for three full paces, but halted in a composed manner as if he had completed a planned military movement.

'Never touch my dog again,' Brémand ordered in a voice like a sword on a grindstone.

'Now, what exactly has happened?' he asked. And his eyes went to Adèle.

'Monsieur Jehan, the master of horse at Crespin Castle, was here,' Adèle explained. 'He asked very courteously that you should wait on Messire le Vicomte de Frébois at the castle, and said that the Vicomte would esteem it a special favour if you would have me accompany you. He said the Vicomte assumed you would bring Rupert, since he was always interested to see how the dog was getting on. That is all I heard him say about the visit, though he made his usual polite remarks about the good order in the farm.'

'So you did not hear him discuss your marriage?'

'Not my marriage,' said Adèle demurely but with a reserve of humour, 'nor the peculiar nunnery founded by William Duke of Aquitaine and Count of Poitiers, nor my future as an abbess, nor anything in my stars.'

'He must have taken your mother aside to pass on all these secrets. Where did he lead you, wife? Was it cold in the dairy? Did he show you how the Lady Eléonore was making eyes at me? Did he mention he fancied you himself? When you were half as thick in the trunk as you are now it was the Vicomte who fancied you.'

'Don't be disgusting,' said Dame Matilda, with no great emphasis.

'I have a good tutor,' said Brémand. 'I must bribe Edmond to keep an eye on you when we go to the castle. When is it to be? No one has mentioned that.'

'On Friday. And you're a fool, Brémand,' said his wife.

'There are two entire suppers between now and then,' said Brémand, 'and I want one of them within five minutes. As for my being a fool, a fool knows more in his own house than a wise man in another's, and even a fool must occasionally be right if only by the spin of fortune's wheel. I'll have you spied on. And I'll have Rupert protected. The rules of war will be an eye for an eye, a kick for a kick. And never forget that you present a far broader target than he does.'

'Supper is ready now,' said Dame Matilda. 'And you're still a fool.' But she tolerated an echoing slap on the upper cliff-face of a buttock as Brémand turned her by the waist and took her inside for a meal.

'What a day!' said Maister Brémand as he took up his soup spoon in one hand and lowered a preliminary slice of prime beef into Rupert's mouth with the other. He glanced round the table to ensure that his audience was all attention. 'Where is Adèle?' he suddenly demanded.

'Adèle? I thought she was here!' said Dame Matilda in some alarm. 'Adèle! Adèle! She was here a moment ago.'

'Where is Adèle?' Brémand repeated, and gazed like an inquisitor at the servants.

'She may have just slipped back to the stables,' ventured Edmond. 'That was where she came from when you rode in.'

'Fetch her,' commanded Brémand sternly.

'I'm very sorry, Father,' said Adèle, darting in and grafting a kiss on the farmer's cheek. 'You came in with such a clatter that I rushed to see you and didn't have time to say "Good night".'

'Good night to whom?' Brémand's eyes went round the table again, counting heads.

'To my owl.'

'Since when have you had an owl?'

'Since he came to call on me. Tonight.'

'Do you have to say "Good night" to him?' Brémand asked, more tolerantly. 'He's in great want of a bird that will give a groat for an owl. Couldn't you just leave him to go and howl on his own?' He was pleased with his facetiousness, and he ploughed on. 'Let him know you don't give a hoot for him.'

'But I do. And, anyway, he's far too grand for that,' said Adèle. 'In fact, I call him Grand-Duc. He's an eagle owl. I owe him all the respect due to a teacher.'

'So he's teaching you,' said Brémand, still striving to be playful, but feeling the prickle of desperation that his great narrative of suspense was about to be drowned in small talk. 'What is he teaching you?'

'Astronomy,' said Adèle.

There was an agonized shout from her father. 'I refuse to take this fantasy any farther. Everyone sit down and get on with your supper.' Brémand firmly planted his spoon in his soup, and swept a slow authoritative stare from diner to diner. He lifted the spoon to his mouth, and his tongue pressed the soup appreciatively against every bud in his palate.

'What a day!' he began, and at last he continued.

6

The Eccentricity of Lulu the Hare

On the following morning all the work at La Tranchée was done within and around the moated walls of the farm. The lambing season had suddenly peaked into intense activity, and the ewes had been brought into folds and shippens for their safety. Rupert had no clear duties when most of the humans were acting midwife, and he decided to go into the country for some exercise.

He made a social call at the retreat of the Little Brothers, who were busy weaving hazel shoots into hurdles which they hoped to exchange with the villagers for food later in the day. Happy-With-Jesus, who was not very handy in the actual manufacture of the hurdles, was chopping the sinuous branches with a billhook in the wood nearby. Rupert exchanged a caress and a few high-spirited barks and professional voicings with the lad, and moved on to further exploration. In the rough land to the south of the forest he hit off the drag of a hare and, following his nose, worked along to her form and put her up from the grassy depression where she had been crouching.

The hare bounded tantalizingly up, sideways, forward, then streaked across the land in a wide arc of a circle which Rupert meticulously followed. At one point the hare stopped and stood on her hind legs to assess the strength of the pursuit. There was little menace or fear apparent in the beginning of the chase. It was almost as if the hare, by nature a solitary creature but perhaps bored in an interval between the chimings of her biological clock, took the opportunity to pass the time by accepting a sporting challenge.

The beagle was bound by his own habits, and worked by scent more consistently than by sight. The hare had an initial advantage in speed over Rupert, particularly when choosing uphill slopes, where the great flails of her hind feet, printing the ground ahead of her forepads, sent her shooting towards the horizon. Occasionally she would deliberately slow her speed, allowing Rupert to get within twenty yards of her, while she made her judgment of the pace at which he could travel.

The hare knew the country by heart, and, when she came to a hare-track she recognized, she decided on a diversion. She increased speed, thundered along the track to the form where she knew another hare was crouching, swerved at the last minute to alter her line of approach and leapt like a virago into the hollow. She took the retreat by storm and forced out its occupant, who sprinted in panic and fresh velocity out into the field at an angle to Rupert's approach course. At the same time the first hare screamed. The noise was enough to make Rupert lift his head and sight the fresh hare pounding through the grass far to the right of his line. He swerved to follow, and finally got a homing course on the second hare. But his nose told him that the quarry was different. He abandoned the line and cast himself to try to recover the original scent. Being a hound of some experience in the wiles of the hare, he did not search aimlessly. After a quick, routine nosing around the point where he had declared his nolle prosequi, he turned in a very workmanlike fashion and followed the fresh hare's trail back to the form from which she had been ejected.

The first hare saw him returning and, with increased respect for her pursuer, leapt out high and fast from the form and set off again at speed. At the empty form Rupert cast himself again to find the scent he was after, and soon the hunt had recommenced. The hare had good reason not to let herself be evicted from this patch of countryside, and she tried a few more tricks. She put on a burst of speed which took her over the brow of a hill well ahead of Rupert. Then she stopped and ran her foil by darting back twenty yards on her own tracks, and made a mighty sideways leap and crumpled where she fell, clapped close to the ground. She watched Rupert pound breathily past, reach the end of the scent, stop to ponder, and again cast himself before returning on his tracks.

At this point the hare decided to rely on diplomacy rather than another exhausting bout of evasive action. She glided, not very gracefully, to put a farther useful distance between herself and the squat from which she had bounded, and when Rupert began to nose around the squat she sat up and hailed him.

'That was good sport,' she said. 'I suppose we could have gone on for hours but I have things to do this morning. We haven't met before. My name's Lulu. What's yours?'

Rupert was completely astonished, caught most uncharacteristically off guard. 'Beagle,' he finally said, very stiffly.

'Of course you're a beagle. I've never seen one of your kind before, but I've heard all about your breeding. The mandrakes are going all jokey with genetic engineering, aren't they? I'm very sorry for you and I know it's not your fault. You're a handsome fellow and I particularly like the line of your head, but you must admit your belly's pretty close to the ground. It may be good for your nose but it rather cuts your speed, don't you find?

Not to speak of that plethora of confusing erotic stimuli you must experience in long grass. If you're a beagle you're new to this country and you must be Rupert. You're very much admired among the free animals, you know. The forest is ringing with your praise. Well met, Rupert. Welcome, Rupert.'

'Thank you very much,' said Rupert, mollified by much of what he had heard but not understanding it all. 'I'm delighted to meet you, Madame . . . Lulu.'

'Anyway, did you like the sport? Did I give you a good run? Of course, I could have shaken you off for good if I had run up that outcrop of scree on the farther hill. It doesn't hold my scent and I could have come into grassland again from any point on its edge. I shouldn't be giving you these tips which may be used in action against me, but I like you. Do you find me attractive?'

'Madame,' said Rupert. 'Whatever your attraction for me, I really should point out that this is the moment when I'm supposed to chop you.'

'*Chop*,' said Lulu. 'Meaning, I take it, to slaughter en passant, to kill in cold blood rather than in the heat of the chase. How crude your professional hunter can be sometimes. I'm sorry it has rubbed off on you. *Chop*. One child of nature is speaking to another child of nature and he casually mentions *chop*! You sound like an axeman-at-arms offhandedly cleaving a peasant by the wayside. Are you hungry?'

'Hungry?' stammered Rupert. 'Not at all.'

'I'm glad to hear it, and you certainly don't look it. You're in glorious condition. That's a really beautiful coat and I congratulate you on it. Have you had breakfast? What did you eat?'

'Porridge.'

'What's porridge?'

'Oh . . . a vegetarian dish.'

'Nothing else?'

'Well, a bone from last night.'

'Whose bone?'

'Not yours,' said Rupert defensively.

'Obviously not mine.'

'Not one of yours. Not anything to do with you.'

'I'd stick in your throat if it was me,' said Lulu with provocative intensity. 'I'd slash your liver. I'd perforate your gut.'

'Never would I put you in the position where you had to be so abrasive,' said Rupert, rather desperately fumbling for some makeshift tatters of gallantry. 'Far be it from my thoughts to upset your natural dignity. It would cut me to the quick.'

'It would pierce you to the heart,' Lulu corrected him with conviction. 'Make no mistake about that. Now what's all this about chopping me when you're not hungry? Why do you want to do it?'

'Well, it *is* done,' said Rupert apologetically. 'I'm not saying I really want to do it. I suppose it's in the rules. It's the sporting tradition. It's good form.'

'By *good form* I suppose you mean mindless fashion. Your *sporting tradition* seems to demand that you kill when you're not hungry. Can't you have a bit of sport without chopping me? Who makes the rules? Who sets the fashion? Do the rules and the fashion run counter to the law?'

'What law?' asked Rupert.

'The law of the forest. Is there any other law? You don't have to learn the law of the forest, it comes naturally to you: Provide for your family until they can provide for themselves; eat when you're hungry, and make as sure as possible that no one eats you; take a bit of sport when you can – every leveret, puppy, cub, foal, kit and whelp instinctively knows the therapeutic value of a bit of sport – but don't bear a grudge if the chap you're having sport with is hungry and means to gratify self and family with your gorgeous body. If you can't stand the heat, keep out of the kitchen. What law do you live by?'

'Oh, the law of the forest, of course,' said Rupert glibly.

'Then what's all this about the rules, sporting tradition and good form? Who says it's good form to kill when you're not hungry? Who made these rules?'

'The mandrakes,' Rupert conceded.

'So there's another law, the law of man. Do you live by that, too?'

'Now and then, I suppose.'

'And man says the rules are to kill when you're not hungry?'

'Yes, if you're out for sport.'

'Sport! How do you define sport?'

'Very clearly, in the mandrakes' canon. Sport is the pleasure derived from hunting and killing.'

'That's a bit one-sided, isn't it? Partisan, and dismissive of the mental factor? What about the party of the second part? Isn't the other contestant considered?'

'With regard to the mental factor,' said Rupert, flummoxed and therefore pompous, 'I understand that sport becomes intellectual when one is hunting and killing fish, which I have never done. I really have no information on the state of mind of the quarry.'

'I'm sorry to insist, but you said "quarry" when I had said "contestant". It's an axiom to us free animals – but has it never penetrated your world? – that the important thing in sport is not to win, but to take part.'

'I can't say it has.'

'That satisfaction is not the triumph but the struggle?'

'Not really.'

'That the reward of sport is not to have conquered, but to have fought well?'

'I say! With respect, that's a bit far-fetched, isn't it,

Madame Lulu? I don't see much reward if you've fought well and lost. You're still dead.'

'You are, if you stick to this fetish about killing when you're not hungry.'

'*I* don't stick to it. Perhaps man does. There is some point in it. Man preserves food, to eat when he's hungry later.'

'Are you telling me that if you had chopped me ten minutes ago a man would have come along and preserved me?'

'Not exactly. Not in this instance.'

'But you've been trained by man to chop me in any case. In the one event of your happening to feel hungry later. In the other event of a man chancing to follow your tracks, come across me, slit my belly, pour out the intestines – and preserve me.'

'Allow me to say, Madame Lulu, that the only way I ever want to see you is unchopped, smooth-bellied, gutsy and preserved until the end of my days.'

The hare Lulu was so affected by this declaration that, not to put too fine a point on her psychosomatic reaction, she farted like a flute. 'Loud sing cuckoo, merry sing cuckoo,' said Rupert with nervous spontaneity, in English, just as he always said *Gesundheit*, in German, when a friend sneezed. He was excruciatingly embarrassed, not by the breakwind but by the extravagance of his unpremeditated tribute that seemed to have prompted it.

Lulu unaffectedly rescued him from his confusion. 'Cuckoo, cuckoo,' she said conventionally, also in English, using the traditional response to the salutation. And she zealously pursued her interrupted argument. 'I was saying that the joy of sport is to participate and do your best, enlarging and relishing your own skill, appreciating the effort of others and not getting desperate if you lose. You said I was unrealistic, because if I lost

I was dead. You're entirely confusing sport with survival.'

'Sport *is* survival. I've seen knights who lost at sporting tournaments die of shame or self-destruction.'

'What is a knight?'

'Among the mandrakes, a lord will call a man a knight, install him and tell him it's a great honour. It really means that the knight must spend heavily on horses and weaponry and turn up with a few followers to fight for the lord on demand.'

'What do they fight for? Food?'

'Honour. The lord's honour. Sometimes he gives the knight a bit, too.'

'What is honour? Very good food?'

'No. And if you can talk about sport as you do, you don't have to be cynical about honour.'

'I'm meeting you on your own ground, the realistic level. If honour carries disadvantages, then there must be some other reward in fighting.'

'Well, there's money . . . loot.'

'Money is very good food?'

'No, but you can buy good food with it.'

'So money means food, though you're not yet hungry?'

'Yes.'

'Like sport means killing, though you're not yet hungry?'

'Well, yes.'

'Why did the knights who had lost at sport destroy themselves? They weren't hungry.'

'No, but they had lost honour.'

'But they couldn't eat honour. I suppose they *could* eat money, if they were hungry later. Is there money in sport?'

'Yes, prize money, side bets. I suppose there's money in honour, if you analyse it.'

'So you can save up honour and save up money, and exchange it for preserved food.'

'I don't see why you're so hoity-toity about preserving food. Squirrels do it. *You* do it.'

'*I* do it?'

'You consume your moist faecal pellets direct from the anus. You crop more vegetation than you can assimilate at one time. You eat when you're not hungry. You eject and take refection while you're resting. It's no different from chewing the cud except that a cow throws up and you pass down. What's that if it's not preserving food?'

Lulu was silent for some time. 'Touché,' she finally admitted with candour. 'I'd never thought of it in that way. But it's only for a few hours. It doesn't make me so depressingly parsimonious and save-for-a-rainy-day as the frugal squirrel, do you think?' She was coaxing in a remarkably flirtatious manner. 'It's my gut, you know,' she confided. 'It holds ten times as much as my stomach. The cow has about four stomachs, so it's easy for her to regurgitate. But my own gastric secretions don't start before the caecum, which I don't have to tell you is at the junction of the small and large intestines, and in addition to being a blind gut in itself goes even blinder with a diversion to the appendix vermiformis. However, I wouldn't call it a dead end, but an extremely lively middle. It produces a most gratifying bacterial fermentation, my dear, literally puts vitamins into my alimentation, and so of course that has to make a second journey through the digestive system for me to get the benefit of it. I'm not boring you with all this dietary chat, I hope. As you say, it's like chewing the cud. The cow drives up a sodden bolus and has a chew. I drive down a moist pellet and do likewise. Bolus schmolus, what's a moist pellet? It's only the first time round.'

'I wasn't criticizing you, only pointing out a fact.'

'And you've made a very good point. I hope you'll concede that there were times, too, when my own logic was unanswerable. Honours even. We've participated and we've both enjoyed the encounter. I'm looking forward to a return match – in the field and in the forum – and I promise I'll give you good sport. Will you make one promise to me?'

'What should that be?'

'Take the edge off your hunger before you set out,' said Lulu. 'Pile up that porridge. It is the bulwark of my liberty and independence.'

Rupert expressed his courtly assent. 'Mark well my bulwarks,' he assured her, 'that ye may speak of peace to the generation following.'

'Gallantry, poetry, and even a modest admixture of religion!' sighed Lulu. 'He is the very *beau idéal*! I'm so glad you spoke of the next generation, which have at intervals rather escaped my mind during our absorbing intercourse, though I have been sharply reminded of them from time to time. Lactation, you know. Or perhaps you don't know, but its pulsing can be physically obtrusive. There is one last thing you can do for me today. Would you be good enough, as you go, to discourage the presence in this territory of the fox Fulgent, who is at this very moment padding around us in a wide circle? I hope I don't embarrass you by commenting on a fact which may have escaped you, but as a working female I have to use eyes, ears and nose continuously even when I'm in the most captivating company. I have no personal fear of Fulgent – it's amazing how even predators respect you if you face up to them with spirit, and although I'm a vegetarian I have very sharp incisors. But I have four leverets not quite weaned in four nearby forms – I think you have been a perfect gentleman in pretending not to notice their existence – and you must certainly understand why I didn't consent to your chasing me right out of the territory, which is why I didn't run up that scree. It is well past suckling time, and indeed I was preparing to start on my milkround when you made your first very sporting and entirely inoffensive passes at me. Now I've been talking to you only for a short time, and I'm convinced I can trust you. But we must face the truth that there are creatures of the kind of Fulgent the fox who, through no fault of their own I'm sure, do not have your restraint and cannot suppress their barbarous appetite for suckling hare. *Please* have the courtesy to escort Fulgent off this ground.'

Lulu's eyes had been restlessly roving throughout these remarks, which, as even the uncritical Rupert reflected, she could profitably have shortened under the circumstances. Suddenly she stamped a hind pad in dismay.

'He's taken one of my youngsters!' she exclaimed.

Rupert glimpsed the fox trotting, at no urgent speed, with a leveret in his mouth.

'He's hungry,' said Lulu philosophically. 'And even if he's not, his vixen Régine and their litter of cubs are ravenous. They lead him a terrible dance,' she explained in a voice all sympathy. 'He was getting on so well, too, at the beginning of the winter. Then his streak of luck ran out. And by that time he was wedded and bedded and the cubs were on the way. He really does work himself to a shadow looking after that family. You have to admire him.'

Rupert had the impression that, unless instant action were taken, the impressionable Lulu might offer Fulgent another of her offspring. 'Shall I see him off?' he suggested urgently.

'Please,' said Lulu. 'Such a pity about the youngster,' she continued, regret merging into resignation. '*C'est la vie.*'

'*C'est la mort,*' Rupert corrected her with English

pedantry, and hurried away to police the fox off the ground.

'A mate and starving family,' Fulgent explained with his mouth full and an exaggeratedly helpless twitch of his whiskers when the beagle caught up with him. 'I don't like doing this to Lulu, but in a way she can afford it. She's far more prolific than we are. She was already pregnant for the second time when she produced this litter. *C'est la guerre.*'

'*C'est formidable,*' said Rupert, sinking into a furrow for a bout of solitary reflection on forest law, sporting principles and survival.

7
The Bowl of Night

Lambing-time was always laborious, but the summons to Crespin had brought additional preoccupation. There was uncertainty, speculation, insecurity at La Tranchée over the significance of the next day's journey, and in the courtyard behind the farmhouse peace came dropping more slowly that night. Adèle coaxed and cosseted Plantagenet, Rupert and Sobrin around the manger, aware that she herself was distrait. 'I'm like a nursing nun in a hospice,' she told herself, 'tucking up patients with an armoured good humour so that I don't acknowledge, and therefore don't answer, their fears that they'll die in the dark.' She laughed at her dramatization, but still knew that the usually clear distillation of the grace of the evening retreat was stained at the end of this day with faint imperfections of confusion and doubt.

Plantagenet, more proprietorial than any mother, was keenly worried by Adèle's impending visit to the castle, and had repeatedly begged Rupert to give her every possible protection. Rupert, although he always gave a serene impression of imperturbable savoir-faire on grand occasions, achieved this composure only after agonized bouts of apprehension beforehand. He was in a full flurry of agitation, compounded with a mental restlessness which he recognized as the aftermath of his meeting with

Lulu the hare. The preoccupations of the pig and the beagle predictably surfaced in unprovoked irritability at the expense of the donkey, but this was absorbed in the beast's timeless benevolence.

Sobrin alone was as placid as ever. He was to make the journey to Crespin, but had been spared any nagging from Plantagenet, and took no offence whatever at the implication that the pig considered him an ineffectual guardian of his mistress.

Adèle herself was expectant, but as yet with no thought for the morrow. She relished her enthusiasms in full savour, one at a time, and she had reserved her gusto for the promised visit of the eagle owl Grand-Duc. She had had a heavy enough day at the lambing, but calmly declined to attend any more deliveries for the hour around Vespers, which at that season of the year, with the time of the sunset plunge creeping towards the equinox, coincided well with nightfall.

The structure of the farm buildings was shaped like a big H with the farmhouse on the horizontal stroke, its main doors and windows facing the principal courtyard and the great gate beyond, which was the only break in the continuous exterior wall. In the lower courtyard, where Adèle and the animals were grouped, all the inner doors of the surrounding farm buildings had been closed, and temporary hurdles cut off the bottom of the H, enclosing the yard against frightened ewes who might bolt during the uncertainties of giving birth. When it was necessary, the sheep were brought into the stables and shippens through doors on the other side, and the glare of crude torches within could be seen from the yard through cracks in the timber. There was a continuous bleating from lately born lambs but no unnerving clamour of human voices, only a gentle roughness of low, encouraging words as a farm servant pulled off a lamb which its mother could not manage to deliver, or dealt with an occasional twin which had been entirely ignored by the ewe as she busied herself licking her first-born. It all made a rounded, unaggressive murmur, Adèle reflected, which should not deter Grand-Duc from dropping in as he had promised.

Drop he did, seemingly from nowhere. She neither saw nor heard his approach. She only felt the airflow as he folded his great wings – as broad across as she, lying in that manger, was long – and alighted in the bowl of an old stone drinking-trough, a sort of rough-hewn font, which stood by her head. The velvet dampers on the leading edges of his wings had filtered away the swish of his flight. The one sound was the grating of the four-square claws on his enormous feathered feet as he settled on the stone. He stood there, very high against Adèle's recumbent body, and in the glow of the unclouded night he was almost luminous. He sounded two very low booming notes, without introduction, as though a fidgeting organist had momentarily let his foot trail across the pedal bass, and followed them with a deep, throaty chuckle.

'I'm early,' he said. 'Or earlier than I promised. No credit to me, but all thanks to Athena. I sprang into the evening fully armed and bagged my entire supper in one swoop.' When Grand-Duc spoke, his body was vibrant with expression. He felt no compulsion to convey his noble descent through a stiffness of communication, oracular aloofness or bored majesty, with its indication that it was unnecessary to project life into his remarks since the penalty of any inattention was death. He was vivacious and persuasive, a Byzantine tetrarch interested in the reactions he provoked or encouraged. He did not make gestures, but his whole body was tremulous with undulations of his folded wings, surges in various zones of the deep pile of soft feathers that ballooned his comparatively slim body, and dramatic ripplings and erections in the great tufted eyebrows which projected from his brow like horns – all accompanied by astonishing variations in the modulation of his voice. At the same time, since he was a very alert and astute listener to extraneous sounds even when he was talking, there was a constant scurry of movement along the feathered edges of his ear flaps, which ringed the disc of his face like two half-moons. The evolution of the owl had rejected any spoiling of his aerodynamic efficiency and silent flight through the crude carpentry of ear trumpets, as in mice and men and monkeys. Over the large cavities of the ears behind his cheeks he wore streamlined muffs opening only at the rear. Yet, with need of a hearing ten times more acute than men, he ceaselessly tuned his scanning reception, so that the feathers on the lips of the mutton-chop flaps rose and fell in a curling wave like white spume on the crest of a comber.

'I am *not* a nocturnal bird,' Grand-Duc continued, persuasively undulating his body and his tone with a warmth of egocentric enthusiasm which captured the interest of his audience. 'That is not to say that I won't stay up all night in good company.' He broke off again and bent his head sideways to study Plantagenet. With his head still askew he moved it forward and back, altering the focus of his eyes as he assessed the distance.

'What a peculiar pig!' he said. 'Unnaturally lean, yet no apparent aggression. Ballistic capacity to be determined. My distance to target jugular, 2,619,837 microns. Length of his exposed jugular, 51,411 microns. My acceleration from standing start, 10,416,672 microns per heartbeat per heartbeat. His early warning coefficient, zero. His reaction speed, scale 3. His calculated deterrent potential, quasi-zero. Excuse me, I was computing aloud.'

The pig Plantagenet rose indignantly and glared at Grand-Duc, who made no apparent movement except that his claws grated on the stone. 'Stop talking about my jugular,' Plantagenet fulminated, in what was intended to be a roar but finished as a squeak. 'I came to this place to get away from butchers. "Reaction speed scale 3", my fundament. You know nothing about me. I'm the fastest pig in the forest. Ask my friend the wolf Hurlaud of the Great Woods. Ask him who led the free animals from Les Combles to Chizé, and outpaced a pack of dogs and horses to entice the mandrakes astray. "Potential, quasi-zero" – that's really rich! What did *you* do in the Great Retreat, daddy?'

'Every apology!' said Grand-Duc in genuine concern. 'You must be Plantagenet. Of course I've heard about you, I know every detail of your gallantry. But I didn't expect to find you here. I was told you had stayed on in the forest with Grondin and the wild boyos. Communications! How they let us down. I do beg you to forgive me.'

Plantagenet said nothing.

'You don't know how sick I was that I couldn't fly operationally on that particular party,' Grand-Duc confided. 'Uhlan had seconded me to the Signals Corps.'

'Ah, communications,' said Plantagenet with edge.

'Come on!' urged Grand-Duc, his joviality slightly tinged with a hint of exasperated seniority. 'You're not going to hold this against me for ever, are you?'

Plantagenet still said nothing.

'Tha bugger?' wheedled the eagle owl, sending the most placatory ripples up his soft, brown-flecked breast into the creamy ruffle below his head.

'Tha bugger,' Plantagenet conceded, and slumped down on to his belly again, not entirely renouncing his right to be sullen. Adèle reached out a hand and kneaded his neck.

'I am not a nocturnal bird,' Grand-Duc resumed with impeccably warm spontaneity, like an actor who has surmounted a dress-rehearsal tantrum by his leading lady. 'I am a *crepuscular* bird. The twilight hours of dusk and dawn I devote uninterruptedly to hunting.' He paused. 'It is not in my nature to spend all day grubbing for acorns,' he added in a loaded aside, but he did not glance at Plantagenet. 'I need this period in its entirety, since I cannot always anticipate what will be on offer in the market. Sometimes I take the whole time, sometimes I take less. This evening I was lucky. On my first reconnaissance I glimpsed a delicious dish retiring from his perch in a tree to his nest on the ground, and I took him in full flight. A blackcock.'

'A blackcock!' said Adèle incredulously.

'Black grouse with a curved tail like Maister Brémand's moustaches,' said Rupert informatively to Plantagenet, trying to keep him in the conversation and aware that he was not a bird-watcher. 'Plump, glossy. . . .'

'Succulent,' said Grand-Duc.

'Huge!' said Adèle. '*Can* you take a blackcock, Grand-Duc?'

'Is that a serious question?' the owl asked, and he began to realize that the climate of approval was not so balmy as he had anticipated. 'Action,' he said vigorously. 'I didn't give up my social hours to discuss my supper. Attention. Instruction. Education. Which in your case you have not got. Dead reckoning. Orientation. Astronomy.' Using ejaculations like cogs to wind himself up to good humour, Grand-Duc was soon in a state of masterly cheerfulness again. But he addressed himself only to Adèle.

'Tonight we treat of the Heavenly Twins. Castor and Pollux if you want to be vulgar, Castor and Polydeuces if you prefer to be Greek. The sons of Zeus and yet not both the sons of Zeus. A pretty story. They were born at the same time to Leda, who you may remember was ravished by Zeus in the shape of a swan. But Leda had already been impregnated that night by her husband King Tyndareus of Sparta. They were born together, Castor the mortal son of a king, Pollux the immortal son of the greatest of the gods. They were very loving in their lives and they fought side by side for the honour of their sister, who became Helen of Troy. The mortal Castor was killed. The immortal Pollux prayed to Zeus for mortality, not to outlive his brother. And the father god set them together in the sky as an emblem of brotherly love. You can see them up there now, very upright, very soldierly – and yet pleasingly simple and childlike, for they are hand in hand, paddling in the Milky Way.

'How to use the Heavenly Twins? First of all, look at them. They're beautiful. It does one good to have beauty as well as duty prompting the study of the sky. It's the same motivation that makes bishops set up statues of the Virgin in church. Or belted knights put portrait miniatures of Adèle by their bedside on the eve of a tournament.' Here the permanently rippling Grand-Duc became so animated with amusement at his own sally that his coat coruscated and coronated like a gigantic feather duster being twirled and shaken. Plantagenet felt a sudden stab of alarm, not at the sight of the once-majestic eagle owl shimmying like a fat, unbelted lady, but at the suspicions he had confirmed regarding Adèle's summons to Castle Crespin.

'How to find the Heavenly Twins?' Grand-Duc continued with tireless enthusiasm. 'If you can't find them you can't admire them. So go back to basics. Use the saddle on the back of the Great Bear, which I defy you to call the Dipper or the Plough. Dip a ladle that shape in a cauldron of soup and you'd find even your elbow scalded. And you've never seen a plough like that in your life. A plough starts as a wedge to lift earth before it uses a blade to cut earth. Where do you see the ram-share up there? Drag that celestial coulter with its dead vertical blade through an earthly field and you'll be bogged down within three ox-lengths. No, the shape is clearly, and always has been, a shafted square cart of the type very well known to the Babylonians and the Greeks and the Arabs as well as to us.' Grand-Duc paused and added quietly, with spurious modesty: 'It was a feature in the great processions to the Parthenon which celebrated the festivals of my patron Athena.' He was still, and apparently overborne by a flood tide of great reverence.

'Basics,' Adèle reminded him. 'The saddle on the back of the Great Bear.'

'The cart,' agreed Grand-Duc. 'Call it the Wain. A wain has a front and a back. The back is bounded by the backboard, to stop the load from falling out. The front is finished with a buckboard, in this case vertical, to stop the horse kicking the driver if he bucks. The backboard is marked by the Pointers, which we considered yesterday: Dubhe at the top and Merak at the bottom. The Pointers point to the Pole Star one way, from Merak to Dubhe, and backwards to the Lion the other way, with the bright star Regulus as the Lion's raised forepaw. The buckboard has the star Megrez at the top and Phecda at the bottom.

'*Now*, draw another line across the Wain, from where the shaft hits the cart to the bottom of the backboard – Megrez to Merak, the twin M's, twins twins twins, remember?, and you hit the Heavenly Twins with the raptorial accuracy of an eagle owl. See for yourself!'

Grand-Duc slumped in patent exhaustion, like a magician who had risked all to achieve a rare transformation, and had succeeded.

Adèle gazed at the sky in silent absorption. Sobrin and Plantagenet had their eyes on Adèle. Rupert stared reflectively at Grand-Duc, who was beginning to boil with another spate of animation.

'Hand in hand, paddling in the Milky Way,' he said. 'But look at Orion on the other side of the stream. "Keep out of my territory," he's shouting. He was a bully boy of a giant, you know. He's raising his club over the stream. I'm sure he was left-handed. He has his club in the left and his shield or a lion-skin in the right, and it's a dagger that hangs from his sword-belt. If he's right-handed he must have his back to the Twins and he's shouting at *us*.

'Orion's belt points down towards Sirius the Scorcher, the medallion on the collar of the Big Dog and the brightest star in the sky. What's useful about the Twins and Orion, apart from their good looks, is that they are reliable guides if the Wain and the Pole Star are obscured. If you can see the Heavenly Twins, and they are *not* standing on their heads, you are facing roughly south. This works nearly all the time. If they are standing on their heads you are looking north. There is one short spell when they are lying on their backs, and you are looking north if you see them then.

'But of course all these stars are of much more use to me than to you. Half the time when *you* need them you'll be in the forest and won't be able to see them. Now, take a tip from an old owl.'

'You're not old, Grand-Duc,' said Adèle politely. 'You're in your prime.' She did not really want to say anything at that moment. She had accepted the owl's idiosyncrasies and had let his language charm her into utter captivation, as like a skilful glassblower he swiftly dilated the bowl of the night and let the fire glint on chosen highlights among the stars. But she was aware that he had paused for the conventional compliment.

'Of course I'm in my prime,' Grand-Duc answered decisively. 'That doesn't mean I'm not old.' His breast humped and heaved as he resolved an internal struggle over whether he should reveal his exact age – he was in fact older than Maister Brémand. He decided against exposure.

'A tip from an old owl,' he said. 'Day or night, you can do without the stars for much of the time, and check with the stars or the sun when you come to a clearing. In general all trees have richer foliage on the south. Their southern branches tend to grow horizontally so that they can bask in the sun. But the northern branches struggle to grow straight upwards so that they can get their share of sunlight. I'm exaggerating, but the typical attitude of many trees is like a man making standing signals with his arms – one arm thrust out to the south, the other arm raised high; and the high side is the north. If you try to get your bearings in this fashion, look particularly for a horse chestnut tree, which is quite extreme in this respect.

'If it's too dark to see the trees, feel them. In this part of the country the prevailing wind is north of west, and it's damp from the sea but drained of the salt. If you feel the trees and you find moss and lichen on the bark flourishing consistently on the same quarter, then that bearing is towards the northwest, because that's where the mosses have learned to settle for moisture.

'And one last tip for tonight. If it's a really grey day and you can't see the sun for direction . . .' Grand-Duc broke off in jagged alarm. The gentle bustle of the lambing operations and their bleating descant had masked the sounds of action in the farmland beyond the moated defence. Now there came the ruffle of horses' hooves on the thick planks of the drawbridge, which had not been raised, and a double echo as a heavy metal mace was beaten against the iron armour of the main gate and the oak groaned in response. Shouts and some screams mingled from outside and inside the farm, and Grand-Duc soared swiftly to cover under the barn eaves. The bowl of night was shattered.

Maister Brémand hurried to the gatehouse and holla'ed to know who was there.

'Jehan de la Tour de la Sénéchaussée de la Vicomté de Frébois,' shouted the master of horse at Crespin Castle, awarding himself an entirely fictitious title in the intoxication of frightening a household in the dark. 'With one sergeant and three men-at-arms. All hungry, and seeking beds as well as supper. We have come to escort you to Crespin in the morning.'

'Supper!' wailed Dame Matilda. 'At a moment's notice and in the middle of lambing! Escort you to Crespin! Adèle, Adèle! Brémand, you unimaginable fool, what have you done? You're under arrest!'

8

The Court of Love

In the courtyard next morning, not particularly early after Brémand had given his farmservants general instructions to cover the following days, the party assembled to go. 'You're taking the beagle?' the lord's master of horse queried in a casual tone.

'I never go anywhere without him,' said Brémand.

'Then that's all right.'

Brémand considered this acknowledgment for a moment and said slowly: 'I never will go anywhere without him.'

Adèle trotted Sobrin round from the stables. Lightheartedly and with some skill, she cast the noose of a rope halter over her father's head as he sat on Lancier. Brémand angrily dragged it from his neck and threw it on the ground. Adèle realized that, in spite of her father's derisive dismissal of Dame Matilda's dirges and his acceptance of Jehan's bland disclaimers, the man was uneasy and her clowning had gone too far. She pulled Brémand's hand towards her and kissed it.

The little troop left La Tranchée – five mounted retainers, Brémand and Adèle, with Rupert reflective after a last, anxious lecture from Plantagenet. They were to follow the long arc of the edge of the forest running west and then north to Crespin. Adèle asked if she could delay them for five minutes by calling at the retreat of the Brothers, for whom she had prepared a basket of food. Since this involved only the slightest diversion Jehan made no objection, though his face set in an enigmatically blank expression. In the more open borders of the forest the solitary white blooms of wood anemone rose as they passed from the green carpet which the plant was laying, and thicker bunches of the purple-veined flowers of wood sorrel tufted upwards in the inner shade. The trunks of the trees occasionally glowed in the luminous light from the misty south with the pale, oval leaves of climbing honeysuckle, offering the first greenery to reappear in the forest.

They came to the retreat. Adèle cantered on ahead. When the party caught up with her she was talking to Sylvester alone. 'Robert and the lad have been summoned to Castle Crespin,' she said.

'Yes, I gave them their orders last night,' Jehan conceded.

'Why are they called?' Adèle questioned with faltering steadiness.

'It was not my duty to ask,' Jehan answered evasively.

'How are they to get there?'

'They are walking, of course.'

'Robert will relish that, the dear nesh tenderfoot,' said Adèle. 'We must ride on so that we can take them up. Are you going to be all right, Sylvester?'

'Never better,' Brother Sylvester replied sturdily. 'I've plenty to do and two days' food secure since you kindly asked me to make those hurdles for La Tranchée.' Brémand looked sharply at his daughter, who smiled demurely. 'And when I get there, if there's any help I can give with the lambing, Sylvester's the man. "He shall gather the lambs with his arm, and carry them in his bosom, and shall gently lead those that are with young." There, you never thought I could speak a

Scripture, did you? But when I hear a Scripture that tells of what I know, I remember it. These rough hands too-long busy with sword and battle-axe were made strong by the plough-haft and deft by the lambing. And while I'm working there I can talk without idleness, talk to the men and the maids about the Lord and the good shepherd that gave his life for his sheep.

'I had a good meditation last night,' Sylvester continued companionably, entirely ignoring the restlessness of Jehan's horse which its rider was doing nothing to control. 'That will surprise you too, dear sister Adèle, my having a good meditation. It has all started since we took that young man in, and Robert reminded me of when Francis said that as far as he was concerned the best friar should be an idiot.'

'An idiot!' said Jehan, who had been following the monologue in spite of his impatience.

'That's what I said,' Sylvester cheerfully affirmed. 'An idiot and subservient in all things to all men. He said a learned man who joined him should strip himself of learning and offer himself naked to Christ. Then the Lord will invest him with new armour.'

'Armour now!' said Jehan rhetorically, less angry with Sylvester than with himself, for giving the friar attention.

'That's what I said,' nodded Sylvester unperturbed, eyeing the horseman. 'Look at you, now. You've got a tidy tunic, leather back and fore with a few bits of iron facings. It'll guard your guts against arrows, but you'd never stand up to a knight, and you well know your lord would never put you in battle against one, except to sop up the gravy before he took on the meat.' Sylvester suddenly spun up the mattock he had been leaning on so that the sharp pickaxe of the head circled towards Jehan's face. The horseman flung up his hand in protection, and Sylvester neatly reversed the mattock in flight and gently jabbed the smooth, wooden shaft into Jehan's exposed armpit. 'See what I mean?' said Sylvester. 'Your defences are poor. But I'm installed as a knight of Francis' Round Table, and the Lord has given me a full suit of armour. So it's as difficult to wound my faith as it is to humiliate an idiot. But I'm keeping you from your errand. Be well, little sister Adèle. Thank you, Maister Brémand, for the chance to serve at the farm. A cheery good morning to you all. The Lord give you peace.'

The party rode on in silence for a long time. The mist cleared and the sun shone stronger. Rupert, ranging through the route with his excess of energy, came across a recent scent of the fox Fulgent, but did not voice his discovery. A succession of birds flew high and wide abreast of the riders as if they were scouts passing on to the adjacent sector reports on the party's progress. But when the birds converged and, with reinforcements, flew low to the side to squawk in anger, Rupert knew that they had combined to scold the roving fox. 'It's his penalty for hunting in daylight,' Rupert reflected. 'His family must be driving him hard.'

'There they are!' Adèle suddenly called, pointing ahead to a clearing where two figures in grey were sharp in the sunlight. 'But whatever has happened to Robert? He must have cut his foot!'

Brother Robert seemed to be skipping like a child, but with far more controlled artifice. He held his hands with grace, level with his shoulders but raising them at times to clap them over his head. For most of the time he was moving round Happy-With-Jesus, who was continually slumping and raising his body as though he were blowing into the bellows of some very demanding bagpipes.

'They must be drunk,' moaned Jehan. 'The festival of Flora two months early. Great God, let them be drunk! I cannot stand another dose of idiocy today.'

They caught up with the two in grey. There was no

doubt about it, Brother Robert was dancing, his gown swirling and shifting with the rhythm. At the same time he was singing, in a pleasant but far from ecclesiastical voice. Happy-With-Jesus, very grave in an extreme of concentration, was reproducing the harmonies of an entire consort of instruments, playing an air which he must have practised many times before.

Brother Robert smiled warmly at the party as they rode up, but did not stop singing or dancing. He seemed to be absorbed in the construction of a work of art as his graceful gestures spelled out to Happy-With-Jesus something of the sense he was singing:

Amor de caritate
We sing the Jubilate
And dance the Exultate
  Loud sing
  Merry sing
    Love

The sun begins so tender
The leaves uncurl so slender
But soon the woods surrender
  Sprouting
  Shouting
    Love

Robert made a sign to Happy-With-Jesus who, by some means, either called in more instruments or varied the drone on his bagpipes so that the diapason widened and the accompaniment became more sonorous, as majestic as Robert's fresh gestures.

And then the sun in splendour
Sets man and flower to engender
And buds and babies render
  May's due
  Praise to
    Love

And birds and beasts in summer
Portray for each new comer
The life that will become a
  Rite of
  The might of
    Love

The singer and consort softened their brio and diminished into affettuoso.

Dear Lord your bright perfection
Was scarred by man's rejection
And yet in your affection
  You sought him
  Brought him
    Love

The dole of the denying
The agony of dying
Transformed to beautifying
  Shameless
  Blameless
    Love

With joy I soar to greet thee
In pain you sink to meet me

Here the accompaniment ceased altogether and Robert's voice was raised in an ardent a-rhythmic cry:

Blend passions I entreat thee
  In mingled
  Single
    Love

Happy-With-Jesus resumed the simple melodic dance tune with which he had started.

For joy still bids Cantate
A joyous Jubilate
A dancing Exultate
  Loud sing
  Merry sing
    Love

Robert and Happy-With-Jesus joined their raised right hands and circled in one trim measure. The lad was not well adjusted on his feet, and in any case was still busy making music, but chuckles exploded from him at each rest and at the end of the tune he gave up all control and laughed aloud in long exhilaration. Robert glanced shyly at Adèle.

'Did you write that song?' she asked with her eyes shining.

'Oh yes, I had a gift for song in the old days.'

'And for the dance, I see. Now there's blood on the grass.'

Robert looked down. The trampled herbage was indeed smeared with red but there was fresh blood running from a wound on the top of his foot and flowing between the tendons to his toes. He smiled and said, 'I didn't know that it had opened up again. I didn't notice. There's joy for you!'

'Happy-With-Jesus,' said Adèle now that the lad had stopped laughing. 'Beautiful, beautiful. Something new, something beautiful.' She looked Robert in the face again. 'And you never cease to surprise me,' she said.

'I was just teaching Happy-With-Jesus. Isn't he good? Really you shouldn't be surprised. Francis is always singing, and in his own cajoling way he almost demands the company of musicians. It's probably why he promoted me. His last words when we said goodbye were "Go round the world singing, then preach a little." '

'You're not going to preach now,' Jehan, master of horse, interrupted very firmly. 'You two Grey Friars have pilfered far too much of my time this morning. Now the young lady said you should be taken up, and I don't dissent except that you're not going to get a ride on a military horse. If Maister Brémand is willing, just you bunk up behind him and set the boy up on the donkey. And we are now going to advance at the trot.'

Adèle would not have Happy-With-Jesus riding pillion, guessing that with his uncoordinated balance he would soon fall off. She set him up on Sobrin in front of her, and in this manner they came to Crespin.

They kicked up the brown dust in the broad track which gradually tidied itself into becoming, first, an avenue, then the straight village street leading to the drawbridge and the menacing stone bastion which was the gatehouse to the castle. The first work of man they came to on the confines of the village was a massive gibbet with two heavy nooses swinging from the top beam. A dirty fringe of black and grey pelts drooped from the beam, occasionally blooming into a tassel which was recognizable as an animal skeleton with tufts of sodden fur adhering to it. The formal purpose of the gibbet was for the ignominious execution of underlings who had offended the feudal lord, and particularly poachers. But Messire de Frébois had not hanged a poacher for a considerable time. Needing to maintain the symbolism of his deterrent, he accordingly sent out his archers from time to time with orders to shoot a few cats, which were promptly nailed to the crossbeam where the carrion birds made short work of them, and this humanitarian leaning earned him warm approval in the village. It also provided the bowmen with valuable competitive exercise in marksmanship, and subtly sharpened the woodcraft of those surviving poachers with the courage to continue in practice. These were well known to the lord, and generally found themselves conscripted for forty days at a good rate of pay in command of scouting parties or flying columns whenever Messire amused himself with forays, raids and other opportunistic hostilities not classified as war.

The houses stood well back from the village street, giving room for private gardens which were desolate enough at this time of year except for a touch of colour from rockery plants and herbal beds; but bare vines and the wood of well-shaped fruit trees promised summer abundance. Behind the houses stretched the vast manorial lands, unfenced except for the enclosure of the grazing areas.

The master of horse rode ahead across the drawbridge to the gatehouse and spoke to the sergeant of the guard. 'I want receipts for four bodies,' he said. 'Farmer Brémand, his daughter Adèle, a Grey Friar named Robert and an idiot. And I want a special note that they were alive when delivered.' This soldierly humour was well received by the sergeant, who was illiterate, though appreciably more glumly by the visitors. Jehan winked at Brémand to indicate that there was still hope. 'I'll take them through to the great hall now,' he said. They rode through the stepped arches of battlemented courtyards, and at the stone stairs of the central keep the visitors dismounted and their beasts were led away by the men-at-arms.

'Rupert!' came an authoritative cry from the vaulted vestibule above. 'Rupert! Good boy! Come on, boy!'

Rupert cast a questioning glance at Maister Brémand and, receiving no veto, paddled stiffly up the steps to Messire le Vicomte de Frébois, a very dark-complexioned man, muscularly lean rather than youthfully slim, who came two steps down to meet him. 'Rupert, you old rascal,' said the viscount. 'How is it going? I've been looking forward to seeing you. You must come straight round to the kennels. I've got some friends I want you to meet. Brémand! I'm glad you could come. Step round to the kennels with us. Adèle, my dear. You're growing prettier every day. Welcome.' He looked at Robert. 'And you're the freak! No, *he*'s the freak and you're the friar. Well, there are plenty of people who want to meet you. Go in, go in. Adèle knows the way and you'll find them all somewhere inside. Now come along, Brémand, you're going to be very surprised at this, but I know you'll be interested and I hope you'll want to help. What do you think I've had sent over from England?'

'Beagles,' said Brémand flatly.

'Good guess! Full marks!' said the viscount, privately resenting his tenant's insight. 'I've brought in fifteen couple. A very mixed lot, you know, they're not a pack, it's up to us to make them a pack, but with breeding and training we'll make something of them. We're lucky in one respect. I've had them out a couple of times, and they're real psalm-singers. Quite by accident their voices are tuned so that in chorus they make what I think the English call the cathedral note. Whether you can actually breed voices is something that at present I know nothing about, but if we go on as we've started I shall be putting them in the choir stalls at Fontevrault. But that's all in the future. What we've got to do now is to get them working. We need an old hand, a hound who can use his experience to train them to respond to the horn, unravel a difficult line, ignore sheep and cur dogs; a hound who can cut through the babble and overrule a false cry – I've already seen that we have one bitch who is a born liar.'

'Ay, they sometimes are, Messire,' said Brémand.

'So what can we do to give the pack some backbone?'

'Ah, perhaps you should send to England for 'n, Messire. 'Tis strange they did not send 'un.' Brémand's speech had become remarkably rural and he impressed the viscount as being far more slow-thinking than he had seemed with his first observation. 'I wonder they didn't send 'n, partic'larly when they must 'a knowed and you must 'a said as you needed a good old veteran with experience to train a pack.'

'Yes, Brémand. The fact is . . . well, the details are unimportant, but they haven't sent one and now it would be months before they could. So we've got to try something else. I suppose we could always use Rupert.'

'Ah, but Rupert, he's a trencher-dog now, used to the house and the kitchen, probably forgotten everything about life in the kennels and how to make himself felt with a pack.'

'Nonsense, Brémand. You're not telling me he's not the most knowledgeable dog in the county?'

'He's clever all right, I couldn't say he isn't, but in an individual sort of way, not like one of a pack at all now. Very individual, he is, very proud with his collar and badge and his little chamber that I painted in your lordship's colours after your lordship was so good as to give him to me. I doubt that he's got the nature now to live along of others in the kennels teaching new whelps old tricks that maybe he's forgotten.'

'He's forgotten nothing,' said Frébois hotly. 'He was born in a pack and he can live in a pack. *That*'s his nature.'

'What you're saying, Messire,' said Brémand slowly, 'is that you gave him to me as a gift but you'd like me to give him back to you now.'

'Nothing of the sort!' the viscount was stung into exclaiming. 'Well, that's to say, perhaps I shouldn't mind borrowing him, and he'd jump at the chance to show off some of his old skills.'

The pair gazed at the beagle, who sat upright and expressionless, certainly giving no hint of jumping.

'You have a lord's right to all my possessions,' Brémand said steadily. 'Even, some say, to the disposition of my wife and my daughter, though there is God's honour and your own honour to be weighed along of that. Certainly you can repossess my dog and my land, which I have nursed and tended with a single heart to the glory of the Seigneurie de Frébois, so that you have been pleased to say that the very fields and the vines were smiling, and a proper credit to you, and a proper. . . .'

'And a proper goldmine to you,' interjected the viscount with rough good humour, aware that there was no immediate advantage in pressing the farmer more strongly. 'You make a very comfortable living out of my fief. Do shut up, Brémand. You're the best tenant I've got, and you know it. Stop trying to wring tears from the stones with all this talk about God's honour and smiling vines. All I want is to start a good pack of beagles. I'm not repossessing anything . . .'

'Thank you, Messire,' Brémand over-promptly acknowledged.

'. . . *yet*,' Frébois concluded. 'And, talking of smiling vines, I saw you carefully lay a keg at the bottom of the steps. I see now that it has duly disappeared.'

'A small one, Messire. My daughter will have seen to its proper placing. It will have settled by suppertime.'

'What is it?'

'The Pinot.'

'Black or white?'

'White.'

'That shouldn't take until suppertime. Come on in now.'

'We were going round to the kennels, Messire.'

'**** the kennels,' said the Vicomte de Frébois, postulating an impossible premise. 'We'll go and tap that keg.'

He bounded up the steps to the hall. Brémand followed more slowly. One of the features of a great fortified castle like Crespin was its reliance on constant changes of level as a system of in-built defence. The man who was two steps higher than his adversary in combat had an immediate superiority. All communication, even from courtyard to courtyard, utilized this advantage of height, so that progress from the outer walls, and particularly into the central defence of the square, stone keep, was like ascending a pyramid. Brémand, a strong man well used to traversing the sticky loam of ploughland, still found it an effort to negotiate the constant flights of steps up which his lord sprang athletically, two at a time. Rupert, who was determined to stay with Brémand and Adèle until he was explicitly barred, managed to give the totally counterfeit impression that he was jauntily taking everything in his stride.

The vestibule led to a utility floor like a quartermaster's store, partitioned into specialized areas for weapons, battledress, hide and saddlery workshops, and cubicles for inventory and accounting, with internal ladders going down to repositories of staple foods kept in sacks and barrels of brine. Frébois bypassed this and took a dark, circular stairway which led eventually to the battlemented roof, but which he left at the atrium to the great hall.

The hall was spacious, surprisingly bright from the narrow but numerous high lancet windows, and suffused a pleasant smell which mingled with and improved the odour from the kitchens. Boys were busy in their regular task of sweeping and renewing the green reeds which strewed the floor, paying particular attention to the corners fouled by the few dogs privileged to use the hall, and they scattered dry herbs which scented the air when they were crushed underfoot. The hall was only sparsely occupied and the atmosphere was leisurely. From the centre of a small group at one table there came the *trictrac* of the dice for backgammon. Adèle, Robert and Happy-With-Jesus were sitting, the latter rather restlessly, in an alcove where a man was talking. Frébois, with Brémand following uncertainly, crossed to join them. Rupert allowed the resident hounds to examine him, then joined the party and slumped to rest.

The man had not risen when the Vicomte approached, though he paused for the briefest interval in the middle of a remark as acknowledgment that his circle had been widened. He was very strikingly dressed in bright-coloured clothes of contrasting hues, the collar and sleeves and hem of the tunic having a scalloped border decorated with single beads of a gold metal. The same small gilded balls glinted on a buckram cap with its brim built up to rise into the peaks of a crown as conventionally represented in armorial bearings. He frequently raised a hand to the rim of this crown, not disturbing the way it sat but assuring himself that the blond hair below it was falling in good order. His speech was animated, pointed with mannerisms and emphases, but with an undercurrent of strain or ennui. He was like an actor, rocketed to sudden fame, who has unexpectedly encountered in his dressing-room people who were not aware how fast he had risen. He was the troubadour Gérard, who had sung in the funeral procession at the far village. The Lady Eléonore, châtelaine of Crespin, after briefly receiving her lord's guests on their arrival, had asked Gérard to entertain them for a spell. Though his words were now mainly addressed to Robert, his eyes often strayed towards Adèle to assess the impression he was making. The Vicomte de Frébois paid little attention to what the minstrel was saying, but regarded him speculatively like a nouveau-riche appraising the potential of an expensively acquired status symbol.

Robert was listening to him in a most unrelaxed, guarded fashion. Once, when Gérard made some play on words, the equivalent of associating *rape* with *rapier*, Robert clenched his eyes tight shut in what could have been shame or, alternatively, apprehension. Gérard noticed the reaction and exploited it. 'You would never imagine, Messire,' he said, 'that this retiring, tonsured Grey Friar has served his time with the licentious soldiery. He was my comrade-in-arms in Lombardy. He was a knight, no less.'

'Much less,' Robert broke in hurriedly. 'I was not a knight and neither were you, so don't try and rub my rank off on yours. I was a sergeant.' This statement was as much a diminution of the truth as the other had been an exaggeration, and Robert realized that he would have to define himself more precisely to the Vicomte de Frébois, who had few interests beyond military precedence. 'I was *mediocris nobilitas*, Messire, not *miles primi ordinis*.' Frébois appreciated immediately that Robert had served as a subaltern knight, wearing lighter armour and riding a lighter horse than the élite shock troops. But his attention was caught and he pressed the point.

'Nevertheless, you held some parcel of land in fee for your military service. Where was that?'

'It was near Assisi, Messire.'

'Ah,' said Frébois. 'That accounts for your grey gown. What became of the land?'

'He sold it and gave it to the poor,' said Gérard sarcastically.

'He could not have done that,' the lord said with cutting authority. 'The land was not his to sell.'

Gérard realized that, transposing his bourgeois experience of private property to feudal tenure, he had made a damaging faux pas. 'Anyway, here's a real knight,' he said sulkily, as another man joined the group. 'Down on your knees, you scum, for the flower of knighthood, the most honourable and gentle Sir Otto of Lübeck, of the Eastern Marches, of Hungary, Poland and Bohemia, and of Jerusalem.'

No one had been aware that Happy-With-Jesus had been following the exchanges particularly closely, and perhaps he had not. But the extraordinary force with which the troubadour made his presentation, and the appearance of the knight himself, had a formidable effect on the lad. He plunged to his knees like a falling boulder, teetered and found a rigid balance, joined his palms in supplication and bowed his head over them like a carving on the side of a tomb.

Sir Otto glared, decided that the boy was a collaborator in impudence with Gérard, and kicked him with no discernible gentle or flower-like lenience until Adèle had helped him scramble to his feet. The knight presented an arresting figure. He wore an elongated tabard, almost as deep as a priest's alb, once white and still startling with the stark, black cross of the Order of the Teutonic Knights, as menacing as the quaking darkness of that death which rent the veil of the temple. This mantle, crumpled and badly laundered so that it showed old stains of either rust or blood, dominated the eye of anyone of normal stature as the man approached, and no doubt had invested him with a holy significance in the sight of Happy-With-Jesus. Above the tabard the impact was wholly fiery. His face was broad and red, with eruptive blue eyes. His hair was rust-red and uncrushably bristling. He had a thick, straight ginger moustache which spat with undeviating discipline to right and to left. In Adèle's perception he looked irretrievably unhappy, no more composed or secure than the lava seething in a volcano's crater.

'Have you been hawking?' the viscount sociably asked the knight.

'Hell-cat. She-devil. Night-hag,' said Sir Otto in disgust. 'She moult. Refuse to bind.' He stamped a foot which Adèle noticed was remarkably ill shod.

'A saker falcon in moult at this time!' said Frébois in surprise. 'That's very unseasonal. Where did you acquire her?'

'In Prussia,' said Sir Otto savagely, defying his host to name a better source.

'Oh,' said Frébois noncommittally.

'No good for two, three weeks. I stay for two, three

weeks. Only thing now is the fighting. When is the tournament?'

'Tournament?' said the viscount, who had not invited Sir Otto to stay three weeks. 'I'll give you one of my merlins. Now that's a tidy falcon, eh? Neat but not gaudy. You can go out tomorrow. Tournament. H'm. I hadn't planned one. That will take organization.'

'Big tournament, big prizes.' Sir Otto defined his requirements with a succession of positive nods. He blew his nose into a corner of the alcove and wiped it with the hem of his tabard.

'Perhaps you'd care to head the subscription list,' Gérard suggested with calculated insolence. 'Or endow one joust in your own name. The Jerusalem Chalice, the Otto Bowl, the Teutonic Cuspidor?' He eyed the mucus on the floor with distaste.

'Sodomite,' said Sir Otto, using a term which then had overtones of heresy as much as perversion. He crossed himself in a reflex action. Speaking very fast in a military lingua franca which was intelligible only to Gérard, the knight intimated that he was no more inclined to lay out his money than Gérard was, that they were both milking the circuit for as much as they could get out of it, but that at least he, Sir Otto, was a professional prizefighter rather than a prostituted pimp. Gérard responded by speaking with equal rapidity in Provençal, of which the Teuton had less than a smattering.

'Sir Otto has asked me to explain,' he mistranslated smoothly, 'that in the course of an active career which began with the sacking and looting of Constantinople, was invigorated by the ravishing and massacre of 20,000 Christians, and was continued in the Holy Land, at Damietta, and in territories to the east of the Holy Roman Empire, he has acquired the considerable amount of booty necessary to maintain him in the station to which he aspired but, mainly owing to his patronage of the brothels of Acre, Antioch, Beirut, Jaffa, Nazareth and Bethlehem, he has not put enough aside to provide himself even with a decent pair of shoes.'

There was a silence which Adèle, in charity, felt impelled to break. 'Sir Otto of Jerusalem!' she said with genuine goodwill. 'Tell us about Jerusalem.'

The knight glanced suspiciously at her, evaluating her dress, which though of fine cloth was drab in colour and very simply decorated. He studied her face, and began to speak with more warmth than he had previously shown. 'Kingdom of Jerusalem,' he said. 'Ver' big, sea to sea, Great Sea to Dead Sea and Galilee. Ver' long, Beirut to Gaza, ver' long. In Acre is der Hospital and Chancellery of Order of Teutonic Knights. Ver' brave men. Good fighters.'

'But Jerusalem,' said Adèle. 'The Holy Places.'

'City of Jerusalem. Not now in Kingdom of Jerusalem. Not yet again. Saracens capture Kingdom. Knights take Kingdom. Saracens keep City. Saladin said Christians go to Holy Places – Bethlehem, Gethsemane, Holy Sepulchre – only as pilgrims. Not armed.'

'Have you been?' Adèle asked with a face half in rapture.

'Never,' said Sir Otto decisively. 'Give up mein sword? Never.' He spat on his finger and ran it over the black cross on his breast. 'I fight for der Kreuz all over Holy Land, in Acre, Antioch, Beirut, Jaffa, Nazareth – you heard what der minnesinger said. I never give up mein sword. Not for Bethlehem, not for Gethsemane, not for Golgotha, not for Holy Sepulchre. Soldier of Christ am I. Always I fight. So I practise. When is there no Saracen, no pagan, no heretic, I practise in tournament. Lieber Christus!' he suddenly burst out in inspiration. 'I fight for you!'

'For me?' Adèle asked, in utter incomprehension. 'You said you fought for Christ.'

'That is right in der Holy Land,' said Sir Otto complacently. 'At Crespin I fight for you.'

'Thank you very much,' said Adèle faintly, with visions of sitting in a pavilion of honour. 'What do I have to do?'

'You give yourself.'

'Give myself what?'

'Give yourself to the winner,' interrupted Gérard like a viper. 'The Holy Terror can't afford to endow the Gallowsbird Goblet in this year's competition, so he substitutes the Scrubbers Stakes, at no expense to himself and at some possible profit. For if there's gold in the offing he'll auction you off. You're a selling-plater, my dear. Sell now, rape later.'

'How remarkably alien to the ideals of *cortezia*,' said a very cool, feminine voice. Eléonore, Vicomtesse de Frébois, had approached unnoticed with three ladies in attendance. She glanced, with an attractive but aloof smile, round the group individually, noticed Maister Brémand as a newcomer, and when he rose from an undemeaning bow she nodded to him quite informally as a well-liked vassal. Her eyes were effectively outlined with charcoal. Her high forehead was milkily pale. Her cheeks were skilfully coloured. She was scented with a strong floral perfume. Her dress was monumentally rich in the blue and gold of the Virgin Mary, and the ecclesiastical hues of crimson, green and cream, which were the colour motifs of the gowns of her three attendants, heightened the impression that here was the Regina Coeli.

Yet the Lady Eléonore's reception was markedly more earthy than celestial. Gérard immediately burst into song, with a recurring jerk of his head to emphasize the rhythm and with a teasing look in his eyes:

Soft breasts
Firm arms
And a strawberry mark in the middle of her charms

Now you oughtn't to be sure
Which lady I adore
But if you are I'll kill you

The Lady Eléonore smiled tolerantly and took a seat that had been cleared for her. Hearing the music, the men and women grouped round the backgammon game abandoned the dice and ran laughing to the alcove. Among them was Gérard's jongleur, the companion minstrel who had been with him at the funeral (as was customary, a man of lesser attainment, who did not compose but sang the troubadour's songs and acted as his aide and confidant). He brought a vièle, a sort of lute, and put it in Gérard's hands. 'More! More!' called the castle company, but Gérard shook his head with a smile, indicating that there was all the time in the world, and basked quietly in the attention he was receiving.

'He's off again,' said the Vicomte de Frébois to Brémand with resignation. 'We'll slip out and broach that Pinot. Quietly, now. I'm not bringing Sir Otto in on this.' The two men moved unobtrusively away.

'Now, you said this is the bird-boy,' said the Vicomtesse to Adèle with faultless protocol, indicating Happy-With-Jesus. 'Gérard had mentioned that I might like to hear him. What does he do?'

'What a question!' drawled Gérard, giving each syllable a range of musical notes so that he injected a world of innuendo into a phrase that said nothing at all. 'I'll thank you not to ask what *I* do!'

'He sings bird-songs, Milady,' said Adèle politely. 'That's not all he does, he's a very fine worker, but I expect that's what you were told about him. Would you like to hear him?'

'Of course.'

After a little preparation and prompting from Robert, Happy-With-Jesus sang the song of the blackbird.

'Fascinating,' said Lady Eléonore.

'La-la-la, far-far-far,' said Happy-With-Jesus, who was beginning to enjoy himself.

'What does he say?' enquired the châtelaine.

'He would like to sing a lark-song for Francis.'

'Francis who?' asked the lady. 'I thought we should slot in the yodelling some time after supper. The Vicomte will be here. Never mind.' She nodded to Robert. Happy-With-Jesus sang the lark-song, laughed with delight, and immediately tuned up his orchestra to play the air which Robert had sung that morning.

'He seems a little excited,' the lady said doubtfully to Robert. 'Perhaps you should take him for a walk while it is still light.' Robert ushered the lad away.

'Now, Gérard,' said the Lady Eléonore with the decisiveness of a justiciar taking up the main policy document at a royal council. 'I want to hear more of your views on the pain of love. At various Courts of Love instituted here in Poitou by my kinswoman Queen Eléonore, the conditions, effects, sanctions, warranties and prohibitions of courtly love were thoroughly examined and discussed. Very fortunately there was remarkably little ground to cover by the time the Queen was imprisoned by her impulsive husband, King Henry II of England, Duke of Aquitaine and Normandy, Count of Anjou. Present throughout this great assize were the Queen's daughter Marie, Regent of Champagne, and her chaplain Andreas. Andreas the chaplain has codified the conclusions of Queen Eléonore's commission in *De Arte Honeste Amandi*. In a striking introduction to this book he insists on the inseparability of love and pain. What are your considered views on this, Gérard?'

Gérard began speaking with fluent ease as if he were

expounding a familiar subject. But he avoided any suggestion of lecturing, phrasing his points with freshness and enthusiasm, and catching the eyes of individuals in his audience as if personally persuading them: 'I think the basis of the identification of love with pain is encapsulated in Countess Marie's historic dictum, delivered after an authoritative Court of Love, that love cannot operate between two people who are married to each other.' Here the Lady Eléonore nodded approvingly. 'For lovers must give love freely and not by reason of rights or duties. . . .'

'Would you like to come and see my horses?' Sir Otto asked Adèle in a low voice from the outside of the circle.

'He has two horses,' said Gérard, who had not been intended to catch the remark, but made no alteration in the tone of his comment, as if it were part of his discourse. 'One horse he rides, the other he is trying to sell. Ask yourself or your father whether he is the man you would buy a used horse from. Now, although love is given freely, it is this very freedom, the absence of duty, which gives rise to suffering, for the suffering of love is, at the heart of it, fear.'

Gérard emphasized his points on the fingers of one hand. He was now concentrating his meaningful glances on the Lady Eléonore, but with an intensity that seemed to be an actor's exaggeration of reality. 'Fear that the lover will not gain the love of the beloved. Fear that their love will be exposed, for an essential of courtly love is secrecy. Fear that, even if their love is consummated, love may still be lost.'

Quietly but unselfconsciously, Adèle moved away from the group. Sir Otto, taken by surprise, hurried after her. 'If that is love, I'll take horses,' she said, and led the way to the stairs.

'These fears compound into a mental torment, which is nevertheless a part of the ecstasy of love,' said Gérard.

'Who among you, having experienced that searing pain of longing, will deny the rapture that is within it?'

With eyes closed and lips parted the Lady Eléonore seemed to be living remembered or hoped-for rapture. Slowly she came round and smiled at the company. 'We shall inaugurate a formal Court of Love in this hall after supper tonight,' she announced. Attended by her ladies she walked towards the high table at the end of the hall, ascended to the gallery, and went to her own apartment among the private quarters to which the gallery gave sole access.

Sir Otto uttered a shriek of sudden pain, threw himself sideways off a bale of hay, snapped his feet like a wrestler before he fell, and stood up, not straight but crouching in angry menace.

'Vampire!' he said, brushing a flow of dark venous blood from the fleshy part of his neck.

'Your taste is as disgusting as your touch,' said Adèle, cleaning her lips. 'Go back to the Dead Sea.'

Robert came hurrying from the bright courtyard into the stable and puckered his eyes in the sudden gloom.

'Is anything the matter?' he asked.

'Nothing,' said Adèle.

'I've lost Happy-With-Jesus. I thought perhaps the soldiers were baiting him.'

There was the sound of a whinny from a farther stall. It was followed by another whinny and then a gurgle of delighted laughter.

'Ah, thank goodness,' said Robert. 'He's in with the horses. Did you know?'

'We never got to the horses,' said Adèle, 'although they had been promised.' She turned her head to examine first Sir Otto and then her surroundings with a long distasteful stare. 'It's a hard choice,' she continued. 'But, on second thoughts, if this is horses, I'll take love.'

Happy-With-Jesus came out of the stall and moved towards the voices he had heard. He hurried to take Adèle's hand, then looked round and saw that Sir Otto was bleeding. He could not bear to see pain in others and, shambling forward to give sympathy to the sufferer, put his arms round Sir Otto.

'Hurt, hurt, hurt,' he said consolingly. Because he was not tall, his level arms did little more than encompass the knight's waist, so that he had to press his head sideways against the chest with the black cross on the surcoat. The effect was that he seemed not to be comforting but to be asking for comfort.

Sir Otto put both elbows behind the lad's throat and threw him to the floor.

'Hurt,' said Happy-With-Jesus.

The Court of Love plainly bored Messire le Vicomte de Frébois, who rapidly increased the rate of his drinking. He used Brémand as a judge uses his clerk, to make audible comments on the proceedings without halting them, and he otherwise eased his boredom by waking Rupert as often as possible to get some notice taken of him. At the end of the communal supper Brémand had been invited to the high table with Robert and Adèle, and Happy-With-Jesus had been left to idle until called on. The considerable number of castle retainers stayed in their places because they knew there would be a song, but kept their voices down as they were expected to, except on nights of high revelry. For a short time Frébois discussed farming matters with Brémand, but he found the feverish discussion of amorous trivia progressively more intrusive and vexatious.

'There is no requirement for a lady to reveal to a would-be lover the state of her heart,' enounced Gérard, and there was an excited murmur of questions as ladies discussed whether they might not at least hint that their affections were not otherwhere engaged. 'The kiss that is called the *merci* is a true exchange of hearts through the transference of breath and saliva.' A tremulous flutter accompanied giggling retrospections to determine whose heart was in whose bosom now. 'A state of pure love can still exist if the lovers contemplate, caress or even embrace the nude bodies one of the other.' Sensation in court!

'It's all in the mind!' shouted the viscount as the company contemplated the contemplation of nude bodies.

'A lover who is unwary enough to become enamoured of a peasant,' Gérard persevered, 'should flatter the girl and, in a convenient place, ravish her, because he must use a little compulsion to overcome her shyness.'

'She's not a peasant,' Frébois roared. This momentarily stopped all discussion. 'She's not a peasant,' the viscount bellowed again across the table at Sir Otto. 'I decide the peasants around here.'

The Lady Eléonore had had her own motives for calling the Court of Love, and she had no intention of dissolving it. But she did see reason in steering for a temporary change of mood. She glanced down the hall towards Balthasar, Gérard's jongleur, who had been sitting at a far table with his eyes constantly on her. She nodded, and Balthasar ran to the high table with a vièle, which he had kept tuned all through the evening. 'A bow!' ordered Gérard, deciding to play the instrument rather than pluck it, and a bow was handed to him.

'Not the *balada*!' Lady Eléonore insisted in a deep, urgent tone.

With a wide-eyed look, as if he had not understood, Gérard defied her immediately by playing the theme of the dance tune she had forbidden. He turned to her with exaggerated deference and said: 'It's mine. Why not?' The tune was promptly recognized by the retainers in the hall, who crowded to the dais to enjoy it. Gérard put one foot on his stool and the other on the table and sang, with the castle servants humming the tune they had learned from him:

I love a lady and a lady loves me
But I cannot tell you more by the rules of Courte*see*
For we like what we do and we do when we can
But Milord her husband's a jealous man

Gérard repeated on his vièle the last line of the verse he had sung. Among the retainers some eyes dropped uneasily.

Oh, no
It isn't fanta*see*
I'm calling up a witness to corroborate me

Soft breasts
Firm arms
And a strawberry mark in the middle of her charms

Now you oughtn't to be sure
Which lady I adore
But if you are I'll kill you

It was a thumping bucolic tune of Gérard's, which demanded a response. He played the chorus again and the crowd in the body of the hall not only thumped it but for the most part sang it. But there were some who could not mouth the words.

Now you oughtn't to be sure
Which lady I adore
But if you are I'll kill you

They finished with a great double stamp and waited for the next round.

I love a lady and a lady loves me
But I cannot tell you more by the rules of Courte*see*
For we like what we do and we do when we can
But Milord her husband's a jealous man

Oh, no
It isn't fanta*see*
I'm calling up a witness to corroborate me

Curved back
Clean side
And a mole in the saddle that we cover when we ride

Now you oughtn't to be sure
Which lady I adore
But if you are I'll kill you

The cheers and laughter after the second chorus had an effect at the high table. The Lady Eléonore, yielding nothing, wore a fixed smile which those who knew her well would say concealed a tense disdain – but for whom? The singer or the audience? Gérard, much less schooled in concealing his apprehension, gave the châtelaine an uncertain and questioning tremor of the lips which evoked no visible response from the mask he was consulting. He surrendered to the shouts for another round.

I love a lady and a lady loves me
But I cannot tell you more by the rules of Courte*see*
For we like what we do and we do when we can
But Milord her husband's a jealous man

Oh, no
It isn't fanta*see*
I'm calling up a witness to corroborate me

There was a hush as the audience waited for his next sally.

Hips that twirl
Thighs that cling
And where I have a navel she has a fairy ring

Now you oughtn't to be sure
Which lady I adore
But if you are I'll kill you

'It's all in the mind,' shouted the Vicomte de Frébois to Louis Brémand above the din that followed the last chorus. 'He goes to bed with his jongleur.'

'Enough! Silence! Go away!' he shouted at the crowd below the dais. 'Finished. Go away.'

The retainers realized that the party was over, sooner than they had expected. They streamed to their dormitories. Except for the duty guards, only a few were permitted to sleep in the warmth of the hall, and on this night they recognized that even they must find beds elsewhere. They went, some clearly in bad humour. By this time Happy-With-Jesus, who had been disturbed by the thumping and stamping, was curled on the floor of the dais playing with Rupert.

The Lady Eléonore waited until the hall was clear, then spoke with some deliberation. Her voice did not employ its full range, as if there were chords in her throat that were still tightened, but it was by no means strained, and her manner was presidential but not austere. The Court of Love had been partly a candid public airing of restricted sexual topics – particularly among the ladies, who esteemed the opportunity to discuss more formally, before men, matters which were normally only chamber gossip – and it had been partly a charade. The charade had been necessary to give the assembly some panoply of credibility, and Lady Eléonore was resolved to terminate the session of the court with the keynote qualities of dignity and judicial bottom.

'In summing up the proceedings of this Court,' she said, 'no radical judgments have been registered, since in the main the Court upholds the decisions reached at previous courts under the presidency of Queen Eléonore and Regent Marie. What has been notable is the vehemence of the objections by one assessor in particular, Messire le Vicomte de Frébois. "It is all in the mind," he has frequently stated. It may well be that love is a reunion of souls that is finer than the union of bodies. The unresolved question has been what part, if any, the body plays in love.

'Messire le Vicomte seems to assert that there is none. Now Messire claims, and legitimately claims, my own body under a sacrament of the Church which assured him that his wife was a fruitful vine and which enjoined the wife to be subject to her husband in all things. This sacrament was preceded by a contract which brought Messire the considerable estates that in part sponsor the adequacy of your entertainment tonight, and which was signed on my behalf when I was six years old. Messire, with an honesty that does him credit, does not claim my mind, and in fact he had my body before I had a mind, in any adult connotation. My mind developed, as far as the recognition of love is concerned, a little later than my breasts. Now, love exists. That is not questioned at all in this court, even, I think, by Messire le Vicomte.

'I have to say frankly that in my own mind, to which Messire restricts it, love concerns a union of bodies as well as souls – as to which is superior I pronounce no judgment. But by contract and sacrament I am forbidden to pursue my concern with that joint union. If I were in the happy position of the Demoiselle Adèle, whose mind has been permitted to develop as unrestrictedly as her body, I should be able to achieve the realistic conception of a fusion of mind and body – at first established in my mind, and later by good fortune expressed through my body. As it is, my imprisoned mind, and the minds of my gentle ladies, can only luxuriate, in a possibly unbalanced manner, in such images as the nudity of devoted lovers, and other colourful obsessions which excite the proprietory protests of Messire le Vicomte: fantasies – or fanta*sees* as the troubadours sing it' (and here she directed a frosty smile towards Gérard), 'an idealization of adultery to which the only alternative is the commission of adultery, yet adultery still yearning for a spiritual consummation. This is anathema to the Church, but the Church has compounded it by ignoring the reality of love. Perhaps the Friar Robert has some comment to make on this?'

In utter surprise, Robert started back in his chair, jerking into confusion the body of Happy-With-Jesus, who had been sitting on the floor asleep, his head on Robert's knee. The friar had never considered himself a member of the Court of Love. He had followed Lady Eléonore's reasoning with intellectual interest. He had had no intention of contributing. But he felt he must respond to the challenge, and so he rose to his feet, his thoughts all unmarshalled.

'Not all the servants of the Church ignore the reality of love,' he began hesitantly. 'I have myself . . .' he paused for a phrase, but in panic abandoned the theme. 'Let us be clear that it is passion we have been talking about, and the Fathers of the Church never came to reconcile passion with marriage. Indeed, Peter Lombard, the Blessed Gregory and more than one of the Popes have said that passionate love within marriage is adultery: *omnis ardentior amator propriae uxoris adulter est.*' He paused. 'It is a pity,' he said drily, and added: 'I shall not dodge that issue. I shall come to it later.

'May I tell you a story? All preachers like to tell stories, but they have a good model, for Jesus preached with stories.

'When I first put on this grey gown I tried to be what Francis called a new-born fool, *novellus pazzus*, which is really no different from the Lord saying "Except ye become as little children ye shall not enter the kingdom of Heaven." Children are simple, you are sophisticated. Love is simple, passion is sophisticated. As a fresh child I first knew love. I saw love behind the Creation. I saw love *in* the creation of the complex beauty of birds and beasts and man and flowers. And since love, however selfless, is itself enriched by being recognized, I thought love would be richer by a response from what love had created. I thought I saw this response to love from birds and beasts and man and, yes, from flowers. I was a new-born fool. I had thrown away my books. I was simple enough to think that if God became incarnate as a man, God might also lend himself to a flower.

'Then, from love, I learned to know passion. Passion is suffering, but it is also an ecstasy. Passion is not smooth, like a tide, but tempestuous as the sea. Yet amid all the currents the tide still runs strong, through battles powered by free wills and proud resistance. I saw in Creation a love that would not let me go and I strove to meet that love. Love's arms drew me, my joyful response impelled me, the intellectual world posed every possible conflict, and in that final union with love I found passion.'

Robert paused and said, very diffidently: 'I said that I should not run away from consideration of human passion. But I cannot pronounce on it. The Fathers of the Church are appalled by it. It is not harmonious or dutiful. But then, neither was the passion of my reunion with the love the Church approves.

'I could postulate human passion as a presage of the divine, the statement of a theme not thrown away but embodied in the final symphony. Then I could plead for the ultimate union of human with divine passion:

Contentious yet persuasive
Emollient, abrasive
Merge me in your pervasive
  Debonair, ebon-haired
  Thorn-crowned, grief-drowned
  Shameless, blameless
  Mingled, single Love.

But to develop that would require deep philosophy. And I have little learning now. I am lost.'

Robert smiled apologetically. But before any reaction from the Court became apparent Adèle was speaking combatively. 'I will be contentious immediately,' she said, repudiating any pretence that she did not understand Robert's allusion. 'When will you understand that you *need* conflict? You need it in love. You need abrasion – as you call it – for subsequent purification – as I call it if we're going in for all these long words. You need the flesh and you need the spirit, and they are fused by love. Love is a yearning for a final state in which any distinction between the lovers is absent. Love is a progress. Love craves physical union as an intermediate pledge. Beyond intercourse it seeks something – oh, Plato put it better than I can – "something of which the soul has only a dark and doubtful presentiment." It's a way to God. . . .'

'With all that to play for, why don't you make love with me?' The interruption came from Gérard, who had lost his place as arbiter. Adèle looked at him steadily and answered:

'Because I have been observing you and I have no yearning for a final absence of distinction between you and me. Why don't you let me get on? You had the stage for an hour. If you're bored, comfort yourself that I want only two minutes.

'Love is a way to God. Sexual congress is the beginning of a long progression, but the passion must be there, because the soul needs the flesh to fire it in the crucible. Robert said God made this beautiful world with love. Robert says that, after torment, he gets back to God in love. To get back, he abandons his body and his intellect. Didn't God make my body with love, my intellect with love? I'll use all I've got to get back to him. How are *you* all reaching him?

'You've accepted the invention of sacred and profane love, two statues installed to accommodate the Church's incompetence to deal with passion. You unwillingly believe that the flesh is evil and will never get you to God. You've further invented courtly love as a mystic, consoling union which is a substitute for consummated love. That's supposed to be all in the mind, but it doesn't stay there, so when you fall to the flesh you have another artificial sin afflicting you.

'Why don't you at least consider that desire, passion – love – may be the God-given first kindling of your desire for God? Learn to educate and exploit desire rather than handle it timidly like a snake. Speculate that the path of passion is a tough climb upwards to salvation, not the broad slope to perdition. That will set the bones rattling in Peter Lombard's coffin. But not in Peter Abélard's, I fancy. Eloïse taught him passion and from it he learned wisdom. In that furnace the image of the Avenger was molten and the loving God perceived, so that he was able to declare: "By the life and death of God he has so bound us to him that love so kindled will shrink at nothing for his sake. We do his will from love and not from fear." '

'Scholar!' Robert affectionately mocked her. 'Proud, peacock, Platonic scholar!'

'Idiot,' said a voice from the other end of the table.

It was Brémand, and the observation stirred Messire de Frébois into amused wakefulness. He had followed the argument of his wife with complete attention, even smiling at her sallies, but during the remarks that followed he had sunk into an attitude of brooding. The altogether unexpected entry of a tenant farmer into a Court of Love diverted him.

'Idiot,' repeated Brémand. 'That's the key. I've heard more about love this evening than I ever reckoned to hear in any night of my life, any night with my wife. I want to put a very simple thing to you, just as it's come to me. I want to put it to you that there's no love in this world that's better, or deeper felt, or a kindlier influence on the souls of all who see it, than the love of a man for his dog and a dog for his man such as what exists between me and old Rupert down here. Now very likely you think I'm a turdy great fool for thinking and saying a thing like that. But put it the other way round. Say that the *dog* is a turdy great fool. Then it's all right, isn't it, because he's allowed to be the fool, he gets the credit for it, he's the lower end of the leash of love and he's supposed to do better the more of a fool he is. Brother Robert just said so. I met Brother Sylvester on the way here this morning and he said the only good friar was an idiot. Why? Because he gets more credit for loving God if he's an idiot. All he's got to know is that he loves God and God loves him, and the less said about proving it the better. That's perfect love. That's what my dog Rupert's got for me. I'm his god and he doesn't know why. And, come to think of it, that's what I've got for my dog Rupert. I'm his god and I don't know why I love him. Call me a fool and I don't mind. Doesn't make my love any littler, does it? Doesn't spoil life for anyone else, but rather makes it better. I don't ask why, I just see that it's so. Perhaps God is like that. Call him a fool and he doesn't mind. He just loves his creation, doesn't know why and doesn't ask why. So nobody needs to speculate.'

Messire de Frébois burst out laughing and clapped Brémand on the shoulder. 'Bravo!' he said. 'But you're no fool. You're a cunning old lawyer. Sitting here quietly and working out that defence! As if I were going to snatch Rupert from you! Really, you take things too seriously.'

'Every vassal has to take his lord seriously,' said Brémand. 'Because a lord can take things lightly. One day his dog, lightly, another day his wife. . . .'

'Nonsense, nonsense! I never intended to take Rupert back. But you will bring him over to help with the pack? What's that boy doing?'

Happy-With-Jesus, who was always relieved when people laughed, was talking to Rupert in his own language.

'Ah yes, the bird-boy,' said the viscount. 'Let's hear him.'

The mood of the company at the table was jaded, but the lord had spoken. Robert prepared and encouraged the lad, and he sang the song of the nightingale. The pure notes, the amazing variations and the spendthrift finale captured the sympathy of the audience, and they praised the boy warmly. Unbidden, he promptly launched into the song of the skylark, and he was applauded so strongly at the end of it that, in full enjoyment now, he started another song. Robert intervened and gently conveyed to him that this was enough. The boy stopped singing, but mischievously mimicked Robert's remonstration with him, using sounds that were not words and copying Robert's gestures so skilfully that he caused spontaneous laughter. With growing excitement Happy-With-Jesus gave a version of Robert's statement to the Court of Love which was almost cruel in its reproduction of the friar's initial diffidence, his increasing sincerity, and a pattern of tender glances towards Adèle which had either been previously missed by the company or were being intensified to the point of caricature by the lad's keenness of observation.

The unreserved amusement which this caused set Happy-With-Jesus laughing loudly with appreciation and made him virtually unstoppable. Suddenly he rose and, with his face and bearing completely changed and a series of jerky guttural noises issuing from his throat, he began an appallingly accurate mimicry of Sir Otto. Approaching Adèle, he made some crude, leering sounds to her which he answered on her behalf with short and very cool replies. With an unexpected movement he twisted her in her chair and had half her body on her back across the table, with his hand high under her skirt. With the speed and sound of a whipcrack the troubadour Gérard vaulted over the table, pulled the boy away and began to beat him. Adèle struggled up and caught at Gérard's hammering arms and fists. Sir Otto had made no movement but sat clenched in his chair, muscles knotted in his cheeks below icy-blue eyes. But the viscount was standing over him.

'She's not a peasant!' Frébois shouted.

'You filthy cretin!' said Gérard, attacking Happy-With-Jesus again.

'Leave him alone,' Adèle ordered.

'Why? He's a brute who must be taught his manners.'

'He's telling the truth, isn't he?' demanded Adèle.

Breathing heavily, the troubadour dropped his fists. Happy-With-Jesus seized Adèle's hand and covered it with kisses from a mouth dripping with saliva.

'Supper is over,' ordered the Vicomte de Frébois. 'Everyone go.'

'Your daughter will sleep with my ladies,' Lady Eléonore assured Maister Brémand.

Long before midnight there was utter silence in Castle Crespin. The fire in the hall was banked down to a low glow. A single flambeau in a bracket on a wall served the guards who, on occasional patrol, brushed through the reeds on the floor. Under the tables a few dark shapes were sleeping.

From somewhere outside, some quarter in this populated castle where the array of circular stairways rose like boles in a forest and echoed like organ-pipes, there came a long, low cry with a liquid ending. Silence succeeded. Perhaps nearby there was a following slither of feet on stone.

Sideways on a pallet, seeming almost to be looking over his shoulder, lay the troubadour Gérard. A broad dagger breaching windpipe, jugular vein and carotid artery pinned him to the bedboard. The spout of blood had hit high up the wall and was trickling down the stone.

In another bastion, and now with no attempt at stealth, footsteps ascended stairs in relaxation, like a man coming home contented after labour. Half-hummed, half-whistled, the tune of Gérard's last chorus piped breathily down a circular stairway.

Now you oughtn't to be sure
Which lady I adore
  But if you are I'll kill you.

9

Pride and Plantagenet

'Goddam the mandrakes,' said Fulgent the fox. He cursed with no particular animosity. But it was the end of a long tour of duty. He was tired and dejected. And it was safer to swear like a soldier at targets out of his range, than risk a rational focusing of his bad temper, which he knew was provoked by his mate.

He snaked imperceptibly through the glossy leaves of the evergreen shrub which grew in profusion around one of the entrances to his earth. He regarded the patch of daphne laureola almost with the contentment of a husbandman who had deliberately planted it, and he had indeed chosen to dig this particular entry because of it. Well over shoulder height, it gave magnificent cover, and the tips of his ears brushed perfumed green flowers which would fruit into choice black berries later in the year.

At the mouth of the tunnel he readjusted in his jaws the body of the young rabbit he was carrying, and wormed his way through the long excavation to his den. Within the earthen burrow a vague mass, as indefinable as spawn, heaved and subsided with a variety of sounds. Dominant was the primeval snuffle, that battle-grunt of the first conflict which every young creature must resolve – how to co-ordinate sucking with breathing, and when to sacrifice blind greed for greater efficiency by lifting the nostrils from the udder. As counterpoint there came the fast sweeping and scouring of a grating tongue on soft fur, and the muffled protest as a sharp nose momentarily drove the breath out of a yielding body. Régine, Fulgent's vixen, was suckling some of her cubs as she groomed others, combing matted hair, flushing eyes and ears and anuses with workmanlike speed.

Fulgent stood upright in the vaulted den with the rabbit in his jaws, and waited unhopefully for recognition. His instinct was correct. He got none. He dropped the rabbit and stood quietly, neither importunate nor sulky. He knew that, as soon as he had left, Régine would dive onto the carcass, eat her fill, dismember the rest and bury it in various parts of the den for future consumption. He would have liked an amicable gesture of appreciation, perhaps the invitation to munch a morsel companionably at her side, and he was sorry. 'This defeatism will get me nowhere,' he told himself. 'But friendly acknowledgment is all I ask. Goddam the mandrakes.'

He turned back towards the tunnel to leave the den. A litter of bones and refuse offended his habitual sense of tidiness, sharpened by survival drill. With one skilful shove of his muzzle he rolled them up in a chewed pelt and carried the parcel out like a toolbag. Back above ground, he went out of his way to drop the refuse at the foot of an elm tree, among the pellets cast there by a barn owl who had recently begun roosting in an upper fork. 'Fetch and carry, bring in the flesh and take out the garbage,' he commented philosophically. He came back and settled comfortably for a spell of watch and ward, half in and half out of the daphne laureola.

Soon he heard, some distance away, a sound which was both recognizable and puzzling. The entire absence of stealth, the dry twigs crackling underfoot, the swish of shrubs taken head-on rather than decently side-stepped – these indications marked the approach of the boar Grondin. But everything seemed to be happening at half its normal speed, as if the torrent which ran the wheel of a waterclock had suddenly lost its spate. Grondin was moving at the rate of a cow at milking-time rather than with the energetic bustle he normally adopted in spite of his great bulk. Fulgent wondered if perhaps he were ill.

A juniper, which had struggled for longer than Grondin's lifetime to reach the meagre height it had achieved, prostrated itself like a slave and sprang back with a decreased expectation of life as the boar passed through it and came into Fulgent's range of vision. The reason for Grondin's sluggish approach was clear. He was accompanied by his cousin, the runt of a boar brood who had been domestically adopted as the pig Plantagenet. In extremes of terror Plantagenet could call on bursts of speed which were superstitiously regarded as out of this world, and were confidently expected to get him there if sustained. But maturity and a certain reputation for heroism had heightened Plantagenet's threshold of terror, and he had cultivated the deliberate stroll which was now holding Grondin back. Their progress seemed even more retarded by an atmosphere of gravity in the conversation which the boar and the pig were exchanging. They were like two statesmen pacing a path in a grove while agreeing the terms of a joint ultimatum. But Grondin smelled Fulgent, located him lying like a sculptured lion in the undershrub, and perhaps in some relief switched to an air of joviality.

'*Couchant gardant,*' he said. 'What a magnificent profile! You'd look superb on a mandrake's shield.'

Fulgent was in no mood to be mocked, but he was a creature of princely courtesy. He recognized that Plantagenet was an honorary rather than a hereditary member of the forest aristocracy and would appreciate immediate masonic acknowledgment in the ritual of the period. 'Ah do, tha bugger?' he therefore inquired of the pig as a suitably arcane friendly greeting, and then he turned to deal with Grondin.

'I wouldn't stoop to ask what you mean by that peculiar salutation,' he said, 'except that I want to know.'

'Have you ever tried stooping when you're *couchant*?' asked Grondin pleasantly. 'It's heraldry. It has amused me since we came up with the mandrakes in the Long March. Surcoats and shields, and all that spurious panoply. I don't know what effect they had on the enemy, but, by God, they exhilarated me. There was a fat over-armoured banneret, dismounted by Plantagenet, too heavy to run, who could do no more than shake his shield at us and pray for thunderbolts. The only blazon he had on his shield was a griffin, and that was supposed to frighten us. Frighten the lords of the forest with an eagle-headed lion! *They*'re supposed to be the experts in breeding and they don't even know practical genetics. But some of the pictures they paint are pretty.

'There was a shield with a portrait that was the spitting image of Flandrin the bear. Well, of Flandrin on the one historic occasion when he came across that barrel of mead that rolled off a wagon on the way to St Andrew's Fair. He thought it was honey, which of course it had been before the mandrakes put the devil in it. There he was on the shield, half as large as life, standing on one foot, forepaws all over the place, *rampant* they call it. Now you were *couchant*, lying on your belly with your front pads extended . . .'

Fulgent allowed himself a slight, covered yawn. Grondin paused politely to allow him to re-engage his attention, and went on with undiminished enthusiasm.

'. . . and *gardant*, looking straight ahead, or, if I know you, scanning right, left and centre, but certainly not turning your head to your tail, which would be *regardant*.'

Fulgent yawned again, more openly. He began to wonder whether the effervescence of Grondin, who had a reputation for being morose, indicated that he had found his own barrel of mead or metheglin. Yet Plantagenet seemed remarkably sober. The boar perceived the fox's reserve but still finished strongly:

'Altogether, a most attractive and alert posture. Accept my congratulations.'

'On making a pretty picture?' Fulgent asked irritably. 'No thank you very much. I was handsome enough in my time, and much good it has done me. Beauty vanishes, beauty passes, and while I crumble all I've got left is duty. Namely, to keep a weather eye open for two and a half pounds of fresh meat a day. Stuff your attractive posture. I wouldn't last long in the open near a recognized cross-route if I wasn't alert. How did you expect to see me? *Couchant dormant*? Senile I may be, but I can still remember my lady mother's maxim: "Forty winks, belly shrinks, half a glance, guts a-dance." '

'Wise old Mother,' said Grondin in vague admiration. 'What did she mean? I don't get the connection.'

'Sound sleep doesn't raise dream dinners.'

'Oh, very good, yes, of course, yes,' said Grondin tolerantly, and swang back into animation. 'Well, well, well, there's a glorious smack of spring in the air. And, talking of connection, when last?'

'When last what?'

'When last connection? How's your love life?'

'About as dreary as you told me yours was going to be.'

'Dreary, eh? I thought I sensed a certain gloom.' Grondin winked at Plantagenet, who did not respond with great vivacity. 'But you've got me all wrong. I'm not down in the dumps at all. Having wonderful time. Wish you were with me.'

'Wonderful time? Charging brother boars? Blunting your agricultural machinery?'

'I'm afraid I don't quite get you, old man. Blunting my machinery? Possibly so, but nothing is permanent. Time's a great healer. I'm really enjoying myself. Taken years off my life.'

'I distinctly remember you cursing what you were pleased to call the Curse. Swelling your bristles at the prospect of having to paw the ground to consummate a doubtful pleasure. Shrinking at behaving in a manner unbecoming to a gentleman.'

'Did I say that? How extraordinary! It just shows what a different creature you are when you're depressed. It all balances out. No, I'm definitely living the good life. Spent a few days sorting out the men from the boys, you know. Formed my own club. We range about and have a rare old time. We spar a bit, of course, if two of us get the same ideas about the same bit of fluff and gristle. But no harm done. Blood all over the place, you understand, but nothing serious. Not as long as you win.'

'. . . "And all for nothing," ' Fulgent solidly continued his indictment. ' "For the ever-loving and unfortunately ever-living Albaine." How *is* Dame Albaine?'

'She's all right,' said Grondin defensively. 'Happy enough. Why shouldn't she be? She's a great family character, you know. Just dotes on a family. Well, there's a batch on the way. All she's got to do is build herself up. She's got no worries at all.'

'Not about you?'

'We've an understanding,' blustered Grondin. 'I'll see she's all right.'

'Does she understand about the club? The bits of fluff and gristle?' Here Plantagenet groaned perceptibly, but converted the reaction into a discreet cough.

'Why not?' Grondin protested. 'She's got no option.

Good Lord, it's just a spree. It's nature taking over. You can't fight nature, can you? I'll settle down again. That's nature, too. I'll probably go back to being all introspective. Pity. We think too much, old boy. That's solitude.'

'You can always think about the palmy past. But you and Dame Albaine have an understanding about the future?'

'W-e-l-l, yes. I don't know why you keep on about this. I'll do the decent thing. Just as you would.'

'I don't have any option about doing the decent thing,' said Fulgent. 'That's nature, too, so far as it hits me. Goddam the mandrakes.'

'You're miserable!' said Grondin in concern. 'Things not going too well? How's . . . er . . . , how's . . . ?'

'Régine,' said Fulgent.

'Yes. How's Régine?'

'Fine.'

'Cubs arrived?'

'Yes. Four. Don't know yet whether they're dogs or bitches.'

'Of course. You get it over faster than we do. So everything's all right, eh?'

Fulgent took a deep breath and exploded in a burst of candour. 'Everything is all wrong. Oh, it was fine when we were courting. I felt magnificent. I felt real pride. And she was as individual, as provocative, yet as loving and confidence-building as you could have wished. And I had fixed up the cosiest earth I have ever prepared and, to give her credit, she toiled away at making it a real home as hard as I did. Comes pregnancy, and she gradually turns. Have you ever been rejected? I don't think you ever have, for once you've splashed the club blood all over the place you're a pretty brutal lover. That's nature, as you'd say. Funny that there's a different nature for you and me – wonder what it's like with the mandrakes? Well, I was rejected all right. And by the time she was digging herself in for the birth she was vicious. She chucked me out. Expelled me neck and crop and brush. So, like a dumb fool, I carry on doing my duty. Forage all night and half the day. Sleep up aloft in the gale. She deigned to hunt with me for a time, but in the last stages she went completely to earth. I continued doing the necessary. Brought in the food, got sworn at, first cuffed and then bitten until I knew my place. One morning I staggered in with the flesh, and the cubs had come. Just in innocent curiosity I went to have a look at the litter and got a gash in my flank that will mark me for life. She's never stirred from the earth since. Except no doubt to stir up a bit of mutiny with the mother's milk. While I stir my stumps pounding through this poxy forest for two and a half pounds of meat a day. Stirring times, eh? Families delivered daily, but not next year nor any other year, if only I can stick to what I've learned in purgatory and now recited in your confessional. You know, we foxes have a reputation for being very clever characters. You'd think one of us would have worked out a way by now to escape from the pregnancy trap, wouldn't you? Thank the Lord you came. You've restored my sense of humour. *Vive l'amour*, but count me out.'

'You should leave her,' said Grondin.

'Leave whom?'

'Great God, do I have to remember her name? Leave *her.*'

'Régine?'

'If it's Régine, leave Régine.'

'You haven't the slightest conception of what you're talking about or whom you're talking to,' said Fulgent, very rapidly losing his new-found sense of humour. 'I thought better of you than that. I don't expect my dependants to fare for themselves. I have principles. I am a fox.'

'Ah, the master race!' said Grondin belligerently. 'Milords, I give you the foxes. Furred, fussy and fastidious. The prima donnas of principles. Principles, my fundament. Principles are nothing but heredity and environment. So I have principles. For most of the year they say "Get out of this rat race, Grondin. Launch yourself into the cool forest. Have a long think about life. You've thirty summers to get through. You won't go hungry. Nature will provide. You're leaving a good fat sow behind and she will see to everything the brood requires. . . ." '

'Oh, you *do* remember that! How convenient!' said Fulgent.

'I remember it as sharply as you remember – if only you'll be honest with yourself – the depression you got into a year ago, and how you slowly climbed out of it. I also remember that on last Midsummer's Day I met you on your own, fantastically high, as foxed as a newt, because at last you'd taught the cubs to hunt and you were up and away. You were only three months later in the year than I was, so that's how perpetual you considered your principles. Since it takes you longer as a couple to train your whelps as predators than it takes my sow to demonstrate the insertion of snout into soil, the interval is hardly surprising. The only holy Joe around here that I have any respect for is Hurlaud the wolf and his lot. And if you ask him why he's monogamous I'll guarantee he'll scratch his head in ignorance and privately wish he wasn't. So cut this talk of principles. You're stuck, man. Stuck with nature, and you moan. I'm stuck too, stuck with two or three months of randiness, and when I see it coming I also moan. We moan because we refuse to remember, and we kid ourselves we are not free. Freedom is the recognition of necessity, but we won't make the effort to accept it. We don't welcome change, though change is life. Soon they'll make it respectable and call it "progress". It isn't progress, it's a turning circle. I don't see you or me spiralling up to higher consciousness. In nine months' time you'll be fooling around with a vixen and ranting about magnificence and pride and confidence – and in twelve months' time you'll be on your knees again. That's not progress, it's life. Ask Plantagenet. He moves in the best circles, where they do imitations of life. He knows all about progress. He's in with Church and State, where they invent all the principles.'

'I'll ask Plantagenet one thing,' said Fulgent doggedly. 'Does he think I should abandon Régine? Does he think Grondin should abandon Albaine? Does he think the sexual link is a blind force of one moment, or a mutual assumption of rights and duties that can at least be requited by friendly acknowledgment?'

'Friendly acknowledgment?' queried Plantagenet. He was making an academic attempt to secure clarity of phrase, but Grondin misinterpreted his reaction as extreme embarrassment.

'You've scuppered him,' said Grondin crudely. 'You've asked the one question he knows nothing about. He's got no experience.'

'Why? Are you a virgin?' Fulgent asked Plantagenet directly.

'I'm . . . I'm saving myself,' said Plantagenet.

'*Sauve qui peut*,' said Grondin. 'I surrendered long ago. And don't ask who he's saving himself for. That will get us into very deep waters. He has a touching intellectual belief in fairy stories, where wicked witches transform beautiful sows into nut-brown maidens, and he's researching madly for the reverse spell. But press on, all the same. Cousin Plantagenet is a great philosopher. It comes from all this mixing with the mandrakes.'

'Goddam the mandrakes,' said Fulgent conversationally.

'Why do you say that?' Plantagenet asked quickly.

'Oh, it's automatic, really. I've learned to blast them and not lift a paw at Régine. You'd call it sublimation. It screens me from future remorse. And why do you ask?'

'I was interested,' said Plantagenet evasively. And for some time he was silent in thought.

'Come on, snap out of it,' said Grondin impatiently. 'You're the oracle around here. Fulgent has shot a set of questions at you. Surely you can answer one of them, even if it included a four-letter word for connection.' He burst coarsely into song:

> 'The sexual link
> Is inclined to make you shrink.
> But don't be shy,
> You can't deny
> That what you never do-o-o-o
> At least you think.

There, I made that up as I went along. How lyrical you get when you've conquered your repressions.'

'I have no reserve at all about discussing the sexual link, Cousin Grondin,' said Plantagenet, rather severely for a pig of his size. 'What interests me is your own rough rhyme relating "link" with "think". This surprises me because, from the vivid accounts with which you have flooded my ears over the past few weeks, when you're engaged in one of these activities you have no inclination at all for the other. That leads me on . . .' – Plantagenet's manner was rapidly becoming elevated to the egoism of a consultant – 'to Messire Fulgent's antithesis between the blind force of the urge and the allocation of rights and duties, with Fulgent's plea that it should be mollified by friendly acknowledgment.

'Now Régine is rigorously fulfilling all her obligations under natural law. Fulgent cannot fault her on the observance of her rights and duties, only for withholding friendly acknowledgment. It may well be that there is no interpretation of natural law which prescribes an obligation for friendly acknowledgment between paired parents. Perhaps there is even an insistence – under natural freedom – that friendly acknowledgment cannot morally operate between mates, but is only virtuous when it is freely given elsewhere, between individuals who have no rights or duties towards each other.'

'What pretentious rubbish!' roared Grondin. 'Where on earth did you pick up such trash?'

Plantagenet giggled in an entirely disarming act of self-deflation. 'From the mandrakes,' he said. 'Rupert told me all about it. That's the sort of thing they say at their Courts of Love.'

His mood suddenly darkened.

'Goddam the mandrakes,' said Fulgent in a formal religious response.

'I wish you meant that,' said Plantagenet.

'I do, I do. It's good to have a spare hate. It takes your mind off your frustrations.'

'It's therapeutic,' said Plantagenet.

'After all, I scored well against one mandrake. That yellow-livered Henriot. He's still lighting candles for that bit of fur I asked Rupert to deliver.'

'You could score against another,' said Plantagenet. 'It would give you something to do. Take your mind off your frustrations.'

'It's an idea,' said Fulgent. 'Have you anyone in particular in mind?'

Plantagenet paused. Then he said fiercely, 'Sir Otto.'

'Why him?'

'You don't know what happened at the castle.'

'Tell us what happened at the castle. Tell us everything.'

'I can't.'

'You mean about Adèle?'

'Well, yes.'

'For God's sake,' said Fulgent crossly. 'He made a pass at her. It happens every day. Ask Grondin. She came out of it all right. You'd expect her to. Tell us everything that happened at the castle. If you want to have a go against Sir Otto, I'm game. But you've got to give me a good briefing. Know your enemy. Now think hard and give me every detail. Conversations and all.'

'It will be an effort,' said Plantagenet. 'I wasn't there. It was Rupert who told me all about it.'

'If I know you,' said Fulgent ungraciously, 'you've been boiling up every last detail in your fevered mind until you know it all by heart. Now make the effort. Start talking.'

Plantagenet started talking. Fulgent listened keenly to the long narrative without interruption. Then he put a series of questions on details that seemed unimportant to Plantagenet. 'His saker falcon is in moult, you say? He'll be there for some two weeks more? Frébois is giving him a merlin?' The fox lapsed into a long period of reflection.

Grondin had been growing increasingly uneasy. He broke the silence.

'Look here, you two. You don't think this is beyond us, do you?'

'Beyond us?' Fulgent was beginning to laugh.

'Out of our scope,' said Grondin. 'Why are we doing this?'

'For fun,' said Fulgent.

'For pride,' said Plantagenet.

'Pride? Are we supposed to have pride?'

'I've got pride,' said Plantagenet.

'We're not being too anthropomorphic?' queried Grondin. 'Pride? Planning? Trying to fix the future? Do you think the Council of Animals would sanction this?'

Fulgent gave a great guffaw. 'Oh, don't let's be anthropomorphic!' he said. 'Our critics would never forgive it. Pride? As an animal I'm allowed anger, as long as the emotion is not termed indignation but debased to aggression; I'm allowed compassion as long as it is classified a by-product of lust or parenthood. Why should not my vibrant sense of individuality be admitted as pride? Planning? With one good fox in partnership I can hunt a hare and drive her to a gully where there is a single way through and my fresh colleague is waiting at the end of it. That's planning, and Hurlaud Lord of the Great Woods, with his brother wolves, is far more skilful at pack-hunting than I am. He can lecture on the unplanned free enterprise of his manoeuvres any evening at the Grand Council of the Forest, and I shall afford him the keenest attention. Influencing the future? Every action I take in the struggle to survive is an attempt to shape my future. I must be an anthropomorphic freak!'

'Excuse my ignorance,' said Plantagenet. 'And it's no great boost for my pride to admit it. But I don't know what *anthropomorphic* means.'

Grondin measured him with a disapproving eye. 'Well, just anthropomorphic, of course. Behaving like a mandrake. *Anthropos*, man; *morphe*, form. I'm just going back to my roots.'

'I see. What roots?'

'Greek roots.'

'*Beet* roots,' said Fulgent, who seemed to be afflicted with facetiousness as a result of the release of tension. 'He's far more at home with his beet roots.' The fox collapsed in light-headed laughter.

'Ho, ho, what jolly banter,' said Grondin in a tone that was entirely unconvinced. His lack of ease was enough to turn Fulgent serious and practical again.

'The simple lad,' said the fox. 'How well does he do the cry of the merlin?'

'I can find out,' said Plantagenet. 'He's pretty good at all the predators.'

'He'd better have a crash course,' said Fulgent in a businesslike manner. 'That gives me quite a shopping-list. I can shove some of it over to Puissard the sparrow-hawk. Item, one merlin, talkative if not tame. Item, one peregrine, preferably savage, with acclimatization to forest terrain as well as mountain country – well, the obvious candidate there is that cantankerous old curmudgeon Erémite. But if I engage Erémite I shall need my own heavy for self-protection because the peregrine would butcher me before we went into conference. Thank the Lord I'm in credit with the eagle owl Grand-Duc. Item, one maverick forest animal to put the fear of God into the Teuton. How about the bear Flandrin?'

'He should be fine for you,' said Grondin maliciously. 'At this moment he will go anywhere, do anything, all shady offers given special consideration. After seven months' fractious pregnancy his mate has just been delivered of two bouncing bear cubs.'

'Then he'll be desperate for friendly acknowledgment,' said Fulgent. 'I shall recruit him.'

Plantagenet had been jumping and coughing as he tried to penetrate the bustle of military logistics, and finally he was heard. 'What are you after, Plantagenet?' asked Fulgent.

'Just one assurance. The simple lad – you won't let him come to any harm, will you?'

'God looks after his own,' said Fulgent glibly, with his mind on other matters entirely.

'It was you I was asking,' said Plantagenet disconsolately. 'I can catch God any time, but you always seem so busy.'

But Fulgent had not heard him.

10

Spring Manoeuvres

It is difficult, but not impossible, for a hare and a beagle to climb a short distance into a favourably disposed cypress tree. What they do when they get there is their own affair. But in the case of Lulu and Rupert the object was neither slaughter nor mental seduction.

Messire le Vicomte de Frébois reserved the true dense forest in his territory for the exclusive art of hunting noble game. The fringes he exploited for timber and charcoal, his bailiffs directing fairly haphazard operations in areas where the cartage was easy. To an extent these sites were governed by the pattern of heathland, some of which was on a chalk base, and dry, some of it on a peat base, and boggy. Consequently the countryside for a league around the Castle of Crespin, except for the permanently cultivated lands, was an untidy stretch, always sloping down to the west, of plantation, marsh and rough open country, but still broken occasionally by thick belts of woodland.

This was perfectly satisfactory to Messire le Vicomte, who did not look on his estates with an aesthetic eye. Beyond the arable and grazing, they were to him an enclosure of the beasts and fowls of forest, chase and warren granted to him for his athletic delight. His delights included hawking and falconry, much of which was best done in parkland or fairly open country. They were now to embrace hare-coursing. In his day the efficient killing of the hare was done by greyhounds. But although they were swift and keen-sighted, their powers of scenting were poor. The custom was being introduced that beagles, with their magnificent noses but somewhat ludicrous though remarkably tireless legs, should be used to smell out and track down the hare, put her up and leave it to the nimble greyhounds to finish the chase.

For this reason Frébois had imported his motley group of beagles and was striving to make a handy pack from them. He had persuaded Brémand to bring Rupert to the castle on a succession of days to initiate the new crew into some disciplined habits, always on the understanding that the farmer took the hound home with him at night. As a conscientious objector, Rupert managed to be as inefficient as possible at Crespin without demanding too great a sacrifice of his master's pride. But he could see that the skill of the pack was inexorably increasing, and he had met Lulu in conferences designed to work out blunter forms of a veto on the success of the new sport. It was as a result of these discussions that they were now conducting a tactical exercise which they were controlling from a novel observation post.

A rough forest ride, part scrubland and part tufted turf, ran round the flank of a long slope in a general north-to-south direction with the slope going down to the west. On the lower edge of the ride was the solitary, hardy cypress which brought the narrow cone of its foliage all the way down to the ground. Rupert and Lulu had managed to clamber up the drooping forks to give them an altitude of three or four feet. In the distance on the left they could hear the baying – by no means as tuneful as Frébois had previously boasted – of the awkward squad of the pack recruited to Crespin. A solitary hare lolloped dutifully along the ride, making good speed but displaying that lack of application which marks the unconvinced long-distance runner. It passed the cypress and went on to the right. Lulu watched it with some dissatisfaction.

'Control to Quarry Target,' she screamed. 'Ease your speed. You are getting out of range. You are pursued by beagles, not greyhounds. Control to Red Squadron. Are you receiving me? Bandits massing nor'-nor'-east at beagles-lengths seven-fifty, repeat, beagles seven-five-zero. Advancing at low speed, owing to the bloody Quarry Target going too fast. Enemy speed now increasing. Scent now taken. Bandit impetus now mid-speed beagle, repeat, mid-speed beagle. Immediate orders now follow. On the scream "SODOM" Red Squadron will sweep direct east to west at maximum speed. After two-fifty hares-lengths, repeat, hares two-five-zero, Red Squadron will regroup on the stone outcrop, but below horizon level, for emergency action if diversion by Blue Squadron fails. Message understood? Roger.

'Control to Blue Squadron. Are you receiving me? Bandit disposition as reported. Immediate orders follow. On the scream "GOMORRAH" Blue Squadron will sweep at maximum speed sou'-west to nor'-east, slowing to optimum cruising speed after hares-lengths five hundred, repeat, hares five-zero-zero. After hares-lengths fifteen hundred, repeat, hares one-five-zero-zero, Blue Squadron will veer right on a radius vector, radius hares one thousand.'

Lulu dropped her voice without taking her eyes off the terrain, and commented complacently to Rupert, who was gazing at her in open admiration: 'That should send the bastards back roughly where they came from, but two points east and, once Blue Squadron starts the arc, going ever more easterly.' She coughed. 'You don't know how you're ruining my reputation as well as my throat with all this screaming. I'm not supposed to scream until I die. I wouldn't do this for anyone but you, and you'll tremble when I tell you what I'll screw out of you in exch . . . SODOM!' she suddenly screamed. 'SODOM!'

From out of the scrubland on the upper side of the slope a force of hares emerged, running in three separate flights in tight echelon formation. Red Squadron raced at top speed over the hummocky turf, broadside across the trail which had been laid by Quarry Target, and which the pack of novice beagles from Crespin Castle had been laboriously following. The hares disappeared over a ridge which led to a rocky outcrop, and presumably re-formed on the stone. The beagles came up to the massive cross-trail and dwelt, halting in complete confusion. Individual hounds circled, cast back, feathered, gave cry and began to follow a loudmouth who was urging a direct change of course to the right. As the pack went to cry and was picking up a corporate direction Lulu screamed, 'GOMORRAH!' A fresh force of hares emerged from over the ridge, well south of where Red Squadron had disappeared, and sped up the hill, but at a northerly angle to the course taken by their colleagues. With the tremendous pace that their strong hind legs gave them on the uphill run they stormed diagonally across the trail that Red Squadron had laid. They were in full sight of the beagles, who after further confusion had no option but to turn and follow them, but with no immediate hope of getting anywhere near them.

The sprawling chase disappeared from sight going in the rough direction of Crespin Castle before Blue Squadron began its calculated turn on a wide right-hand circle.

'A magnificent beginning, Madame Lulu,' said Rupert. 'Beautiful co-ordination. Thank you very much. Of course the pack is only cubbing at the moment. We still have to think of a way to deal with the greyhounds.

But you must agree we have made a very promising start.'

Lulu smiled enigmatically. 'I am now introducing you to genuine sport, Milord Rupert,' she said. 'Participation – after taking a good breakfast. A contest of wits and muscle. To strive is better than to subjugate. No one killed. Well, not deliberately killed,' she amended. 'We always lose a few hares who rupture their hearts trying to keep up with the main body, but that's just a question of the wheat and the chaff. Culling, I think it's called. I wouldn't mind dying myself in the élan of a glorious uphill charge like Blue Squadron's. By God, I'd give a scream of consummation that you'd hear in La Tranchée. Listen out for it.'

Rupert found himself so unexpectedly touched that in his emotion he fell out of the tree. 'Dear Lulu,' he said, 'you must never even mention such an end. You must go down in history as the inspiring architect of victory. In England we once had a queen like you who challenged the entire Roman Empire. We revere her name today.'

'What was her name?'

'Boudicca.'

'Boudicca? How barbarous! Couldn't she think of something prettier? What happened to her? Did she win?'

'Well, actually, no.'

'You English love a loser. Did she die?'

'Yes.'

'Did she scream?'

'I don't know.'

'I don't think so,' said Lulu. 'The others would have done it for her. With a name like that, who would need to scream?'

Fulgent padded in a cautious circle in a gulch filled with dry leaves, and prospected a bank above him which still solidly supported an oak, though some of the roots were exposed from a fall of earth in the past. He coughed twice and uttered a restrained bark.

In the sloping side of the bank, what had seemed a gigantic bird's nest of woven twigs popped out like a bung from a barrel, and a head emerged. It was a huge head, broad and brown with widely-set but disproportionately small ears. Twigs and crumbs of earth were embedded in the unkempt fur, giving the general impression of a creature who had retired from the world in negligent disgust after a long bout of debauchery.

'Ah, Flandrin,' said Fulgent jovially. 'It was good of you to leave that message that I could call. And here I am. Everything going well?'

'Let me get out of this blurry pit,' mumbled the bear Flandrin. There was a great heave, and half the bank seemed to collapse as a mass of interlocked boughs erupted into the gully carrying earth and leaves with them. The dead timber, which had been a main door to which the condor's nest was only a wicket, scattered into pieces. Flandrin fell out stiffly and eyed the fragments with satisfaction as if he would not be using them again. 'It's like coming out of solitary confinement,' he said. 'On second thoughts, it isn't like it, it blurry well *is* it.'

Then he stood gingerly on his hind legs, and scratched himself, and inefficiently dislodged some of the debris that was lodged in his fur. Fulgent unobtrusively backed, in case the bear should topple. He was approaching twice the height of a man and still unsteady on his feet.

Flandrin dropped to all fours, and winced.

'Your old wound is still troubling you,' said Fulgent sympathetically. There was a deep hole in the bear's flank over which only sparse hair had grown.

'You know where I got that?' Flandrin grunted.

'Everyone in the forest knows where you got your war wound,' said Fulgent. 'The Long March. The battle with the curs. Your torture, your gentleness, in putting

Hurlaud's brother Fulmet out of his agony. The pursuit. The spear that you had to have torn broadside through your flesh so that you could get to your defensive post in the underwood. Do you think we don't talk about that when you're not there?'

Fulgent turned suddenly, and it seemed that his spine lost all cohesion. He recovered, and looked ruefully down at the red gash in his own flank that had not yet healed.

'Is that a war wound?' asked Flandrin.

'Another war,' said Fulgent with disingenuous dismissal. 'You've been through that, too, but let's not talk about it now. I've come to make you a proposition.'

'If there's anything I suspect,' said Flandrin slowly, 'it's a proposition.'

'This concerns a man with a spear.'

'You interest me.'

'Enough to tell you more?'

'Tell me more.'

Much later, Fulgent left with a supremely satisfied expression.

'Just dance on his back,' said Adèle. 'Dance without moving your feet. Sobrin will use all the feet you need. He loves dancing, in his own way. All you've got to do is float. Don't plunge like Plantagenet, soar like a skylark.' She pretended to kick the recumbent Plantagenet, who was watching from the shade, and she imitated Sylvester's mime of the skylark, though strangely with less grace. Plantagenet grimaced in a formal smile.

Happy-With-Jesus looked down at Adèle from Sobrin's back, where he was lolling at an impermanent angle.

'Float,' Adèle repeated, and looked around her. The enclosure of the Franciscan retreat where they were practising balance was now so neat and comely that there was hardly a weed in sight. She ran to the palisade, put her hand through a gap, and boldly plucked a thistle. It was far too early for thistledown, but she brought the stalk to Happy-With-Jesus. 'Float,' she said, and blew at the thistle. With her arms stretching outwards from her shoulders, fluid and undulating, she followed the imaginary thistledown and finally puffed it over the fence. 'Float,' she said. 'Sobrin, gently, move.' The donkey, in all his indulgence, walked slowly round the enclosure, sometimes delicately increased his pace, responded when Happy-With-Jesus gave obvious signs of lack of control, and in silent gratitude came to a halt when Adèle commanded.

Happy-With-Jesus was delighted with his stint, and slid off Sobrin with a caress for the donkey. 'Ki-ki-ki-ki,' he said in careless pleasure as if exercising a new catchword without particular thought. Then he looked up at the trees with concentration and produced a far more painstaking sound: 'Ki-ka-ki-ka-ki-ki, ee-eep, ee-eep.'

Adèle looked vaguely puzzled, and stood in thought. 'I've heard that call before,' she said. 'But not from Happy-With-Jesus.'

'It's the merlin,' said Plantagenet off-handedly. 'The hen merlin a-chattering to anyone who might be attrackerted, de-da-de-da ki-ka-ki-ka. The lad's been greatly taken with it recently. Practises it all the time. I can't think why.'

'Supercilious superior sarcastic proud fool!' hissed Fulgent from the undergrowth outside the palisade. But he did not reveal himself or admit that he had been listening. His next admitted appointment at the retreat of the Franciscans was not until dusk.

Grand-Duc flew into the retreat within minutes of sundown. Fulgent, who had been taking extremely ineffective cover under a ribwort plantain, was about to come out and greet him when he sensed, rather than heard, the long incoming glide of an aerial creature, and observed the peregrine falcon Erémite make a controlled landing near Grand-Duc. The fox thought he would do well to wait until the birds had made a sociable encounter, but was surprised when almost immediately he heard the grating voice of Erémite.

'Come out, Fulgent. I know where you are. I've got eyes like a hawk, only better. Nothing to worry about. I've just had grouse for supper. Hurry up, now. I'm not at my best at this time of day. What's the contract?'

Fulgent did not stir. At least a few plantain leaves were better cover than confrontation. He peered out and found the black and grey of the huge predator even more menacing in the twilight than he had expected. But he responded to the falcon's direct approach with a reply just as blunt.

'How do you feel about merlins?'

'About the same as I feel about you. Why?'

'I thought you might consider them one of the family.'

'Family! Those midgets?'

'He'd eat his mother, and complain she was tough,' Fulgent told himself. He said aloud: 'I've got a contract for a merlin.'

'No problem. No pleasure, either. Sawdust as far as I'm concerned. I'd take three for breakfast and still regard them as medicinal only. Roughage against constipation, nothing more. Where's the venue?'

'Just south-east of Castle Crespin.'

'What terrain?'

'Scrubland merging into trees.'

'How do you get your merlin to rise above trees?'

'I don't. There are brakes between the copses. Good rabbit country.'

'Good planning, anyway,' Erémite conceded. 'When do you want the job done?'

'Any morning within the next three days.'

'That will cost you. I want a three-day retainer.'

'Agreed.'

'How will I know which morning?'

'Grand-Duc will give you immediate notice. As soon as the merlin is working, you'll know in ten minutes.'

'This is a captive merlin?'

'Yes.'

'Piece of cake,' Erémite muttered to himself.

'What did you say?'

'Hard to take. Very cunning, captive merlins. Know all the tricks. What's your price?'

'Six days' food. Freshly slaughtered. Nothing longer than an hour dead. Prompt delivery. Every day on the stroke of Lauds, at the brake by Stags Crossing.'

'Ten days' food.'

'Seven days' food. Come on, you know you could do with a week off.'

'Eight days' food and no heel-taps. Final offer.'

'My vixen and cubs! They'll starve!'

'Then chuck 'em out at Stags Crossing. Newly dead but not too thin. It will save you labour. Eight days. Done?'

'Done!' groaned Fulgent.

11
The Lure

The Vicomte de Frébois took an elaborate public farewell of Lady Eléonore, but there had been a detailed briefing previously. He was leaving Crespin for a period of up to a month. The official reason was that he was making a visit of almost state importance – certainly involving considerable protocol and demanding the attendance of an imposing force of his subordinate nobility – to Guienne, where he had strong family connections and many unresolved lawsuits over property. The unofficial reason, which Frébois had ordered to be leaked as assiduously as possible, was that he was seeking a rich husband for his nine-year-old daughter Anne-Marie.

The real reason, of which only Lady Eléonore was fully aware, was that a high-ranking kinsman of the Queen of France was making an informal progress through Poitou, and Frébois wished to be out of the way. The French throne had achieved a very strong position in reducing the power of the English Empire within France. The present King was sickly and likely to die. His Queen, Blanche of Castile, would take over the regency for her eleven-year-old son. The French nobility was being obstreperous for its own purposes against the Crowns of both France and England, and the Vicomte had no great wish to be politically identified with the nobility or the sovereigns of either country.

Frébois, on assuming his estates in Poitou, had successfully fudged the swearing of allegiance to his nominal overlord, King John of England, Duke of Aquitaine, Count of Poitou and (on paper) Duke of Normandy although he dared not go there. When John died and left a nine-year-old son and heir as Henry III, King of England and Duke of Aquitaine, Frébois again clouded any oath of allegiance by piously setting out for a Crusade when the homage was due, but making sure he never got as far as the Mediterranean. The advance news that Blanche of Castile was about to start lobbying in Poitou convinced the Vicomte that this was no time to stand up and be counted. He therefore announced his journey to the south.

Lady Eléonore had experienced many absences of her volatile lord, and was used to assuming responsibility. She was a redoubtable châtelaine. 'I am leaving you a force quite strong enough for defence,' the Vicomte told her. 'As for administration, you run the estates better than I do when you get the chance, and the usual staff will be working. I see no great problems. The wretched Sir Otto must leave within a week, if only because I have leaned on that foolish young man Golletières to organize a tournament. He's rich enough, there's reasonable prize money, and Sir Otto got his official invitation this morning. We'll have to extend him the usual courtesies in the meantime, hunting and all that. I'm not particularly happy about it. He has the use of my falcons, of course, but though he's knowledgeable about bloodhounds he doesn't know a damn thing about beagles, and I hope he can be discouraged from taking them out. I'd like to have left you Jehan to come the sergeant major on him in emergency, but I need him too badly. I've posted his number two to be i/c stables – Guillaume – you know, the one with the scar – and I hope he can stand up to him.'

Neither the Vicomte nor Lady Eléonore mentioned the subject that had been in the forefront of their minds over the previous days – the death of the troubadour Gérard. Administratively, that had been disposed of within eighteen hours of the murder. In the solar, the only genuinely private apartment available to the lord and his wife, Frébois had announced the termination of the affair in a judgment which was monumental in its ironic detachment:

'There are a number of people who could have killed this man. The first thought in many people's minds must be that you did it, for reasons connected with his public utterances. Or someone instructed by you did it. Or someone sympathetic to you did it, not instructed by you. Or I did it, on the spur of an interpretation – or misinterpretation – of what he had said and sung. Or I told somebody to do it. Or a loyal servant did it, out of resentment at the indignity to you and to me that had been offered. Or Sir Otto did it – if he understood half of what had been said, he had reason enough. Or the jongleur Balthasar did it, out of jealousy at what had been implied, or after a private lovers' quarrel. In order to end speculation as soon as possible I have decided that, whoever did it, the jongleur will pay for it. And if you care to glance out of the window now you will see him being taken to the gallows as an exemplary of instant justice.'

It was indeed the body of Balthasar, dark and terrifyingly mangled by predators, that swung from the gibbet at the end of the village as the lord passed through on his progress.

As soon as the ceremonial party was decently on its way Sir Otto declared that it was a day for falconry. He would take out the merlin with which he had previously been having trouble, because no obscenely described *falke* was going to get the better of him. A messenger was sent to the mews to have the bird prepared, and Sir Otto went to dress. He took from the castle wardrobe – not having the equipment himself – a plain leather hunting tunic and a high pair of boots, as waterproof as could be obtained at that time. From the armoury he borrowed a boar-spear. He wanted to go out alone, since his unorthodox treatment of falcons excited comment among the castle servants. But since the forest was hardly innocuous parkland and he did not know what he would meet, he took adequate protection.

Puissard the sparrowhawk had based himself in a spruce, the nearest useful tree to the castle walls. From it he was able to beat off and undertake regular glides, though he had to keep at a greater altitude than his usual cruising height. When he saw the beginnings of activity at the falcons' mews he was alerted. He waited impatiently to identify Sir Otto and saw him leave the castle. As soon as he was sure of the area where the knight intended to hunt he flew off to Fulgent, who had established himself at a command post in a dogwood shrub offering the best communication with his many outstations.

Puissard delivered his report and received the expected order: 'Right. Tell Grand-Duc immediately.'

This was the first link in the chain of operations, and it was the most hazardous. The eagle owl was most at home on heights, and did not favour the comparatively level flight-base of the crown of forests. Fortunately there was a bleak rocky crag pushing clear out of the trees near the forest heights at Les Combles, and Grand-Duc had agreed to take a temporary lodging there. Fulgent had persuaded the owl to adopt this residence because the peregrine Erémite favoured the same country and could be easily alerted. Puissard dared not make direct contact with Erémite because of his uncertain temper. The sparrowhawk had military dash, but also military caution, and was convinced that his own life was far safer with Grand-Duc than with Erémite. But the great objection was that the eagle owl was a nocturnal bird, somnolent in the daytime and also genuinely troubled by daylight. Puissard located him but had great difficulty in rousing him. He found it even harder, since he lacked Fulgent's smooth power of persuasion, to persuade the owl to move. At last, grumbling mightily, Grand-Duc laboured off to Erémite's haunt, and Puissard flew down and away in great relief.

In the meantime Fulgent set out in search of Happy-With-Jesus. For the past few days Adèle had consented, after subtle prompting from Plantagenet, that Happy-With-Jesus should perfect his new skill at balance by riding Sobrin peacefully through the glades of the forest. Plantagenet, who knew almost every track in the great expanse, escorted them. Fulgent located the trio, was satisfied with their course, and had a short conversation with Plantagenet. Plantagenet made a suggestion to Sobrin. Sobrin cheerfully agreed to continue for a further spell, and Fulgent doubled back to keep a rendezvous with the bear Flandrin, whom he was reserving for the last stages of the coup.

The two key characters, unconscious of their part in the drama, gradually approached. Happy-With-Jesus ambled peacefully onwards riding Sobrin and singing bird calls. Sir Otto moved forwards, prospecting good ground for falconry.

The merlin was a low-flying bird, but capricious. He had been temperamental in the past, and Sir Otto wanted to take no chances, but to be assured of success in order to imprint his domination. In previous expeditions he had located a brake of heathland, beyond the first banks of trees in the outer forest. It had been colonized by rabbits, who had found the stretch of country so unmenacing that they had established an empire there.

Sir Otto came to the edge of the brake, planted his boar-spear in the ground, and stood still for five full minutes. Very cautiously he eased the restraints from the merlin and began to tease it into hunting awareness.

The lad and the donkey were only half a mile away, with Plantagenet idly routing for food quite near. And at this point Happy-With-Jesus fell off Sobrin. He tried once or twice to remount, but in his clumsiness failed, which set him laughing. Sobrin expressed all his good intentions, but could do nothing to help him. Plantagenet began to feel that he was sinking out of his depth. Fulgent, who was observing from the undergrowth without declaring his presence, did nothing at all. He was absolutely delighted with his good luck and speedily applied his mind to turn it to his best advantage.

Sir Otto, having roused the merlin, saw a likely target and quickly launched the bird. But his main experience was with the heavier saker falcon, well over twice the merlin's weight, and he jerked too vigorously. The merlin was badly launched, and fluttered. The rabbit sprinted for a hole and disappeared with yards to spare. Sir Otto swore. The merlin rose to perch in a tree. It presented an extremely bad-tempered appearance. Sir Otto swore again.

Happy-With-Jesus, never long frustrated by any accident, accepted that he was now dismounted, sat against a tree, and rehearsed a few more bird calls. He progressed to the call which had recently taken his fancy, and worked hard at it: 'Ki-ka-ki-ka-ki-ki-ki, ee-eep, ee-eep.' Plantagenet indicated that it was a great performance and should be continued.

Sir Otto made what he thought were enticing noises at his merlin. But, since he was not good at true seduction and had never lived with a baby he had fathered, they were not productive sounds. Sir Otto then threw a piece of rotten branch at the bird to show who was master. The merlin rose quite high to show that the subject was in dispute, and came down in much thicker woodland out of sight of the Teuton. It uttered a cry of 'ki-ki-ki-ki' which could have been interpreted as derision. Sir Otto took up his boar-spear and plunged in the direction of the calls.

Plantagenet, who had bad sight but good hearing, heard the call and moved towards it. Sobrin sauntered to keep pace with him. Happy-With-Jesus, never a solitary character, got up and followed. He was still calling: he liked to do one thing at a time and do it well.

Sir Otto traced his merlin and again spoke to it in tones which were by no means wheedling. He reached down for another missile. The merlin rose in what was intended to be a modest zoom over the crown of the tree into the next glade.

As it lost height, prospecting where to perch, it was aware of a hissing, reverberating rush of air, a massive jolt at the back of its neck, and nothing more. The peregrine Erémite, diving at phenomenal speed, had stooped on it, killed it, and, according to contract, kept well below Sir Otto's sight-line as he devoured his prize.

From a little deeper in the forest there came the call of the merlin. Sir Otto grimly followed.

Farther and farther he was lured by the call, until he blindly departed from tracks that were there for a forester to see, and in sweating rage became trapped by creeping growths that seemed to have no order. His spear was now impeding him because of its height. He shifted it to his left hand and drew from its sheath in his belt the short, curved falchion, a combination of sword and cleaver, which he had brought back from the Holy Land. Useless for thrusting, and with only one edge, it was still the handiest steel to use in woodland.

He freed himself, and listened. Still the call mocked him. But suddenly it changed. The sound of the merlin ceased. The song of the blackbird followed. It continued for a considerable time. Sir Otto took little notice of it, waiting again for the merlin's call. But what he suddenly realized he was hearing was the ecstatic song of the skylark. Larks sounding so loud and clear through thick forest growth puzzled him. Then he heard an honest, simple human laugh. Happy-With-Jesus, who always enjoyed his own recitals, was congratulating himself during the first interval.

In one flash of recognition Sir Otto realized the possibility of what could have been happening. The scene in the hall of Crespin Castle, with its final insulting humiliation, sprang into the Teuton's memory. He uttered a great roar of anger and crashed through the impeding undergrowth towards the source of the sounds.

Fulgent, who had been listening from under a patch of his favourite daphne laureola in serene appreciation of the call of the merlin, had jerked up and was nervously pacing the undergrowth in alarm. Events were passing out of his control. His apprehension turned to panic when he heard the lad bubble into laughter. He raced towards the copse of beeches where he was keeping Flandrin in reserve. As he ran he heard Sir Otto's shout.

There was no immediate sign of Flandrin. He began to search in desperate rushes, but was suddenly halted by a hoarse croak from low in the undergrowth:

'You filthy scum! All high and mighty, now, aren't you? Too good for your family, I suppose. Your own flesh and blood means nothing to you. You've never even looked out for me. Family! They're all the same.'

In utter astonishment Fulgent looked down and saw a fox in the undershrub, but lying in an entirely unnatural position. His rear quarters were flat on the ground. His forefeet were poised and straining, but they held up his shoulders only with difficulty.

'Fléton!' gasped Fulgent. 'What are you doing here? I haven't seen you for days.'

'Oh, brotherly concern!' said Fléton bitterly. 'You could have looked for me.'

'You're sick,' said Fulgent.

'Observation!' said Fléton. A stream of thick saliva ran like honey out of his jaws.

Fulgent had never been anything but the firmest of friends with his brother. He was disorientated by this additional crisis. 'Fléton, old man, you've got to give me a little time,' he pleaded desperately. 'Have you seen a bear around here? Flandrin?'

'Bear? Yes. Idle bastard. Mooching around to the west. Why not? It's a free forest, I suppose.'

'I've got to find him,' gasped Fulgent. 'To the west? I'll be back just as soon as I possibly can. Give me a few minutes.'

'I give you your lifespan. It's brother bear now, is it? I don't care if I never see you again.' Fléton's forelegs collapsed and he sank to the ground.

Fulgent raced away. After three speedy circles he found Flandrin. 'Get to the lad, quickly,' he ordered, and gave the bear a course. At his highest speed, without regard for cover, he streaked back to where he had left Fléton.

Plantagenet had heard Sir Otto's shout and the crashing brushwood as the Teuton plunged towards the voice he had heard. He ran at his top pace to where he had left Happy-With-Jesus. But the knight had seen the lad at fifteen paces while Plantagenet was still homing in.

'So it's you!' said Sir Otto, and crouched slightly, automatically feeling the edge of his falchion with his left thumb. He advanced at a slow pace towards

Happy-With-Jesus, his eyes alert for any movement of escape to right or left that the lad might make.

From well behind Happy-With-Jesus, Plantagenet charged directly at Sir Otto.

The Teuton was taken by surprise. He saw Plantagenet racing at tremendous speed, but could not appreciate the situation. This was a small pig, not a forest boar. Boars charged, and were enemies to respect. Their attack was more than dangerous. It could be fatal. But this was a pig.

Plantagenet came straight on, at a speed Sir Otto could not apprehend. The knight swung his falchion and missed completely. Plantagenet took him straight in the legs, below the knees, knocked him over and sprawled himself. Even as he fell he gathered himself and jerked the side of his snout up the shin of the Teuton. Sir Otto felt a shaft of pain. He looked down and saw the snout jabbing upwards again. He saw his own blood and the weapons the animal was using. They were tusks. Ridiculously small tusks, but dagger-sharp and skilfully used. This was a boar.

Sir Otto sprang up vigorously, threw away his sword, and transferred the boar-spear to his right hand. He thrust, while his enemy was still floundering. The spear took Plantagenet on the breast, was diverted by the bones of the thorax and jerked out short of the shoulder. The Teuton drew back the spear for another blow.

He felt the shaft of the spear firmly gripped behind him. Then it was clumsily wrenched from his grasp and thrown yards away. Light and blood glinted on the blade as it circled.

Sir Otto turned round and saw Flandrin, towering half a span above him. He turned again, took off from the blocks of his ankles, and ran.

Flandrin went after him, shambling fast on all fours and chattering with a rage that he had sustained since his last encounter with spearmen, in the Great Retreat. He had every advantage over the Teuton. He could have caught him at any time, torn him apart with his claws longer than treenails. But he was under orders not to kill, and he respected these, knowing that full retribution could provoke the battue of retaliation from which all the forest animals had suffered before. He contented himself with menacing the knight to the extent of his powers – pursuing him so closely that his breath could be felt, relaxing, speeding, weaving so that he could control the direction of the retreat.

At a satisfying location, almost within sight of the end of the village, Flandrin carefully ushered the fleeing knight into a peat bog.

He then closed on his victim. He drove him into the marsh until the man was gasping far above his previous exhaustion with the extra effort of traction through this terrain.

Then, with one easy lunge of his huge head, Flandrin sent Sir Otto curving face down into the bog.

The knight lay helplessly spreadeagled in the ooze. If he had been insensible he would have drowned. In terror he forced up his head, entirely black with the rich sediment of the bog. He scrambled to his feet and turned for the next bout with his aggressor.

Flandrin was yards away, ambling towards home, with never a backward glance.

Fulgent was at the side of his brother Fléton. The sick fox seemed unconscious. Uncontrolled tremors rippled over his flesh, and the mucus still dribbled from his mouth. Fulgent could only wait.

'Fléton, Fléton,' moaned Fulgent. 'I'm here. I've come back.'

There was one convulsive movement. Fléton seemed to gather all his strength. His forelegs weakly arched, and his shoulders came up a little. Fulgent looked closely to perceive some communication. Fléton slowly raised his head, and buried his teeth in the soft side of Fulgent's neck. Then he relaxed, and made no further movement.

12
Man-Hunt

Sir Otto of Lübeck, of the Eastern Marches, of Hungary, Poland and Bohemia, and of Jerusalem, sometime (until unfrocked) Prior and (until debarred) Grand Cross of the Order of the Teutonic Knights in the Holy Land and elsewhere, had brought six mounted retainers on the tour that had reached Castle Crespin. Strictly speaking, he did not retain them, since he had not the means. At no expense to himself he quartered them on his current host. In return they provided the muscle he needed for status. In between castles they catered for immediate requirements and future pocket money by discreet highway robbery. They were, in fact, mercenaries and bandits who needed Sir Otto's title as keenly as he needed their presence.

Early in the morning after his encounter with Flandrin, Sir Otto summoned his men for daily orders, delivered in their military lingua franca in a courtyard of the castle small enough for the meeting to be inconspicuous and open enough to give protection against eavesdropping.

In the untidy group the knight looked at least superior, though shabby. His face was even redder than usual from the rescrubbing it had just endured. He had made a memorable progress down the village street on the previous evening, with a head like Satan and the squelching gait of a drowned revenant, and those of the castle servants who occupied houses in the village had been careful to hide their faces over their spades as they mimed work in their front gardens when he passed. Once in the castle, he had thrown away his clothes, which did not belong to him, and submitted to long agony under the cold pump. He had repeated the ablutions at dawn but, owing to a constitutional failing in finesse and the lack of a mirror, his ears showed streaks of black as formidable as his fingernails. But, after a long night's thought, he was ready for action.

'I want all the Vicomte's bloodhounds and talbots got out of the kennels and out of the castle,' he ordered. 'Immediately. The word is that we are going hunting. The word is that we are going hunting very early – now. But the fact is that there will be a certain delay. I don't want those hounds inside the castle while the delay is being discussed. Get them all to the other end of the village. Round the gibbet would be a good place.'

'That will mean we must use kennelmen, hunt-servants,' said one of the retainers. 'That means authorization,' he added with soldierly caution.

'Authorization, my arse. I've already told that stand-in – Guillaume, isn't it? – that we've got Frébois' blanket permission.'

'Huntsmen, then.'

'As few as possible. And as dim as possible,' Sir Otto directed. 'Choose the real *bonshommes*, tell them they've a good chance of a full day off if they'll get the hounds out to the gibbet and hold them till we slip off.'

'What's it worth to them?' came the practical question.

'What do you mean? It's worth a day off.'

'Where do they go to get out of the way? They'll want more than time off.'

'Meaning what?'

'Baksheesh.'

'*Coins*?'

'Yes.'

'They wouldn't recognize coins if they saw them. All right, give 'em some.'

'Coins?'

'Yes.'

'I wouldn't recognize coins if I saw them. We've been here a long time, you know.'

'Well, liquor, then.'

'No go. It's all locked up. The lady has the keys. She's tighter than the lord.'

'For God's sake! All right, I've got a few kegs stashed under my armour. Take two. No more.'

'Right.'

'*Are* we going hunting?'

'Of course we're going hunting.'

'Deer? It's a bit late in the season, isn't it?'

'What we're hunting is always in season.'

'What's that? Woman?'

'Man.'

'Cor! No! Really?'

'It's a long time, isn't it?'

'Where's the man?'

'You're going to fetch him.'

Robert and Sylvester were working in the garden of their retreat when two men-at-arms rode up. They asked brusquely for the idiot.

'He's asleep,' said Robert.

'Asleep? At this hour? Get him up.'

'Why?'

'He's under arrest. Orders to take him direct to Crespin Castle.'

'You can't do that,' said Sylvester.

One of the men spat full in his face. 'Asleep!' he said. 'Lying low to get on the run, more likely.' He went into the dwelling and came out pushing and kicking Happy-With-Jesus in front of him.

The lad blinked in the sunlight. He had got back to his home very late. Plantagenet was the only one who knew the way, and he was wounded and shocked. The boy had not been able to mount the donkey, and it had been a tortuous trail in the dark. Plantagenet could go no farther than the retreat. He was cowering, tense under cover outside the retreat, at that moment. Sobrin was equably grazing on the meagre herbage of the enclosure.

'You're under arrest,' said a man-at-arms, and tied the hands of Happy-With-Jesus behind. 'Get up on that horse.' He spoke to his confederate: 'Tie him to my waist when he's up.'

Robert protested. 'He'll never get up with his hands tied. He hasn't the skill.'

'We'll see,' said the man. He frogmarched the lad to his horse and threw him at the animal. 'Get up,' he said. He punched and cuffed him.

Happy-With-Jesus gave an extraordinary smile, not of bewilderment but of understanding that the other man could not be expected to know how difficult the operation was. The answer to the smile was a direct punch in his teeth. 'Hurt!' Happy-With-Jesus protested.

'You'll never do it,' said the second man. 'Untie his wrists.'

'By whose authority is this lad arrested?' Robert asked.

The first man-at-arms paused. 'He's wanted immediately at Crespin Castle,' he said with caution.

'By the Vicomte de Frébois?'

'He's gone away.'

'By the Lady Eléonore?'

'She'll do,' said the man, and gestured to his companion. 'Get these ropes fixed quick.'

Sylvester stood at the horse's head with his hand very

firm on the bridle. 'By what authority?' he demanded squarely.

'By this authority,' said the man-at-arms, and struck him full on the head with the flat of his sword. The friar fell to the ground. 'Hurt, hurt, hurt,' said Happy-With-Jesus in sympathy, and tumbled both himself and his escort sideways as he almost fell off the horse to try to comfort Sylvester. But the stirrup took the strain and the ropes held. The soldier roughly jerked him upright and the men spurred away.

'They can't do it,' said Sylvester, picking himself up and testing his tonsured crown for the depth of the cut. 'We are both going to the castle. Separately. I can move faster than you. Get to the castle as soon as you can and speak to the Lady Eléonore. I can't do as much, but I'll have done something to drag the lid off this cesspit by the time you arrive. By God's bones, I will.'

'You're swearing,' said Robert in gentle confusion. But Sylvester was away.

'Dear sinner!' said Robert. A thought struck him. He looked around and saw that Sobrin was watching him, but decided that it did not matter. He went into the retreat and came out wearing a pair of sandals. 'Adèle did give them to me,' he excused himself to Sobrin. 'For use *in extremis*. I *will* tell Francis when I see him.'

He hurried off, with forgotten youth in his stride.

Sylvester had adopted what he called his feather-light infantry quickstep. He ran for two hundred paces, walked for two hundred and ran again. He took cover as he approached the village. There was a large crowd around the gibbet. A few horsemen were prominent among a number of restless dogs who were being held by foot-servants managing multiple leashes. Happy-With-Jesus was tied to an upright of the gallows. Sylvester could not determine any details of his face, but he was clearly not slumped as a result of violence or despair. He seemed to be taking a lively interest in what was going on, and was trying to fondle the dogs who were allowed to smell him.

Sylvester ran round the frontier of the cultivated land and came from the side to the castle entrance. Before he got to the drawbridge he was stopped.

'Who are you?'

'Brother Sylvester.'

'What do you want?'

'To see the Lady Eléonore.'

'**** off.'

'Ask the sergeant!'

'**** the sergeant. **** off. Which way did you come?'

'Across the fields.'

'Why the fields?'

'I'm used to fields.'

'Ah, you're one of these working friars. I can get you some work, old man. Why didn't you say? We're short for the spring sowing.'

'I must see the Lady Eléonore.'

'Lord bless you, brother, the Lady Eléonore doesn't see the likes of you. She has men who do that for her. But you're lucky you met me. I can get round the bailiff, you don't have to bother to lick his arse. Let's see, you don't take money, do you? Never mind, I can fix it. Day and a half's food for a day's work. How's that?'

'Listen, squaddie. I know you mean well, but I've got to see the Lady Eléonore.'

'****off. And down the street this time. I'll have my eyes on you.'

Sylvester turned down the street, and after four houses dodged between two buildings and ran out into the grazing. The soldier watched him and did nothing.

'Bonkers,' he said. 'Religious mania.'

Robert, having made very good time, came straight up to the village street and tried to take in what was happening. He saw Happy-With-Jesus and went to speak to him. A man-at-arms, not one of the pair who had made the arrest, peremptorily ordered him away. Robert had an air of authority and was not barred from the village street. He came to the drawbridge and was stopped for interrogation.

'Allo, allo! Another of you? You want to see the Lady Eléonore I suppose. It's too bad, isn't it? Well, take my sincere advice. Just pick up your skirts and. . . .'

'Let him in,' said a voice from the courtyard.

The guard looked up and saw Lady Eléonore.

'I humbly beg your pardon, my lady,' he stuttered, and said not a word more.

'It is very good of you, Lady Eléonore,' said Robert as he entered the castle. 'I came . . .'

'Something is happening,' said Lady Eléonore. 'What is going on at the end of the street?'

'I go hunting,' said Sir Otto, hurrying along in a new hunting suit.

'My lady, have you given orders for the arrest of the simple lad who was here some nights ago?' asked Robert.

'No, of course not. What reason would I have?'

'He has been arrested and brought to Crespin. He is tied to the gibbet at the end of the street.'

'What does this mean?' demanded Lady Eléonore, turning at once to Sir Otto.

'I arrest him,' said Sir Otto calmly. 'I go hunting.'

'What has that got to do with the simple lad?'

'I go man-hunting,' said Sir Otto, as if the explanation were enough.

'Man-hunting? Hunting whom?'

'The idiot,' said Sir Otto.

'It's impossible. You can't. It's illegal. It's sacrilege.'

'Sacrilege!' said Sir Otto scornfully. 'Have dispensation from Pope. Not dispensation, plain permission. All Teutonic Knights have permission from Pope. Hunt from Prussia. When no good game, hunt man. Good sport. Heretics, pagans, good sport.'

'But this is Poitou. This is a man. It's inhuman.'

'Not inhuman. This is not man. Is subhuman. All subhumans east of Prussia. Some subhumans in Poitou. I hunt him.'

'But this is a soul,' said Robert, as if the argument were still academic. 'God loves him. He loves God.'

'Not soul. Not man. Subhuman,' said Sir Otto complacently. 'If God loves, that God's business. I hunt.'

He paused. 'God loves deer. God loves dogs, they say. Deer loves God, dog loves God, perhaps. . . .'

'And they don't know why, God doesn't know why, but they're creation,' Robert burst out, with a searing memory of Brémand's puzzled credo at the Court of Love.

'Nor I know why. Not important. I hunt deer with dogs. Today I hunt man with dogs. Subhuman. Pope says "Yes".'

'I forbid it,' said Lady Eléonore imperiously. 'As châtelaine of this castle and regent of this fief I forbid it. Have that boy released, get your men back to this castle and leave within the hour.'

'You have no law,' said Sir Otto complacently. 'You have no right, you have no law. I call Guillaume.' He beckoned masterfully to a man who had been standing holding a horse, watching the encounter with horror. 'Guillaume, stand here.'

The man shrank as he came forward.

'I am Holy Prior of Pope's Order of Teutonic Knights,' lied Sir Otto. 'I put you on God's honour to answer one question.'

The man mumbled.

'Is that idiot boy at end of street true vassal of Messire le Vicomte de Frébois?'

The man could not speak for the dryness of his throat.

'Is he true vassal of Vicomte de Frébois?'

'No,' said the deputy master of horse.

'What!' exclaimed Lady Eléonore in amazement.

'His holding was repossessed by Messire le Vicomte. His tenancy was annulled. He was expelled from the estate.'

'Is outlaw,' said Sir Otto. 'I hunt him. Horse!'

He climbed into the saddle and trotted down the street without another word.

They bloodied Happy-With-Jesus. They started with a knife in his leg. 'Don't cut the tendons,' ordered Sir Otto. 'Not good sport.' He swung a fist against the lad's face, and the head was held by the post of the gibbet. A stream of blood gushed from his nose. 'That helps,' said the Teutonic Knight. 'Let the dogs smell.'

Happy-With-Jesus cried. The bloodhounds and talbots, tight on their leashes, were allowed to approach the lad and sniff him all over. The boy was pleased by this and gradually came out of his misery. He laughed when the dogs licked the tears on his cheeks, and he tried to fondle them.

'Let him go,' ordered the knight.

The ropes were released. Happy-With-Jesus began to smile as if to ingratiate himself. He was pushed down the track. He dawdled and then looked back. He seemed to think that it was all over. He was whipped down the trail until at last he began to run. Then the whipping ceased.

'It will take long time,' said Sir Otto in great discontent. 'One hour, one hour and half. Else no sport.'

'Open the barrels,' he commanded. 'Kennelmen stay until dogs slipped. Then holiday. Then finish barrels.'

At the first grove of trees which placed the lad out of sight of the village Sylvester dropped from a branch and joined Happy-With-Jesus. 'Come along, youngster,' he said cheerfully. 'We've a long way to go.'

The disturbing news of the beginning of the man-hunt was hurriedly given to a body of the principal animals, who were meeting in extraordinary session.

In the deep forest the fox Fulgent was being arraigned before a Court of Inquiry consisting of a committee of the Council of Animals. In an opening speech the wolf Hurlaud gravely condemned him for overweening pride in attempting a feat of organization which was beyond the powers of animals. 'He has not accepted the natural law that we, the animals, are locked into our environment,' he said in his indictment. 'Freedom is the recognition of necessity. We have not the potential to make dynamic changes in our circumstances, to manipulate objects, to manipulate animals – above all, small power to manipulate men – so that the natural consequences of our actions may be evaded.'

No sentence was imposed, precisely because the law of the forest did not sanction rewards or punishments, but only recognized consequences. It was clear in any case that no award of the Court would have been accepted by Fulgent. In a spirited defence the fox stoutly denied the validity of the orthodox law of the forest.

'We do manipulate each other,' he claimed. 'We can to a certain extent manipulate men. The irony is that it is the least of this trio, it is *objects* that – apart from a few simple tools that many of us can master – we find difficulty in manipulating, because of a weakness in our capacity to plan for the future. But I will not believe that this failure is permanent. We can overcome it. And if we really set out to *plan our planning*, perhaps we can even do better than the mandrakes. Grondin admires what the mandrakes call a work of art – a painted shield. I myself prefer a stone statue. We don't yet have the potential to make art because we can't fully enough envisage the future form of the paint on the shield, the statue within the block. But since, as I claim, we *can* manipulate each other, we *can* manipulate men, my faith is that in time we shall manipulate objects into art.'

A slight convulsion shook him and for a moment he seemed to lose the flow of his thought. A gummy stream of saliva dripped from the corner of his muzzle. He shook his head, and said with an attempt at a smile: 'Who knows? If we concentrate on works of art, we may do better for the forest world than the mandrakes for theirs. I'm sure they'd be quite happy to specialize in making crossbows.

'In the meantime,' he concluded, 'I confess that I have overreached myself. I admit to pride. I concede defeat. I am truly contrite, and I make without reserve an offer to do for the free animals of this forest whatever they require of me for their good.'

The Court noted the offer, but adjourned without further comment. The wolf Hurlaud had been closely watching Fulgent during his final speech, and he came up to him in a comradely fashion when the session was dissolved.

'Are you in good health?' he asked sympathetically.

'I . . . I think so,' said Fulgent hesitantly.

'A little excited, perhaps?'

'Excited, yes.'

'Both up and down?'

'What do you mean?'

'Fits of deep gloom? Ill temper that you secretly fear?'

'That's life.'

'Nothing out of the ordinary – beyond that cock-up with the Teuton – has occurred to you lately?'

'Great God, no!'

'How is Fléton?'

Fulgent looked hard at Hurlaud.

'He's dead,' he said.

'You'd better tell me about it.'

Fulgent told him.

'You know what it is, don't you?' said Hurlaud. 'You know what it means to you?'

'I think I do.'

'Where did he bite you?'

'In the neck.'

'Then you haven't long.'

'To live?'

'Not long.'

'No works of art!' said Fulgent, to exaggerate self-pity.

'We shall have to avoid you. And you must not go back to your family.'

'I understand. A bloody pariah. Any consolation at all?'

'There is one thing.'

'What's that?'

'If this man-hunt gets serious – affecting the free animals, I mean – and these events do spread like forest fires. . . .'

'Yes?'

'If we have to defend ourselves. . . .'

'Yes?'

'Take one or two with you, eh?'

'I will. Thanks, Hurlaud.'

'And there's one thing about rabies you ought to remember.'

'What's that?'

'It's not something you should leave until you're raving delirious.'

'No. What is it?'

'The higher you bite, the nearer the head, the faster they go. Aim high.'

'I'll remember that. Thanks again, Hurlaud.'
'God take you into his holy keeping.'

When Sylvester dropped from the tree in the grove Happy-With-Jesus was in elemental need of physical comfort, a palpable demonstration that not all human contact was aggression. But the friar resolutely avoided touching him. Instead, he promptly put a distance between them. Talking very slowly but continuously and persuasively, making little sense but all sympathy, he extended a stick and encouraged the lad to grip it. Then, still talking, he edged away from Happy-With-Jesus, always indicating that the boy should hold the end of the stick, while he himself lightly continued to sidestep and the stick seemed to grow miraculously so that they still had this wooden link between them. Happy-With-Jesus was so fascinated by this magically expanding yoke that it took up his entire attention and he laughed in his enjoyment of the novelty. What he had not seen was that Sylvester, before vaulting down to greet him, had first dropped to the ground a long strip of hazel cuttings which he had been busy binding together while he was waiting for the lad, and this was to be the tie beam between them. When he had paid it all out and was holding the other end, the two were ten paces distant from each other.

Sylvester moved gingerly forward, tensely encouraging Happy-With-Jesus to keep a tight hold on the other end, and took a sinuous course until he had worked the pair of them out of the grove so that there was a long stretch of rough heath in front of them. He wheeled back until they were in line abreast, and then he began to trot forward. Happy-With-Jesus kept up with him, ten paces to the right. Sylvester's great difficulty was to run as fast as he knew their situation demanded yet keep the lad going and always maintain their distance. They did not make impressive speed, and Sylvester was in some desperation when they reached the end of the first stage he had set them.

It was a small, rocky pool below a sharp slope in the terrain on the edge of the true forest. The trees had grown thickly so that they plunged in confusion from the upper shelf and stopped abruptly on the border of the heathland. A clear rivulet poured down, bouncing brightly over rock into the pool, where it apparently disappeared, feeding some underground conduit that would later disperse into marshland.

In swiftly co-ordinated action Sylvester steered Happy-With-Jesus, like a circus horse at the end of a long whip shaft, to the edge of the pool. He wrenched the hazel yoke from the lad's hand and sprang up the escarpment with it. At thirty paces' depth into the forest he thrust the bound hazel high up the trunk of an ash, inside the growth of ivy that sheathed it. He ran through the trees to the top of the brook and gestured to Happy-With-Jesus to come towards him into the pool.

The lad was distrustful of water and moved forward only a few inches. Sylvester pulled his grey gown over his head and threw it on a branch above him. He stepped out of his short breeches and climbed down the rocks into the pool. Happy-With-Jesus, seeing the naked Sylvester coming towards him, perceived that another game had started, laughed, and threw away his own gown and breeches. Sylvester, laughing with unconvincing energy, suddenly leaned forward and gripped the lad's wrists in a wrestler's hold. Happy-With-Jesus rose in the air with the clumsiness of a panicking pheasant. He was twisted on to his back in a victory roll. He was firmly held, and then delicately lowered into the pool. Sylvester laughed with ferocious insincerity as he rapidly probed with his fingers in the water, washing the blood from the lad's legs, ducking his head and rubbing his face clean with the vigorous precision of a masseur. Making far fewer encouraging noises – for he now had the lad's confidence and could not spare the draining mental energy that every nurse must generate – he darted to the heathland side of the pool, grabbed the boy's clothes, slung the meagre breeches high to a bush above the waterfall and carried the gown back into the pool. He plunged it under the water, brought it up limp and disposable, tied it securely round a loose boulder as thick as his waist and dropped the shrouded rock to the bottom of the pool. Then he fiercely washed his hands and forearms.

With a showman's '*Allez-oop*' to show that this was still only a game, he ducked his own head and shoulders deep into the water and came up with his neck under the crutch of Happy-With-Jesus, who rose in the air like a drunken Ganymede at a Bacchanalia and, after a pause for assessment of the situation, laughed. Sylvester then climbed up the waterfall with the naked lad on his shoulders and, by a mixture of speech and firm manipulation, induced him to hang from a bough at the top. Supporting him with one hand under his pelvis, Sylvester swiftly dried him with the grey gown he had himself discarded. Reaching to the bush where the lad's breeches hung, he slid them up the dangling legs as dexterously as a nursing mother. He took the lad's weight again on his shoulders and threw the damp grey gown upwards, telling the boy to put it on.

The entire operation had been completed at extraordinary speed and with obligatory good humour. Sylvester found himself standing in the forest with a tousled young man of considerable weight sitting on his shoulders in comparatively decent array, while he himself stood damp and stark naked. He walked the pace or two to where his own brief breeches were hanging, raised a foot and almost fell prostrate. Then for the first time that day he burst into a belly laugh of absolute spontaneity.

He held the drooping garment in both his hands, carefully elevated his knee, tried to slip his foot into the hole, and staggered wildly as Happy-With-Jesus plunged forward and would have hit the ground if Sylvester had not dropped the breeches and wrenched the lad backwards. He bent both his knees slowly and felt with his hands to retrieve the underlinen. He grasped the cloth, raised himself, and blindly explored the breeches with the toe of his other foot, hoping for better luck that side. Squinting down, he could not see beyond his belly, and all his probing could not achieve a penetration. He laughed, long and full-heartedly, and Happy-With-Jesus joined in ecstatically from above him. With a regal gesture he flung the breeches away and strode forward. Within two paces he had second thoughts and retrieved the linen from the bush where it had landed. No additional scent was to be left near the place where the cleansing had been made.

Jovially he draped the breeches over his head. A sudden sensation made him turn back to look across the pool to the heathland over which they had run, then down at the drying hair on his chest, which was distinctly rippling in the breeze. 'The wind has changed,' he said. 'Turned almost dead south. It couldn't be better. We shall be downwind of them all the way.'

Sylvester turned again and plunged into the forest on the track he had already determined. The strange tableau merged into the underwood, a lolling youth in a grey gown precariously riding the shoulders of a resolutely striding man, with stocky flanks reflecting in the play of their outer muscles the strain he was taking, and a blur of black hair sweeping into the cleft of his buttocks. And thunderrolls of crashing laughter sent the birds reeling from their roosts in the trees.

The one eventuality which the Vicomte de Frébois had not anticipated when he left a depleted garrison in Castle Crespin was the quasi-military defiance of his domestic order by a piratical guest, and the temporary shock subversion – at least into unreliability, though not into mutiny – of his weakened retainers. Lady Eléonore realized that she could not immediately regain control of the situation when the group of Teutons, with the hounds and hunt-servants, were outside the castle. Yet immediate action was necessary to save the simple lad. The extreme recourse of an armed arrest, possibly after a running fight in the village street, could not be organized before the hunt was started. She had to assign the rescue of Happy-With-Jesus to some improvisation by Robert. She sent to the stables for a horse to be prepared for him at once, and saw him mounted. Since he could hardly be expected to gallop down the village street, a recognized ally of the boy and riding in the direction he had taken, without being stopped by the Teutons, she ordered a mounted man-at-arms to lead him to a forest ride on the east of the castle, and conduct him on a trail well known to the natives which would put him on a direct path to his retreat. It was a faster route, given the certainty of local knowledge, than the lazier, safer path round the fringe of the forest. But it could be remote from the expected action since it avoided not only the track down which Happy-With-Jesus had been whipped, but the probable course of the hunt which Sir Otto intended. For horsemen were far slower than hounds in woodland of any density, and the knight of Jerusalem had somewhat blindly gambled on a cross-country course, with appropriate sporting interruptions from copse and bosk, such as he had been used to on the steppes of East Prussia.

Robert rediscovered an old sensual delight as he settled himself in the saddle. He pulled the skirt of his gown up through his crutch and felt disturbingly military again.

He was kindly, but slightly peremptory to the man-at-arms who escorted him. Riding away from the castle he reflected that an attitude to life varied significantly according to the height at which one travelled. Philosophically – for his mind reserved accommodation for philosophy even when he was riding on a desperate errand – he viewed this flexibility with an approval that surprised him. Humility rotted self-confidence, and he was aware that he was making assessments, judgments, plans with authority and decisiveness. But he prayed earnestly, abrasively, as he rode.

He dismissed his armed guide once he was sure of his route. He arrived at the retreat. It was mid-afternoon. The place was entirely deserted. Even Sobrin and Plantagenet had gone. He wrapped the rough makings of a meal in a napkin of Adèle, put it in a small basket which she had also brought previously on one of her visits, and hung the basket on a bush by the spring of water which he knew any fugitive would seek even if he avoided the house. He rode immediately to La Tranchée. Maister Brémand, uncertain of the effect of this new imbroglio on his future relations with his lord, gave him a gruff but positive welcome, which Rupert etiolated with an extraordinarily un-English demonstration of affection and concern. Dame Matilda stayed darkly silent. Adèle greeted him with grave relief. She had walked to the retreat earlier and found Plantagenet and Sobrin. She had coaxed the pig to struggle to his home farm and ridden Sobrin to escort him. She still had only a confused idea of what had happened. Robert, lacking communication with the animals, had even less knowledge of the complicated plotting which had led to the brutal arrest that morning, but he was as precise as possible about the later events of the day. Even these details added up to little. Happy-With-Jesus was the quarry for an organized man-hunt. Sylvester was missing. Robert and Adèle did not know that the two were together. Robert could plan using only vague possibilities.

'The imperative is that Happy-With-Jesus must be located before the hunters come up with him,' he said. 'That is the most unlikely circumstance of all, yet we know that hunters do fail to find their quarry. And, apart from the chances of ordinary life, he can still be given extraordinary salvation by the grace of an especially loving Lord, or by some accidental – or miraculous – intervention and diversion of the hunt.' Here Rupert pricked up his ears and gazed at Robert in total absorption.

'Once we can get Happy-With-Jesus into our keeping,' Robert continued, 'however temporary or uncertain that may be because of the force of arms against us, the surest way to save him is to get him into sanctuary in a church. But that church and its priest must have an independent standing. If we take the lad to refuge in the parish church of his old village, neither Sir Bernard nor the villagers themselves are likely to stand out against the moral force of what they will see as their feudal vassalage, and there will not be time to bring in Lady Eléonore to tell them what is right. The same sanctions hold, but to a worse degree, in every other country parish. Therefore we must get him to the Town.'

The Town had its own freedoms, which basically in the eyes of its burghers spelled 'Touch Me Not' to the power of the landed nobles. The Town was at the opposite side of the forest to La Tranchée. Crespin was far nearer to it, but the man-hunt had been set in the other direction, round the southern fringes of the forest. Even if Happy-With-Jesus knew what he was doing, he would need to have run a deliberately wide circle to be able to head back towards the Town,

'How can we justify any assumptions about the lad?' said Robert. 'Yet we have got to make assumptions. We can only trust that, if he is not caught by now, he will be trying to reach the retreat or this farmhouse. But both places are obvious targets for the hunters. We must have them covered, but we can't afford to be here ourselves. We have vital business elsewhere.' Robert was speaking urgently and directly to Adèle, but he was alert to a narrowing of the eyes and freezing of the face in Maister Brémand. He realized his tactical error and worked immediately to remedy it.

'Dame Matilda,' he said, turning unexpectedly to Adèle's mother. 'I give you my solemn assurance that there is nothing in my intentions which will expose Adèle in any way to physical danger from any meeting with these wild men. I want to send her to sanctuary first, so that she may warn the priest and others in the Town. The man who leads these savage hunters wears the Cross on his surcoat, but the sign is far more wickedly false than the Cross borne by that crazed youth who in deluded ecstasy seduced your own son, those many years ago, to go to seek Jerusalem. I am trying to save another trusting soul, not intelligent but still loving the Lord, from the death your boy endured. I am asking that Adèle should go to the Town to prepare his sanctuary within the Mother Church. Will you permit this?'

Dame Matilda's face became suddenly swollen and knotted with unshed tears, and she mutely nodded.

'Maister Brémand,' said Robert, 'will you allow your daughter to do what she can, without being set face to face against the hunters, to save this boy?'

'I want to know,' said Brémand stolidly, 'that this will not be in breach of my vows to the Vicomte de Frébois.'

'In my presence,' said Robert, 'the Lady Eléonore, as châtelaine of Crespin Castle and regent of the Vicomte's fief, forbade this man-hunt and ordered the boy's release. She was defied. By the counsel of Brother Francis I do not swear oaths, but I affirm this on my sacred status as a deacon of the Church.'

'Then I am content,' said Brémand. 'What do you want done?'

'A reliable servant to be sent to my retreat, to await the hunters if they come, to give them no information but to collect as much as he can and to report back to you. He must be a man, and tough enough to take intimidation.'

'Edmond,' said Brémand. 'He will surrender no information because he will be given none. What next?'

'Yourself to command this farm. To give no information but to absorb as much as possible. To receive Happy-With-Jesus if he should come here, to conceal him if necessary, and to get him away as fast as possible to the heights of Les Combles. That is where I shall be.'

'Les Combles!' said Adèle in surprise. 'Apart from the Glade of Grace, it's thick forest all the way through from here.'

'The harder to hunt through,' said Robert. 'But you in La Tranchée know the track, and the Teutons don't. The heights of Les Combles are near and above the Town, and in a military sense command it. But if Happy-With-Jesus can reach them he'll be at the end of a long journey, and he'll need someone he completely trusts on that last stage. I shall bring him down. To you, in St Michael's Church.'

'St Michael's?'

'That's where I want you to go now. It's the first church you come to in the Town, almost immediately after you've crossed the bridge. Find Father Célestin. You're a persuasive girl, and you can convince him of the truth. But, in any case, I'll give you a note that you can take with him to the Bishop. I'll do it now. Can I be given writing materials?'

The terrifying request for pen, ink and vellum was a

material requirement that set Dame Matilda into a practical baffled confusion which conveniently fired the explosion of all her deeper emotions. She harried her underlings as she bustled to prise out these rarities.

'The Bishop?' queried Adèle acutely. 'Do you carry weight with him? And would it matter if you did? It was the Bishop who got Happy-With-Jesus expelled from his village in the first place.'

'Different diocese, different bishop,' said Robert. 'And yes, I may carry a little weight. We were scholars at Cluny together.'

'In the midst of strife we are indexed. I didn't know you were a Benedictine.'

'I'm not now,' said Robert. 'That was before there was a Francis. See to Sobrin. We must be going.'

Brémand called for Edmond and went to meet him. As he walked he looked round and whistled automatically for Rupert.

'Ah yes, see to Sobrin,' said Adèle ironically. 'The reliable little donkey. You've got a fine horse now. You think you could make Les Combles?'

'Well, naturally.'

'Have you ever been to Les Combles?'

'Yes, on foot.'

'Poor feet. Not even sandal-shod then. Do you remember the way?'

'Pretty well. I can recognize it.'

'Do you remember the head room? When you were playing hopscotch across the brambles?'

'Not particularly.'

'Darling Robert. I withdraw that, but, all the same – dear Robert. You're turning out to be a magnificent general but you still need a staff officer for detail. You will never make Les Combles on that horse. You don't really know the way, you'll have to pick your path at a snail's pace, and within five minutes of twilight you'll be garrotted by the first low branch you fail to see. By contrast, I know the way, I sit low on a low donkey, and I have absolutely no influence with Father What's-his-name or Bishop Fiddle-de-Benedict, who would probably excommunicate me on the spot. You are going to gallop on your magnificent charger round the rim of the forest to make all the ecclesiastical arrangements in the Town, and I shall keep this vague rendezvous at Les Combles. I'll see you at St Michael's.'

'But I can't. You can't. I promised your parents.'

'An innocent vow. Made in all pious ignorance. I dispense you from it. Come on, we must be moving. See to your horse. What's his name, anyway?'

Maister Brémand was coming towards them with a puzzled, even pained expression.

'I can't find Rupert. There's no trace of him in the farm. I know he goes for jaunts on occasion, but not when I need him.

'That dog has never let me down before in my life.'

Sir Otto, who had no other means of telling the time, waited until the shadow of the crossbeam of the gibbet reached a predetermined object in the dust. This happened to be a neck bone of the unfortunate Balthasar, mistakenly extracted by a carrion crow and dropped as soon as the bird realized it had been picked clean. The knight gave the order to start the hunt. The hounds were unleashed and the Teutons pursued, accompanied by a surprising number of dissolute horsemen and agile hunt-servants, running on foot, who had no desire at all to meet the castle châtelaine in her now well-reported rage, and had conclusively imbibed all the reserve wine to reinforce their decision.

The hunt streamed effortlessly to the first grove. There was a comparatively formal flurry of sniffing and casting. Then it was an easy run on the scent of Happy-With-

Jesus to the rocky pool. Sir Otto was displeased with the direction taken, since it seemed to point to the forest, into which the wind was now driving steadily.

The ending of the scent at the pool itself was doubly disturbing since it seemed to indicate the applied intelligence of an animal rather than a subhuman. Hounds cast ineffectively for an increasingly infuriating time, until Sir Otto chose to dignify the quarry with calculable motives. If there could be no reliance on scent, one had to draw on experience of the habitual evasive tricks of the game being hunted. In this case the sole possibility seemed to be that the quarry had sprinted for home. The Franciscan retreat was known only to the two men-at-arms who had arrested the lad, and they led the cross-country gallop which the bloodhounds and talbots had to tail.

The troop arrived at the retreat before Edmond had reached it, which was perhaps fortunate for him since their mood was ugly. They sacked the entire construction, after presenting what rags of fabric they came across to the bloodhounds to smell. The fresh hoof marks of Robert's horse were discerned, and the hunt plunged through to La Tranchée. Edmond, running fast, had got back there before they arrived. Brémand immediately closed his stout main portal to the farmyard, raised the drawbridge, and waited with the angry anxiety of a practical man caught up in political scheming. The party arrived and reconnoitred the farm. It was walled and moated, but its primary defence was ranged against wild animals. It could stand a siege if it had the requisite garrison, but even a score of mounted soldiers, with bloodhounds baying below them, constituted a superior power which Brémand had neither the force nor the conviction to combat.

Shouted demands from outside were expressed in language incomprehensible enough for Brémand to convince himself that it was foreign and carried no obligation to reply. So he kept quiet. The Crespin retainers understood the status Brémand held in the esteem of the Vicomte, and did nothing to reinforce the menace by translating for the condottiere. Sir Otto's men-at-arms, after riding round the moat, gathered opposite the gatehouse. One athletic soldier dismounted, made a running jump over the water; and finished with a firm grip on the base of the raised drawbridge. He hauled himself up and parleyed from the top of the gatehouse. Short of shooting him with arrows, which Brémand was not prepared to do, he had to be listened to. The farmer grimly planted himself in the front courtyard and Dame Matilda, with ill-timed fortitude, stood in support of him.

The soldier, who had been a sardonic observer at the castle on the night of the Court of Love, eased himself into a comfortable seat on the top of the portico of the gatehouse and spat an entirely unexpected question:

'Where's that fancy teaser of a trollop of a daughter of yours? The girl Adèle?'

He shrewdly noted the unconcealed surprise in Brémand's face, and the almost total collapse of Dame Matilda, who clutched at her husband in utter alarm.

'She's not here,' said Brémand.

'I'm coming down to see,' said the man-at-arms. 'Bring a ladder.'

'Jump,' said Brémand.

'Bring a ladder,' said the man. He rested his hand casually on the head of the axe in his belt.

Brémand signed to a farmhand, who fetched a ladder and propped it against the portico. Keeping his eyes on the group in the farmyard, the man-at-arms stepped on to the ladder and slid lightly down it, face forwards, with the ease of a sailor on a companionway.

'Everyone stay here,' he ordered.

He went swiftly to the house and searched every chamber. He came out, took up a pitchfork and went round the barns thrusting the fork into hay and straw.

'Where is she?' he demanded when he had come back.

'I don't know,' said Brémand.

'Trusting father! Right. Now we come to what we really want. Where's the idiot?'

'I don't know,' said Brémand.

'Has he been here?'

'No.'

'Is he with the girl Adèle?'

'No.'

'How do you know if you don't know where she is?'

Brémand was silent.

'I'm going,' said the man. 'For the moment. Open the gate.'

Brémand signalled again, and a farmhand began drawing the bolts of the great gate. The soldier moved to the ladder, lifted it and stood waiting at the gate.

'Where are you taking that?' Brémand asked.

'Outside.'

'Why?'

'I'll need it, won't I, if it's dark when we come back.'

With a sudden forceful gesture the man drew his axe and swung it at the bole which formed the wooden mandrel of the drawbridge mechanism. The drawbridge rattled down across the moat. The soldier flung the ladder through the gate on to the land beyond the moat. He hit the bole vigorously with three more axe blows in apparent vandalism, but in reality he had destroyed the ratchet system, and the drawbridge could not be raised. He strode out to where the horsemen and hounds were waiting, and said something incomprehensible to Sir Otto, then turned back to the Brémands.

'I want to find that ladder there when we come back,' he said. 'You can bolt the gate if you want to. That will be protection enough against wild beasts at night. You won't need the drawbridge on account of you don't need protection against soldiers of the Cross. Understood? Right.' He leered at Dame Matilda. 'You'd better start preparing all that soup we'll need for supper. A pig would do very well, too. If your girl Adèle doesn't want it you can be sure the rest of us will. We can all have a cosy meal together.'

He put a question to Sir Otto, who confirmed with a growl and a nod of his head. He climbed into his saddle, and the party rode away fast, the horsemen again leading the hounds.

The stricken Dame Matilda looked dumbly at Brémand with a torrent of unarticulated questions in her eyes. Her husband gazed down at her.

'Do you think Rupert could somehow have come up with Adèle?' he asked. But he did not wait for an answer.

Sir Otto and his company, some two dozen men including the running hunt-servants, rode directly back to the rocky pool. The hounds were set once more to search. They still seemed to be in good spirit, by no means listless after what had already been a long day. They were all huge dogs, the bloodhounds at that time appearing not at all ferocious, obviously well bred and well trained so that they gave an impression of being almost domesticated. The talbots were even larger, and much fiercer. Both breeds had been developed from the classic St Hubert, a strain bred for centuries at the monastery of that name in the Ardennes. But the talbots had been bred from them with a concentration on size and strength. Massive but raw-boned in frame, lighter in colour than the bloodhounds, treating them almost as menials who did the routine work before the shock troops were called in, they roamed around the pool, undisciplined and intractable.

A hunt servant gave a shout to Sir Otto from the middle of the pool. He had waded in, and his foot had brushed a different texture from stone. He raised high the boulder with the simple lad's gown lashed around it. Sir Otto swore crudely. The fabric was wrenched away and presented to the hounds. They took little interest until one of the men-at-arms thrust at them the scraps of cloth taken from the retreat. One bloodhound, after sniffing at the pieces with an extreme of ecstasy more understandable if due to venison gravy, ran importantly into the wood above the pool and began urgent investigations into the leafmould of a previous year. He edged forward a few paces, smelling the ground all the time and suddenly cried that he had found the scent. It was Sylvester's, and he had recognized it from the cottage rags. The deep, truly shocking, bay of the bloodhound struck at the instincts of his fellows with the swiftness of mass hysteria. Their voices exploded like choirmen singing the *Dies Irae*. The talbots, alert yet still dependent, responded in a tuneless stridency even more terrifying than the matched chorus of the bloodhounds. The humans, brainwashed from puberty to relate to this thrilling animal sound, shrieked and whooped in reaction, and formed up to proceed in order into the wood. Sir Otto set his horse at the rocks on the edge of the escarpment, turned round once to shake his fist at the south, from where what was now almost a gale was driving the scent of the quarry away from them, and manoeuvred a way into the thickening forest. The squared pupils of two yellow eyes stared keenly from the hollow interior of an ancient chestnut tree, a lively and healthy survivor with bright-green flowers already tossing in the wind, though the same wind hissed through the centre of the base where the old timber had rotted to form double portals like an arch of triumph.

The yellow pupils snapped into obscurity as if shutters

had been dropped over them. A grey shape emerged stealthily from the hollow tree, then leapt into urgent speed. Baclin the wolf, brother to Hurlaud of the Great Woods and deputy leader of his pack, was streaking to report that the invasion of the forest uneasily anticipated by the free animals had indeed occurred. The aggressor had crossed the frontier.

Sylvester had been stumping for a long time with his burden on his back. 'But he is no burden,' Sylvester said aloud. 'He is my dear brother Happy-With-Jesus, and the Lord has sent him to receive my love, which is still the Lord's love just as there is only one sunlight.' Sylvester had been voicing all his thoughts aloud for the past two hours. He knew too well that he was tired, but he also realized that the lad was fractious. With no assured chain of memory, Happy-With-Jesus forgot from time to time exactly what his situation was, and Sylvester did not directly remind him. On occasion he wanted to get down from Sylvester's back, struggling violently when the friar assured him that this was the one thing he must not do. So, like a mother using the music rather than the sense of her voice to soothe her child, Sylvester continued talking:

'I told him, and you should have heard me telling him straight, but you were on your way to the castle at the time with dear Brother Robert. I told him. I said, "Look at you, now. You've got a tidy tunic, leather back and fore with iron facings," I said. "It'll guard your guts against arrows but you'd never stand up to a knight. And your lord would never match you with one unless he used you as the gravy he wanted sopped up before the meat." The gravy before the meat! You should have seen his eyes. He was hurt, you know. But I didn't want to hurt him. I was just speaking bluntly, speaking as I find.'

Sylvester trudged on. His legs were black to the thighs, where the weight of the lad had borne him down in soft bogland. There was a recurring tic in the muscles of his legs and he was moving very slowly.

'Pi-pi-pi-pi,' said Happy-With-Jesus.

'No you can't get down, and you must know it because I've told you so many times.'

'Pi-pi-pi-pi.'

' "But I've got the faith," I told him. "So you'll never thrust through to the real me. It's as hard to wound me as it is to humiliate an idiot." And, idiot or no, it takes a lot to humiliate you, don't it, Happy-With-Jesus, my dear brother in the Lord? You've got the armour and I've got the armour, and it's called Love. "I stripped myself and offered myself naked to Christ like Francis said," I told him. "And the Lord invested me with new armour." '

Sylvester halted absolutely, and allowed himself a dry-throated chuckle. ' "Stripped myself naked," I told him, "and offered myself to the Lord." Now, my dear, do you by any chance see a resemblance between what I told him and what I am now? But, you see, I've still got my armour. He couldn't see it, but both of us, Happy-With-Jesus, both of us know it's there. It's the same with me as it is with you, my dear.'

'Pi-pi-pi-pi,' said the lad.

'Oh, let it go,' said Sylvester with resignation. 'Let it go.'

The urine sprang against his neck and streamed down his chest and his back.

Sylvester sighed and took up his dragging march again.

At a discreet distance from the pair, the man slowly pounding with anguished muscles and the boy now happy in his relief, the free animals of the forest cautiously kept pace, extending vigilant cover to them.

Hurlaud, nominally in command of the wolves, had been by the general will persuaded to co-ordinate the whole operation, and his divisional command had been assumed by the capable Baclin. There was never any difficulty with the wolves, who were by far the most disciplined group. By contrast Grondin was floundering, ineffectually trying to instil some order into the free-booter boars. Flandrin, always unworried, was boisterously raising the corporate morale of the initially sleepy bears until with grunts and chuckles they warmed into relish for the fight that might ensue.

At one point Hurlaud sent his son and personal aide, Grand-Gueule, to summon the three lieutenant generals for a perambulating conference following an intelligence flash. 'Hard news is just in from Puissard the sparrow-hawk,' he told them. 'Adèle with the donkey Sobrin is at Les Combles, apparently resting and waiting. That appears to be a rendezvous. But I have no indication that these two fugitives know of it. It can't be planned, it must be improvised, the route takes in the whole depth of the forest and much of it uphill. Well, at least we know. If the pair need nudging in the right direction we nudge them towards Les Combles. Is that understood, gentlemen? Very well, dismiss. And, Grondin, do try and stamp out some of this maverick individuality your boars are indulging in. You bloody loners all turn out to be rogues in any expedition. You don't seem to recognize the extra impact of a disciplined force.'

'Sorry, Hurlaud,' said Grondin contritely. 'It's just high spirits. All they want is a fight, and I've got my work cut out trying to stop them mauling each other until they get a whiff of the Teutons. It's all good fun really.'

Fulgent the fox had been painfully trying to keep up

with Grondin, but often seized the opportunity to hover in rest while the boar bullied his recalcitrant peers. Grondin finally paused in his sweating labours and slumped down for a chat.

'At the pace we're kept down to I can catch up in no time,' he said. 'How are you? Are you mad yet? Crude, isn't it? But what else can you say between old friends?'

'I can't rely on my endurance,' said Fulgent. 'I can keep going for quite long spells, then suddenly I become useless. My hind quarters fail. I can't now be sure that I shall be in on the mark when the action starts. And I don't want to die miserably under a bush. Especially when Hurlaud has given me a little mission.'

'We can deal with that,' said Grondin confidently. 'But first there is something that must be said.'

'A deathbed confession?'

'Deathbed expiation, Fulgent old boy. We've shared many a high summer morning in the days when we were free. We've seen the strengthening sun burn away dubious mists which in reality held nothing – but we couldn't be sure. It is a time for that now. I shouldn't like you to go without one foggy hollow being exposed as the clearing it always was. I do this, I admit, for my own peace of mind more than yours, for how can such shadows seriously trouble you now? A little time ago I was contemptuous to your face about your principles. In decent humility I withdraw that slur. I respect your principles, whatever roots I trace them to. I honour them the more because I know that, since you first suspected the nature of your sickness, you have resolutely abandoned your mate Régine and your cubs. You have sacrificed a principle of family providence for the higher responsibility of family survival. And Régine, like many one-parent families – I mention this only academically, without polemics – is learning to manage. But what I want you to be sure of is my respect for you.'

'I should like,' said Fulgent, 'to have known those cubs. If only to have sexed them.'

'Feminine curiosity over detail, old man. Entirely understandable, but irrelevant to their survival. You are prince of the foxes. Your line goes on.'

'Thanks, Grondin.'

'And now we must be practical. You distrust your stamina. Can't be sure of footing it to the front line. No problem. You ride.'

'Ride!'

'Mounted assault. You mount me.'

'That's impossible.'

'The only one who has proved that it *is* possible is you,' said Grondin. 'And if I hadn't seen a small part of the action with my own eyes I should have dismissed the whole episode as the spume of your line-shooting imagination which has enlivened so many forest banquets in the past. Do you remember that time when Frébois had his old pack of St Hubert's out, and a couple caught your trail and couldn't be edged off it on to nobler game for all the whips and oaths in Aquitaine?'

'Ah, that was a day,' said Fulgent.

'You only saved your skin by springing on to the back of a sheep and stampeding that dim bewildered beast until it had covered a quarter of a league without leaving a trace of your scent, after which you dropped off and lolloped home as cool as an otter.'

'Dear God, that ewe was terrified,' laughed Fulgent reminiscently.

'Not half as terrified as I'm going to be. You weren't infectious then. But I'll take a chance with you. I know you can ride. But remember, that ewe had wool you could cling to by teeth and claws. My bristly back is a less convenient saddle, and I want no perforations at all. In return, I'll go more sedately until the last charge, but you've got to spreadeagle yourself for balance and give your dying promise – no perforations at all. Is that an understanding?'

'Willingly, gratefully, given. I can never thank you. . . .'

'Cut the gratitude. Talk of the target. You know who it is you want. Can you identify him to me so that I can home in on him?'

'With absolute certainty.'

'Will he be mounted?'

'Not on a boar,' Fulgent chuckled. 'On a horse. Grondin, you don't know what an excellent idea this is. With the state of my legs I'd never have been sure of gaining the extra height for the last jump. Now it's the good old one-two. You bowl the horse over, I go for the man. You'll go hard, of course. But he'll have a spear.'

'I do a double-jink at fifteen paces that beats any boar-spear.'

'But, Grondin . . .'

'Yes?'

'Don't go for the horse when he's down. It's only the man I want.'

'No left and right uppercuts? No swordplay from ploughshares? They're bony beasts, you know, horses, from the belly downwards. An uppercut through the guts pays off a bit for the bruising.'

'Please, Grondin. Last will and testament.'

'If you say so. I've got nothing against horses myself, really. Never knew them chase man or beast of their own will, without a warlord in the saddle. Did you know they were strict, orthodox vegetarians? More kosher than I am, if the truth be told. All right, no hitting above the belt.'

'Grondin, I really am grateful.'

'Save your breath to pump your rabies. Would you like to rehearse that spreadeagle posture now on a short canter? I'm scared into squitters already. Don't know what made me offer to do this. I must have been bitten already by your principles.'

Rupert and Lulu were in earnest conference on the edge of a wide forest clearing near Bel Air which lay on the direct line between the rocky pool and Les Combles. The site was remarkable because an enormous circle within it was fresh with extraordinarily vivid green grassland. It was an ancient fairy ring, centuries old, where the annual growth of the underground spawn of mushroom and champignon, radiating outwards at a rate of two human hand breadths a year, had been undisturbed for so long that a hundred men could lie down in a line across it before they had marked its diameter.

'Apart from the Glade of Grace, farther north,' said Lulu, 'this is the only open space on the line of march where we can operate. I propose to do an experimental sweep here, learn what we can from it, adapt our tactics and bring off the real *coup de grâce* in the Glade of Grace.'

Lulu paused. 'That was meant to be a jaunty, nonchalant, do-or-die witty remark,' she said, pensively. 'Judging by your total absence of reaction, it didn't come off, and on reflection there was certainly something morbid about it. I'm beginning to shiver myself.

'However, to business. I've called out as many of my chaps as I could after the very short notice you gave me. We've been recruiting hard, and I've got well over the strength of the two squadrons you saw on the last exercise. They're all in the undergrowth around this dale now, and if you haven't been aware of their presence it's a tribute to their sense of cover.'

'If it didn't come off last time, you must be joking now,' said Rupert. 'The whole place stinks of hare.'

'Is perfumed with hare,' Lulu corrected him. 'But, however you describe the aroma, that's what we're here for. A strong counterscent. I hope it works. We shall see. I've never been chased by bloodhounds before and I don't greatly care for it. Are they really interested in hares?'

'They take six or seven dozen at dawn and then call for breakfast,' said Rupert genially. 'No, seriously, they're single-minded hounds when they're hunting, and I'm putting much more hope in your effect on the talbots. They really are a set of savages with just enough sophistication to make them vicious. They've renounced the law of the forest and don't take kindly to the rules of the humans without a bastinado of whipping. If you can put up the sort of diversion that will effectively confuse them, the huntsmen will have to pull back the bloodhounds while they sort things out. It gains time, and time is our target.'

Lulu considered. 'We'll carry out the first exercise with a comfortable margin,' she said. 'That is, not in sight of the enemy. We'll wait for the quarry to pass, and after a reasonable interval do a series of sweeps. At least our scent will be the freshest. This first pass is not going to be very spectacular, but we can observe the effect and possibly learn from it. Do you mean to stay and watch?'

'I am yours to the death,' said Rupert gallantly.

'Another unfortunate remark,' said Lulu with a slight tremor. 'This doesn't seem our day for eloquence. Listen!'

With fluctuating volume, but never more than faintly, the baying of bloodhounds sighed up from the south.

'Deceptive, of course, in the strong wind,' said Lulu. 'But worrying, just the same. The quarry has not passed yet.'

She stood on her hind legs and faced first north and then south. 'Parade! Parade! Attention!' she screamed from the centre of the fairy ring.

Adèle waited in a space where the ride slightly broadened in the forest heights of Les Combles, exceptionally uneasy because there was nothing she could do beyond waiting. Sobrin, all sympathy but as taciturn as ever, soothed her with his comfortable presence and even with an occasional nudge from his nose as she lay on a horse-cloth she had spread on the ground and looked up at the first stars piercing the veil of evening.

There was an almost imperceptible stir in the air and a slight pneumatic hiss as Grand-Duc, the eagle owl, settled near her. He boomed like an outsize tuning-fork and chuckled to clear his throat. 'The stars are not going to serve you well tonight, my poppet,' he said. 'The trees are too dense. You've chosen the best platform available and it still gives you no more than a funnel.'

'Grand-Duc! How nice to see you!' said Adèle with new animation.

'Delighted to drop in,' said Grand-Duc airily. 'I live quite near, these days. I tried out an apartment on the crag above. It suits me and I've decided to stay.'

'You don't ask why I'm here,' said Adèle pointedly.

Grand-Duc abandoned his casual manner and spoke seriously. 'I don't ask why because I know why,' he said. 'We have to know in the forest. A reckless sparrowhawk called Puissard woke me up early to tell me. A desperate sortie, but that young short-arse has got so much guts that I decided not to have 'em for garters. Excuse the military phraseology, but this is a military occasion.'

His voice softened into more personal concern. 'Listen, Adèle, I know you're troubled but I think it's going to be all right. The hunt has not yet caught up with the simple lad. The friar – the other friar, not the one who's moony over you – has joined up with him. When last seen, by no less than the scion of Athena who is now extending you an audience, they were holding a very satisfactory course towards you. They are being shadowed by a strong protective force of the free animals. If they deviate, they will be put back on course. It's hard for you, but if you can endure the vigil this is still the place for you.'

'But this is magnificent!' said Adèle. 'It's news, and good news.'

'What will you do when they arrive?'

'Get the boy to the Town.'

'How?'

'On the donkey.'

'Do you know the way?'

'I've never been to the Town in my life. But I'm told there is a well-beaten track.'

'You can still go wrong. Fortunately the direction is almost dead north. Do you remember my last lesson?'

'I think so.'

'Feel the trees, and the moss on the bark is north of west. Look for horse chestnuts, and the spreading branches are southerly, the high-pointing branches northerly. It won't work so well on your way to the Town because the slope to the river is almost dead north, and with that incline the trees don't respond so obviously. But the slope will help instead. When in doubt, choose the most consistent downhill path.'

'I remember now.'

'And I shan't be far away. A little navigational assistance. Would you recognize my call at a distance?' Without waiting for a reply Grand-Duc thrust his hooked bill into his wing-coverts and tromboned his very low, two-toned *to-woo*. 'Sounded once, it will mean "Go left". Sounded twice, it will mean "Go right". Three calls, and it means "Freeze, danger ahead, wait till you hear again".'

Adèle was buoyant with new optimism. Grand-Duc repeated the instructions. 'Have you fixed them?' he asked.

'Indelibly,' she said. 'To think there'll be someone up there hooting for me!'

When Sylvester and Happy-With-Jesus came to the fairy circle the baying of the hounds was sounding strongly in their ears. The sight of the stretch of open space jerked Sylvester into a clarity of thought that in the last hour of exhaustion had been slipping from him. He realized that it was now no accident that the hounds continued to sound from behind him, and that they were following his own scent. There was no advantage in carrying the lad any farther. Under the best conditions, running separately, they could make four times their present speed. He lowered Happy-With-Jesus to the ground and tried to explain this.

As soon as he touched the turf, Happy-With-Jesus, his poor co-ordination worsened by cramp, fell flat and face down. What had looked like grass was in reality a sodden pool where water had run off the clearing, with the rich herbage growing green above it. The prone body of the lad was half-submerged in water. Sylvester pulled him to his feet. With the lack of blood circulation he had had to endure, the boy began to shiver.

'We're going to run,' said Sylvester, and started out across the green. He looked back, and Happy-With-Jesus was still and staring, incredulous that he was being abandoned. Sylvester ran back, already feeling a new strain in his muscles but hoping it was the dregs of the old exhaustion. He took the lad by the hand, and at a far slower pace than he had hoped for they trotted across the clearing and plunged into the trees on the other side.

Gradually they adjusted to a pace at which, each with his physical disadvantage, they could mutually support each other. The forest animals had also passed over the glade and were covering them from the flanks, but they were blankly unaware of that. What puzzled Sylvester was that they seemed to have gained a lead on the hunters which was inexplicable even by their new acceleration – a rate of progress which could not enthuse him, for Happy-With-Jesus was already floundering.

The advantage was, in fact, due to the hare sweeps across the fairy ring, which effected a delay that Lulu found highly satisfactory as she observed it all from distant cover. But there was a sequel to the confusion, the ill temper, the whipping-in and the remustering which she could not understand and which was equally teasing to Rupert and gave him much more anxiety. After order had been restored in the hunt most of the horsemen dismounted. Half a dozen riders remained on horseback. Each took a leading-rein which was knotted to the bridles of the other horses, and they raced away down the clearing to the east. Sir Otto and the remainder followed the hounds on foot into the farther forest, where they could be anticipated to make better speed than when on horseback.

Happy-With-Jesus gradually faltered in his pace. Sylvester still had the endurance to press on, but the difficulty of the route meant that for much of the time he could not even hold the lad by his hand. The cry of the hounds came inexorably nearer. Sylvester realized that he had to make a last stand. The hunters might not yet have realized that there were now two individual bodies being chased in the man-hunt. To find one might be enough.

He stopped, and pointed forward for Happy-With-Jesus to go on. The lad could not understand. He smiled, simply and trustfully. 'Don't smile now!' Sylvester pleaded. 'Or smile at me, but not at *them*' – and he pointed back in the direction of the hunt. 'You don't know the danger you're in from your smile. "Father forgive them for they know not what they do" goes well on the Cross, where nothing more can be done, but in

Gethsemane it will only take you to the Cross.' He pointed ahead, and still the lad did not move. 'Why can't I make you *afraid*?' Sylvester yelled at him. 'Is it your love that will lose your life?' He took up a stick and, merely menacing with it, drove the boy a little forward. He raised the stick to strike him, and he dropped it. 'I am not going to die,' he shouted, 'leaving you to believe that I did not love you.' He kissed the lad firmly, mouth to mouth. He turned, and with all the energy left in him he ran at speed through a bush that promptly set him out of sight, and raced, determined, exhausted, naked, black, towards the hunt.

From out of the surrounding cover the free animals of the forest moved in, almost encircling Happy-With-Jesus but leaving him one outlet to the north. They came up to him until they were pressing him with their bodies. Finally, bewildered, he began to advance.

Behind, the drilled cry of disciplined hounds suddenly lifted into riotous tumult. Sylvester ran straight at them, and the dogs brought him swiftly to the ground. 'Call them off!' roared Sir Otto, and he plunged heavily towards the mangled man.

Sylvester, already butchered, looked up at him and the bloodied lips, drawn back wide over clenched teeth, relaxed into his own forgiveness. 'These last years,' he said, 'I have lived in the faith of things not seen. Now I go to see.'

'Go,' said Sir Otto, and he thrust his spear through the body and into the ground.

From out of the forest ahead of the hunt a black shape charged. 'Man with the spear by the body on the ground,' said Fulgent into Grondin's ear, almost embracing him as he strove to cling to the pounding boar by muscles rather than claws. 'Watch this double-jink,' grunted Grondin as he did his swerve at fifteen paces. He charged straight at his target, launched Fulgent, swung to give the fox an accurate trajectory without collapsing the knight, used his right and left tusks to gore a couple of hunters and, still at his unyielding speed, circled wide and northwards to rejoin the forest animals. Fulgent soared like a true flying-fox, instinctively spread his forelegs to adjust his glide and landed against the left breast of Sir Otto. He raised his head and sank his teeth in the Teuton's neck. He fell to the ground, was immediately stamped on by the knight and his body was severed across the haunches by a soldier's axe.

To the north, the experienced hound who had first scented Sylvester at the pool bayed commandingly. He had retraced the friar's last run, and gave cry that there was still quarry ahead to be hunted.

'Forward!' shouted Sir Otto, tying a dirty rag round his neck. Gore was seeping from the wound, for Fulgent had lacerated a blood vessel as he had intended. But he had done additional damage beyond his wit to devise. Although the neckerchief staunched the flow of blood it did nothing to soothe a heavy throbbing that pounded in the knight's head. Sir Otto pulled the rag more tightly and the throbbing eased.

Happy-With-Jesus moved on at the pace which the bears imposed. Flandrin had brought them in as immediate escort. The boy had no fear of them, and even laughed if they unexpectedly tickled him as they nudged him forward. He was near spent with exhaustion, and was sometimes overcome by bouts of shivering from his last immersion. He moved in a dream, and in his walking dream he saw strange sights. The hounds had soon come up with the quarry but they could not break through the ring of the free animals. A rearguard action of maximum harassment was being fought. The wolves, weaving in and out of the trees at a speed too fast for spearmen to aim, rushed at the dogs to slash them but never to close their jaws on them, and steadily diminished the force of the pursuit. The boars, as undisciplined as ever, used their enormous pace to make individual charges from the flank of the line of hunters so that, as Flandrin noted, they were virtually playing skittles with the men and tore flesh at every attack. 'These bloody boars are having the time of their lives,' Flandrin complained to Hurlaud. 'My men are getting restless. They want to do more than stand in as halberdiers at a royal procession.'

'It will be your turn soon,' Hurlaud assured him diplomatically 'We're not out of the wood yet.'

'Very funny,' said Flandrin insincerely.

But it was no pleasantry. Ahead lay the Glade of Grace, before the last rising ground of forest to Les Combles. Hurlaud had sent scouts forward, and they reported that half a dozen horsemen and many more horses were already there. When the free animals came up to the break in the trees they saw a disturbing prospect ahead: fire.

The horsemen had ridden round and feverishly cut a massive quantity of brushwood which had been crudely bundled into faggots. The sound and scent of the approaching animals was very clearly carried to them on the wind so that they knew where the main body would emerge. The faggots were hastily lined into a V-shaped avenue across the glade, making a funnel of diminishing width through which the animals had to pass to the forest beyond. That exit was piled with more brushwood. The exit and the faggots were set alight, so that there was no way out of the trap. Three mounted men patrolled on each side of the V. They were not concerned with killing the animals, who could be expected to break through, but they felt certain of cornering Happy-With-Jesus. The condition of the timber at that time of year made an extensive forest fire unlikely, but the same conditions made smoke, which was initially far more disabling if not destructive. The direction of the wind, straight into the angle, gave absolute clarity to the inside of the trap though it obscured the exterior. It had been important to time the operation as exactly as possible because the amount of brushwood they had been able to cut had only a critical efficiency. The horsemen waited.

The free animals came to the brink of the glade, and they also waited. To the horsemen it seemed a diabolically engineered tactic. 'All out against the dogs,' Hurlaud ordered his wolves. 'Delay them as long as possible. If necessary, engage *à outrance*, for we have got to take casualties now. Grondin, as a last appeal, get your boars into order. Split them right and left. I want them to be ready to take on these horsemen from the flank, as they have been doing very admirably, but in concerted action now, and under orders. Flandrin, who is jealous, calls it playing skittles. Well, skittle 'em, but only on the command from me. Flandrin, the final advance is up to you now.'

The animals went into action. The wolves now fought to the death when the situation demanded, determined to hold back the hunt from the group on the fringe of the trees. The brushwood fires began to die down, though the approach into the farther forest still blazed and smoked ominously. 'Over to you, Grondin,' said Hurlaud and, in the best order they could keep, the boars charged the horsemen, wheeled and charged again. 'Flandrin,' said the lord of the wolves simply, and the bears shambled forward, shepherding Happy-With-Jesus in the middle of a tight circle. On the southern edge of the glade, their backs to the flames, the wolves still faced the hunters.

The march across the open ground began. One horseman, in full flight from the boars, burst through the burning line and saw the moving nucleus of bears, ungainly but speedy, drifting across the glade ahead of him with his human quarry in the centre. The horseman had set his spear at the ready to defend himself from the boars, and he merely converted his flight into a charge, with his spear pointed relatively low, at stirrup height. The three bears receiving the charge waited until the last moment, then swiftly raised themselves to full stature, which gave them height advantage as well as nullifying the previous target. Literally they fell on the man, and equally literally they tore him to pieces. The rest of the bears closed round their charge and pressed him forward until the farther border was reached. Here the woodland still glowed fiercely and put up blinding smoke. 'Here goes,' said Flandrin. He stood on his hind legs, eight and a half feet tall, picked up the bemused Happy-With-Jesus like a baby, and shot forward. He knew that his greatest difficulty would be to keep his six-inch claws from closing instinctively on the lad, and he hugged his burden to his chest and dug his claws into the opposing shoulders, making a St Andrew's Cross of his forearms. He leapt frantically through the depth of burning wood, found the smoke still intolerable long after the immediate pain from his burned legs, and he plunged on for a long distance before he set down his charge.

Hurlaud barked an order, and the wolves raced across the clearing and re-formed, facing the hunt, on the other side. The hounds came forward, not eagerly now but shaken by the battle and dismayed by the fire. As they came into the open there was a vibrant drumming down the turf of the Glade of Grace. Lulu – and Rupert now keeping pace with her – was leading three squadrons of hares in the sweep intended to be the final diversion. Hurlaud groaned as he realized what was happening.

'It's magnificent,' he said. 'But it is now unnecessary.'

The hares thundered down the glade, through the embers of the brushwood. The hounds were caught by their strong scent, especially attractive since it no longer led into fire. The more athletic turned excitedly in pursuit. There was almost no daylight now, but the going was easy. Casualties were inevitable. Rupert, no longer able to keep up with Lulu, saw a hound pursuing her, heard the snap of a jaw and a muffled growl, and saw her body circle sideways into the air and fall. The hound who had chopped her careered forwards and stopped. He had not seen the arc of her flight, and began to search for her. Rupert sprang ahead and closed his teeth and tore on the most vulnerable of his enemy's organs. The hound, ignorant of what had attacked him, shrieked and staggered off the battlefield. Rupert quickly ran to where Lulu had fallen.

'A glorious charge,' she said. 'I think that's settled it. It's all over now. Lie close alongside me and keep me warm.'

Sir Otto assembled his surviving men and hounds in the Glade of Grace. Two of his men-at-arms had been left gored in the forest. Four remained. 'That's enough for me,' he said to his sergeant, pressing the rag uneasily against the wound in his neck, from which an inflated membrane was beginning to protrude like a bladder, pulsating with the flow of arterial blood. 'Tell all the Frébois horsemen to mount,' rasped Sir Otto. 'We've probably lost enough men altogether for there to be horses for everyone now.'

'We've lost a horse, too,' said the sergeant, indicating the aftermath of the bears' picnic.

'Any hunt-servants unmounted ride pillion,' ordered Sir Otto. 'Send them all back to Crespin. Dogs as well.'

'Aren't we going back to Crespin, then?'

'Crespin! We're going to La Tranchée. Men-at-arms – advance!'

At Les Combles Adèle had become progressively more

alarmed after the burst of optimism inspired by Grand-Duc's visit. Intermittently she had caught on the wind the baying of the hounds. Then she had smelt the smoke. After that there had been two hours of silence, which was the worst of all to endure.

The two-hour interval, which represented an inordinately long stretch for the passage from the Glade of Grace, could have been halved if Happy-With-Jesus had been in any fit state to walk, or even if he had known where he was going. But he was in an extreme of fatigue and fever, and beginning to be demented. The great expeditionary force of the free animals, who were now an almost ostentatious escort, divined that their fighting task was over and in discontent broadly conveyed their view that they should be demobilized. Hurlaud, a cautious general, temporized, privately agreed and eventually dismissed them on the proviso that they would attend a parade of honour for official recognition of their valour by the President of the Council of the Forest. 'Will you stay for the last lap?' he asked Grondin.

'I'm only staying,' said the boar gruffly, 'because I need news of my cousin Plantagenet, and that girl Adèle is the only one who will have it. He was wounded, actually wounded, by that [bleep] of a Teuton, and one spear through that scraggy carcass would do little short of dissecting him.'

'*You'll* stay?' Hurlaud said affectionately to Flandrin.

'Can you think of an alternative?' asked the bear with exaggerated resignation. He was upright and carrying in his arms again the lolling body of Happy-With-Jesus. 'I've got a bitch of a mate who won't even let me play with my cubs, and I get landed with a hundred and fifty pounds of flesh that positively stinks of mandrake.'

'That's life,' said Hurlaud.

'I want liberty and the pursuit of happiness.'

'Happiness!' scoffed a deep voice that seemed to veer

from right to left as Grand-Duc idly soared above them. 'You pansy vegetarians ought to lift your sights above happiness and start aiming at *joy*. Joy of living, joy of achievement, joy of hunting, joy of taking. Genuine rapture! That there Grondin has never taken anything larger than a snail, and I've no evidence that Flandrin's fleshly intake has ever exceeded an ant.'

'Shut up, Grand-Duc,' said Hurlaud tolerantly into the upper air. 'Is the girl still there?'

'Still there,' boomed Grand-Duc. 'I'll take over after delivery. Thanks for all your efforts.'

They came to the forest ride where Adèle was waiting, and Flandrin gently set the lad down at a distance from her. She called his name, and he stood, rubbing his eyes, looking for the source of the sound. He stumbled to her and splashed her hands and arms with kisses. Grondin approached, and stood like a polite but bad-tempered old clubman. 'Plantagenet is not badly hurt, and I will send him to you as soon as he can make the journey,' she assured him in his own language. She conveyed her gratitude to Flandrin and Hurlaud with a full gaze and a tender smile, and that was enough for them. They bowed and left her, not realizing that it was almost beyond her power to get Happy-With-Jesus to the final sanctuary.

He was physically as unmanageable as a loose sack of grain. Finally Adèle got Sobrin to kneel like a camel, and she folded the lad across the donkey's withers, tying his ankles to his wrists. It seemed bestial, but there was no other way. She mounted the donkey with her near-dead cargo fronting her. They picked their way down the forest track to the Town, with Grand-Duc giving rather formal signals and never throughout the transit of the forest sounding the command to freeze. But as they came above the approach to the bridge across the river there was an unfamiliar cry, and the triple call came from

Grand-Duc. He swirled down and perched on a stone wall by the side of them. 'I've had Erémite, the peregrine, posted in the church tower all night,' he said. 'He tells me there may be trouble. It's man-made, out of my scope. I can only warn you. Go carefully, Adèle. God keep you.' And he flew away.

At La Tranchée Sir Otto and his men-at-arms resorted to simple torture. Torture is simple, not ingenious, as the Dominicans, soon to be authorized by Pope Innocent IV to torture for the Holy Inquisition, had already discovered. The soldiers subjected Dame Matilda to agony and humiliation, and held her husband as they forced him to watch. Dame Matilda said nothing. Brémand eventually conceded that there had been a rendezvous at Les Combles. The pair were released, and after their mutual glance of relief the torture was started again. Brémand finally groaned that sanctuary was being sought at the Church of St Michael in the Town. The Teutons sprang to leave as quickly as possible.

But Sir Otto unaccountably staggered as he tried to mount his horse. His men had to lift him onto it. 'I'm giddy,' he said. 'No food.' He pressed his hand below the wound in his neck, where the bulging artery wall was visibly throbbing.

Lulu, lying helpless in a declivity in the Glade of Grace, had been restlessly talkative throughout the night. At intervals she complained of the cold, but nothing Rupert could do seemed to assuage it. Her face, usually so tremulously sensitive, became as calm as if it were frozen. Her eyes, once constantly moving, declined into stillness. She still murmured intimately to Rupert. 'Boudicca!' she said once. 'You love a loser. Love me. I'm lost.'

There was no more than a whisper in the air. A shape

descended, and from the very side of Rupert Lulu was lifted into the air. As Grand-Duc shifted his talons to execute the instinctive strangling which the eagle owl gives to its live prey, Lulu screamed. It was the high, near-human scream which every hare gives at sudden death. And Rupert stood and howled, howled longer than any beagle hound had ever done.

Adèle descended with Sobrin cautiously to the bridge. There was the sound of hooves approaching swiftly on the earthen path along the river. She urged Sobrin into speed. The gate on the farther side was open and as she dashed through it she saw a group of citizen guards, with military accoutrements not very effectively buckled over bourgeois clothing, staring at her like yokels. She saw the church ahead of her and reined in Sobrin in the square. Robert was waiting at the bottom of the steps. He was wearing vestments of a complexity which Adèle had never seen. 'I can't get Happy-With-Jesus free in time,' she told him. 'We are still being hunted.'

'Bring Sobrin into the church,' said Robert.

The donkey climbed the exterior steps, and Robert held the door open for him to enter the church. Robert led him down the nave, and at the foot of the chancel steps they began to loosen the ropes that held the unconscious lad. Robert lifted him and carried him within the sanctuary to the open space before the altar. As the boy sank to the floor the door at the west end of the church crashed open, and five armed men strode in. Robert recognized Sir Otto. Behind his bodyguard teetered a diffuse group of citizen conscripts, indignant but disordered.

With a gesture more appropriate to a bedchamber than a church, Robert put his hands crosswise to his hips, pulled the richly ornamented smock of his dalmatic over his head and placed the robe over the lad. The soldiers stamped down the nave. As they mounted the chancel steps Robert stooped to put one hand on the head of the boy, and the other he raised palm outwards towards the advancing men. 'This man is in sanctuary,' he said with a clarity which was almost entoned. 'I adjure you to respect this sanctuary in the name of Jesus.'

The lad stirred. His hand came up to touch the hand of Robert on his head. 'Happy-With-Jesus,' he said, and smiled and slumped back.

The soldiers hesitated, and the citizen guards grew bolder. They came slowly towards the strangers. 'Get out,' said the most venturesome. The soldiers moved, but towards the sanctuary. Then Sir Otto stumbled. He fell to the floor, and sawed helplessly with his leg as he tried to get up. His men tried to help him to his feet. 'He's drunk,' said the bravest of the bourgeois. 'Get him out. They're all drunk. Get out!'

Happy-With-Jesus was crawling towards them. The soldiers did not move because they could not understand the action, and lacked authority. The lad came to Sir Otto, who was supported at half-height by his men, and began to dab at the wound on his neck.

'Hurt, hurt,' he said solicitously.

Sir Otto suddenly realized that the hand of his victim was lifted towards him. Convulsively he swung back his arm to strike in self-defence. There was a great spurt of blood as the aneurysm in his damaged carotid artery ruptured. His armour tore the fingernails of his supporters as he dropped heavily to the floor. At the same time a soldier raised his knee and sprang his heel hard at the lad's chest. Happy-With-Jesus was thrown in a backward slide across the stone flags. He gave a searing gasp and began to cough. His own blood spat on to the stone.

'Get out!' shouted the leader of the armed burgesses.

The Teutons turned to leave, and then realized that they were abandoning their leader. Not knowing that he was dead, they clumsily carried his body away. Sir Otto of Jerusalem, former Prior and Grand Cross of his Order, was denied the privilege of lying even for a few moments within the sanctuary.

Happy-With-Jesus was brought home to the Franciscan retreat, which Robert and Adèle restored to a decent state. And he did his chores and said his prayers with the sweetness he had always shown since he had met Sylvester and Robert, and through them his Lord. But a veil hung between him and life. His bones were crushed and a consumption was in his lungs. On a summer afternoon he went out into the underwood, tried to make a few bird calls and lay down to die. The animals of the forest found him. Grondin the boar, whose snout and tusks could lay open a trench better than any gravedigger, covered him decently.

'Love and death,' said Adèle. 'We have known something of it. There was Sylvester.'

'We have known Happy-With-Jesus,' said Robert. 'He had love. I don't think he had anything but love.'

'He was the fool,' said Adèle. 'As you chose to be. Dropping learning and finding love. Wilfully simple. Lost, or found?

After many minutes Robert looked and saw the tears in Adèle's eyes.

'Perfect fool,' she said. 'Precious fool.'

But Robert could not be sure of whom she was talking.